TRAPPED

While the officer's attention was occupied, the man called Hugo suddenly decided to run. It was a spur-of-the-moment thing, David could tell, an impulse of such idiocy that only an imbecile or a man frantic to the point of madness would have attempted it, for they were completely surrounded by troops and the nearest cover was at least forty yards away.

Under David's astonished gaze, Hugo began to sprint frenziedly, his long limbs moving in an erratic, unwieldly kind of way. It was plain to see Hugo could never make it.

David saw the barrier, he saw Hugo running, he saw the soldiers, their rifles cradled against their cheeks. Then the shots rang out and he watched Hugo cartwheel into the dust.

With a curse, the officer drew his pistol and thrust it under David's chin. His air of politeness had vanished. His eyes were cold and intense, his features taut as stamped steel. David stared at that face and his heart sank.

"You are under arrest, *señor!*" the officer declared.

Also by Bob Langley
AUTUMN TIGER

FALKLANDS GAMBIT

Bob Langley

BANTAM BOOKS
TORONTO • NEW YORK • LONDON • SYDNEY • AUCKLAND

All characters and events portrayed
in this story are fictitious.

*This edition contains the complete text
of the original hardcover edition.*
NOT ONE WORD HAS BEEN OMITTED.

FALKLANDS GAMBIT

*A Bantam Book / published by arrangement with
Walker and Company*

PRINTING HISTORY
Walker edition published December 1985
Bantam edition / June 1988

ISBN 0-553-27210-1

Bantam Books are published by Bantam Books, a division of Bantam
Doubleday Dell Publishing Group, Inc. Its trademark, consisting of
the words "Bantam Books" and the portrayal of a rooster, is
Registered in U.S. Patent and Trademark Office and in other
countries. Marca Registrada. Bantam Books, 666 Fifth Avenue, New
York, New York 10103.

PRINTED IN THE UNITED STATES OF AMERICA

KR   0 9 8 7 6 5 4 3 2 1

ONE

Buenos Aires, February 1982

Segunda parked his car at the barrier and showed his identity card to the policeman on duty. The man checked it for a moment, then saluted smartly as he stepped back to allow Segunda through. The streetlamps cast pools of orange light across the empty quayside, and Segunda could see the rusting hulks of derelict ships cluttering the narrow harbour as he crossed the dockland, a big man, heavy-shouldered and long-limbed with dark tousled hair and a pleasant, intelligent face. There was no tension in him as he reached the line of gaudily-painted housefronts and turned to the left, moving slowly so that his footsteps would not echo against the concrete pavement. Killing meant little to Segunda. As a boy, he had hunted the predators at his father's estancia on the Argentine pampa. Later, in his teens, he had graduated to people. It had been a natural transition, without trauma. People or animals, he found little difference.

The squad car stood parked in a narrow side-street facing the river. It was a Ford Falcon with an illuminated sign on its roof. Its occupants, four men, shirtsleeved for the heat, lounged around its exterior. They made no attempt to straighten as Segunda approached, took out his ID card and flashed it at them briefly. "Who's in charge here?" he demanded.

"I am," answered a solidly-built man whose belly bulged precariously beneath his ribcage. For comfort's sake, he had opened the lower buttons around his waistband, disclosing glimpses of a faded undervest. His cheeks glistened with

1

sweat, and he chewed steadily as he regarded Segunda with indifference.

"What's your name?" Segunda asked.

"Sergeant Chema."

The man was balding slightly across the dome of his forehead, and he had tried to minimise the effect by combing his hair over the front of his crown. He had a thick moustache which drooped around the corners of his mouth, and his nose had been broken at least twice. He looked awkward and aggressive by nature, but Segunda knew his recalcitrance went deeper than that. Segunda recognised the problem, understood it, sympathised. Nevertheless, he had a job to do.

"You are sure they are in there?"

"They were fifteen minutes ago."

Segunda peered across the waterfront at the line of buildings framed against the stars. La Boca was the old red-light district of Buenos Aires. Once it had been a natural haven for Argentina's most violent criminal element, and many a sailor fresh off his ship had ended his life with his throat slit in the same narrow streets where the tango had been born. But time had changed all that. Now the artists and writers had moved in, renovating the delapidated houses, giving new life to the crumbling bars and tumble-down cafés, imbuing the area with an air of order, legality, respectability. Yet despite this transformation, La Boca's turbulent past still lingered like a forgotten ghost. The houses looked derelict, transitory. They were timber-built, painted in various shades of yellow, green and ochre, their roofs flat in places, sloping in others. The lamplight glinted on sheets of corrugated metal where sections of the decaying woodwork had been replaced.

"These all the men you've got?" Segunda asked.

The sergeant shifted his gum to the opposite side of his mouth. "There's another squad car around the back. Nobody can get out. Both exits are blocked."

"What about the roof?"

Chema frowned. "The roof?"

"There must be a fire escape. If they get aloft, they can follow that line of buildings to the end of the street. You can't cover every door."

Sergeant Chema stopped chewing. For the first time, he looked faintly uncertain. Then he spat on the ground. "What the hell, they're your responsibility, not ours. We don't know what crime they've committed."

Sighing, Segunda drew him quietly aside and, fumbling in his pocket, took out a packet of small cheroots. "You smoke these things?"

Chema shook his head. "They're bad for the health."

"Wise man."

Segunda placed a cheroot between his own lips and carefully lit it. He could sense Chema's resistance like a palpable force.

"Were you the one who put the call through?" he inquired.

"Sure. When we ran the names through our computer, we discovered there was a D.42 on Colonel Hugo Pinilla. I sealed off the area immediately and contacted army security."

"You did the right thing."

Segunda took the cheroot from his lips, exhaling gently, and peered back at the detectives gathering around the squad car. Their faces looked curiously pale in the street-lamps' glow.

"I have to tell you," Segunda said softly, "that what we are facing here is a situation of some delicacy."

"In what sense?"

"The bodyguard, Luis Masetti, is of little importance. But Colonel Pinilla . . ." His voice trailed away.

Chema stared at him. "Yes?"

Segunda shrugged and studied his cheroot in the lamplight. He flicked ash from its tip and placed it back in his mouth. He was trying to look nonchalant and relaxed, but they were always difficult, these moments. There was no way to do it cleanly, gently. No matter how you phrased it, the statement always came out blunt and direct. "He is not to be taken alive."

Chema stopped chewing, but only for a moment. His powers of recovery were really quite remarkable.

"The order comes from the highest authority," Segunda added. "Please believe me when I tell you I find such action

personally distasteful, but I am an instrument, nothing
more."

"And I am a policeman. That's my job. I don't go around
murdering people on the instructions of the bloody army."

"Nobody's asking you to get involved. I merely want you
to give me three minutes . . . three minutes, that's all
. . . then start up your siren, move your squad car into the
centre of the quay and send in your men front and rear. By
then, with luck, it'll all be over."

He raised his eyebrows, waiting for the sergeant's nod of
assent. Chema would like to refuse, he knew. He seemed a
decent man, conscientious and humane, and Segunda
guessed he resented the arbitrary methods of the security
forces, but he was also a realist and he knew the penalty for
failing to co-operate.

"Who are you anyhow?" Chema whispered.

"My name is Segunda."

He glimpsed the flash of recognition in Chema's eyes.
"The Gaucho?"

"Right."

A new wariness entered the sergeant's face. "Tell me
something," he said.

"Yes?"

"What kind of knowledge can a man hold in his head that
makes him too dangerous to live, even in the hands of the
police?"

Segunda's eyes were cold and direct. "Pray to God,
sergeant," he said, "pray to God you never find out."

He threw his cheroot into the dirt and moved off, leaving
the squad car behind and keeping to the shadows as he
edged toward the line of silent buildings. He could see the
house where the fugitives were hiding illuminated clearly.
It stood in the middle of a row of houses, clumps of foliage
sprouting from the wrought-iron balconies which decorated
its windows like intricate black lace. The roofs sloped
steeply, and Segunda could see a clutter of chimneys and
TV aerials in the moonlight.

He found an alley and ducked along it, coming out at the
building's rear. A wooden fence blocked off a patch of waste
ground where the second squad car waited. Dustbins stood

among the shadows and the putrid smell of refuse was overwhelming.

Segunda crept more cautiously along the wall, his movements slow and graceful. In the darkness, his tanned skin blended perfectly with the night. Windows glided by his head, and then, directly in front, he spotted the spiralling metalwork of an ancient fire-escape.

He paused, listening hard. No sound reached him from above. The building, and the alley beyond it, lay in total silence.

Segunda's hand crept to the base of his spine. Thrust crosswise into the belt at the small of his back was his *facón*, a traditional gaucho knife with a fouteen-inch cutting blade, Segunda's favourite weapon. At his father's estancia where he had been born and raised, the *facón* had been his constant companion. Like the other gauchos, he had used it from the time he had been old enough to ride, for mending fences, butchering carcasses and, when the occasion demanded it, settling arguments. Its blade was like part of his right arm, as natural and comfortable as an old and familiar friend.

Gently, he eased out of his shoes and began to mount the fire-escape in his stockinged feet. He made no sound as he moved warily from one landing to the next. He was approaching the second floor when the unearthly wail of the police car's siren reached him from the building's front and he froze in his tracks, one hand lightly clutching the rail, the other gripping the *facón's* handle.

Someone was moving inside the house. Segunda heard the scuffle of feet and the hiss of laboured breathing as the door drew slowly back and a pale blob appeared in the narrow gap. A moment passed, then a figure eased out to the fire-escape, short, thickset and dressed in dark trousers and a light cotton shirt. For a moment it paused there, peering warily into the alley below. Segunda could hear the man's breath rattling in his throat.

A second figure ducked through the doorway, this one taller, thinner, and with a curiously uneven look as if the limbs had somehow grown out of alignment. The two outlines hesitated on the fire-escape landing, then the thickset man began to edge down the narrow stairs, feeling

his way along the rail with his right hand. He was almost
within reaching distance of Segunda before he noticed a
thickening in the shadows and pulled back, frowning
worriedly, his eyes struggling to adjust to the murky gloom.
Segunda saw his face lit by the starlight, his heavy jowls
coarse and unshaven. Excitement rose in Segunda's chest.
Bunching his muscles, he moved, feeling the energy
exploding inside him as he brought the *facón* forward in a
dizzy blur, his body locked into the remorseless ritual he
knew so well, his wrist twisting expertly at the moment of
contact, wetness spraying his face and neck. It took the
thickset man a moment to realise his throat had been cut.
His eyes bulged in disbelief as blood pumped from his
severed jugular and crimson froth bubbled between his
lips. For a full second he stood quite still, his hand still
gripping the rail, then his body seemed to lurch to one side
and he sat down heavily on the step, a terrible gurgling
sound emerging from his gaping windpipe.

Segunda went past him at a run, taking the steps two at a
time. The thin man had turned back and was sprinting
upwards, heading for the roof where the fire-escape ended.
He was up it in an instant, scrambling across the sloping
tiles, clearly visible against the sky. Segunda gripped the
facón between his teeth and dragged himself over the roof's
lower slope, picking his way diagonally across the tarred
boards. He realised his mistake in an instant as his
stockinged feet began to slither on the precipitous incline.
Desperately, he clawed the woodwork, trying to find a
purchase on the slippery surface, but his body skidded
helplessly down the sagging timber.

Cursing, he clattered back to the fire-escape and retrieved his footwear as the air echoed to the clamour of
policemen's voices. He darted into the alley and scuttled
along the line of dustbins, squinting upwards for a glimpse
of his quarry above, but he knew in his heart he was already
too late. The roof offered a dozen exit routes.

For twenty minutes, he checked and re-checked the
rambling houses both front and rear, but in the end, he was
forced to concede defeat.

He made his way back to where the police had rigged up
arc-lamps on the spiral escape, flooding the place with

light. They were photographing the corpse, exchanging details in dull, methodical tones.

Sergeant Chema stood watching as Segunda mounted the steps towards him. He had recovered his composure and was chewing his gum in a calm, lugubrious way. There was a smear of scarlet across the front of his shirt where he had brushed against the body.

"Have you searched their room?" Segunda asked.

"We're tearing it apart. They left nothing behind."

"What about him?" Segunda indicated the bloody figure sprawled on the staircase.

"He's clean. He was carrying a few coins, a dirty handkerchief, a driver's licence in the name of Luis Masetti, nothing else."

He stopped chewing for a moment and regarded Segunda coolly. "Looks like you killed the wrong man," he said in a quiet voice.

Segunda nodded, peering down at the heavy face. The eyes were locked in the blue-marbled milkiness of sudden death, the lips drawn back in a grimace of protest and despair.

He felt no emotion whatsoever.

POLICE DIVISION UNUSUAL OCCURRENCE REPORT
SQUAD: 21. DATE & DAY: 3-2-82. TIME: 0200. PLACE OF OCCURRENCE: 24 Av. Almagro.
DETAILS: 1. Telephone call 0120. Two men tentatively identified as Colonel Hugo Pinilla and bodyguard Luis Fabricio Masetti reported occupying above premises. Area sealed off to pedestrians and traffic.
  2. Army Security notified. Representative arrived 0157.
  3. Entered premises 0214 hours and found body of Luis Masetti on fire escape. The throat was cut. No evidence of further injuries. Masetti pronounced DOA at San Martin Hospital. There was no sign of Colonel Pinilla.

TRANSCRIPTION OF TAPE-RECORDED STATEMENT
TAKEN JANUARY 30TH, 1982, FROM SERGEANT
RAUL CUETO, MILITARY HEADQUARTERS,
BUENOS AIRES.
PRESENT: Cl Ernesto Yuro (Internal Affairs), Cl Jorge
Barrientos (Internal Affairs)

Q: You were on duty on the night of January 29th?
A: I was.
Q: What were your orders?
A: I was in command of security at the special operations
room.
Q: Alone?
A: There were three of us. Myself, and Privates Bravo and
Rodriguez.
Q: What happened to Bravo and Rodriguez?
A: At approximately 01.15 a.m. I sent them to the café
across the street to buy sandwiches and coffee.
Q: Was that a customary procedure?
A: It was not authorised, no, *coronel*.
Q: So you were breaking regulations?
A: (Pause.) Yes, *coronel*.
Q: You were alone in the operations room at the time
Colonel Pinilla arrived?
A: That is correct.
Q: You did not refuse him entry?
A: I . . . he had a PD.3. I saw no reason to.
Q: Is there not a regulation which stipulates no one will be
admitted to the operations room except when it is
properly manned and guarded?
A: (No response.)
Q: Sergeant Cueto, did you recognise Colonel Pinilla?
A: I'd seen him around, yes, *coronel*.
Q: Nevertheless, under Regulation 205, he should not
have been admitted until Privates Bravo and Rodriguez
had returned, that is correct?
A: Correct, yes *coronel*.
Q: Why was he allowed to proceed among the filing
cabinets unattended?
A: I had to guard the door. That was my first consideration.
Q: When did you become aware that Colonel Pinilla was
behaving improperly?

A: I thought he was taking an unusually long time to complete his business, so I entered the security room and discovered the Maximum Secret cabinet open. The colonel was studying the contents of one of the files.

Q: Did you challenge Colonel Pinilla at this point?

A: Yes, sir. I ran forward and called his name. I think I . . . that is, I remember trying to draw my revolver. Colonel Pinilla scooped up the papers and threw them into my face. Then he hit me with something solid, here on the temple. I must have blacked out. Next thing I remember, Privates Bravo and Rodriguez were kneeling over me. I sounded the alarm immediately.

Q: But by this time Colonel Pinilla had left the building?

A: I understand so, yes, sir.

Chandeliers sparkled beneath the vaulted ceiling, and the hum of the diners' voices as they moved along the sumptuous array of food, filling their plates from the tempting display in front of them, almost obliterated the murmur of the danceband playing at the far end of the room.

Colonel Ernesto Camero, head of Argentina's Security Division, mingled with his guests, a small man with a beefy, unhealthy face and darkly piercing eyes who enjoyed holding nocturnal get-togethers for the simple reason that they allowed him to parade in his gold-braided uniform. From his earliest youth, he had been painfully conscious that his body was too long for his absurdly short legs, but the uniform, embellished with medal ribbons and insignia of all shapes and sizes, minimised, he felt, the limitations of his frame and imbued him with a certain dignity and glamour.

He was standing with a group of officers at the punchbowl when he spotted his aide, Major Vieira, hurrying anxiously toward him. Colonel Camero tilted his head, straining to hear above the clamour. He was careful not to allow the smile to slip from his features.

"Señor Segunda is on the telephone," Vieira whispered. "He wishes to speak to you most urgently."

"Where?" Camero demanded.

"In your study, *coronel.*"

Excusing himself, Camero put down his glass and made his way up the broad marble staircase to his private quarters on the floor above. The lights were on as he entered, and he saw the telephone receiver lying speaker-uppermost on the desktop. The noise from the room below was sending vibrations through the polished wood floor.

Colonel Camero closed the door and locked it. Then he moved to the desk, took a cigar from the inlaid box beside the blotting pad, lit it carefully and picked up the telephone. "Segunda?" he said.

He heard Segunda's mocking laugh at the end of the line. "Celebrating again, colonel? What a frenzied life you soldiers lead."

Camero frowned disapprovingly. He did not care for Segunda. The man was both insolent and insubordinate, and operated with an arrogant disregard for regulations or authority. Camero himself belonged to the old school. He believed in status, rank, position, a defined pattern to the order of things. Segunda undermined all that, and in Camero's opinion should have been disciplined long ago, but the ruling junta regarded Segunda as an invaluable weapon in their fight against subversion, so Camero was forced to endure the man's disdain.

"What happened?" he snapped, ignoring the sneer in Segunda's voice.

"He escaped."

"What?" Camero's tone was incredulous. "You swore you had him. You promised he'd be eliminated before morning."

"I know, I know," Segunda answered, "but he wasn't alone in that room. His bodyguard, Luis Masetti, got in the way."

"In other words, you killed the wrong man?"

"An unavoidable mistake," Segunda said. "Pinilla escaped during the confusion."

"Mother of God, have you any idea of the damage that man could do?"

"He has to get out of the country first, colonel."

Camero was silent for a moment. "You're right. He'll head for Uruguay or Brazil, probably try to cross the frontier further north."

He paused, taking the cigar from his lips and peering at it thoughtfully, his cheeks green in the reflected glow from the lampshade. "I want all detachments placed on immediate alert. I don't care who they are or what they're doing, everything halts until the emergency's over. Colonel Pinilla is a very dangerous man. The knowledge he holds could have the most serious consequences. He must be silenced at all costs."

The bus stopped, and the young American in seat 14 watched the new passenger clamber on board and pause to peer anxiously along the rows of weary travellers. He was around the forty-mark, tall and extraordinarily slim with black hair and a chin heavily coated with beard stubble. Something about the man caught David Ryker's attention. He looked nervous and ill-at-ease—furtive almost, David thought, as if the most ordinary things in life filled him with a deep and profound suspicion.

David watched the newcomer pay the driver and shuffle along the aisle, pausing at David's seat to peer at the space beside him. "*Permiso?*" the man muttered.

"Sure," David grunted, shifting along to make more room.

The stranger settled himself down, rubbing his face with his fingertips. His eyes looked baggy, and a series of tremors ran through his limbs as if the sudden act of relaxing had released some spontaneous reflex inside him.

Curious, David offered him a cigarette. He looked surprised. "*Mil gracias*, señor," he said, taking one and sniffing at it tentatively. "American?"

David nodded. "I can't stand Latin tobacco."

The man studied him warily as he leaned forward to accept David's light.

"You are from *Los Estados Unidos*, the United States?"

"Correct."

"But you speak Spanish so fluently."

"Well, Spanish is kind of my second language. On the ranch where I grew up, most of our hands came from south of the border. It was Mexicans who taught me how to speak."

The man drew on his cigarette, letting the smoke curl

from his nostrils, his eyes still dark and cautious. "You are a cowboy then?"

David chuckled. "The only time I ever heard that word was in the movies. We called our men *vaqueros*. Still do." He held out his hand. "Listen, my name's David Ryker."

The man hesitated for a fractional moment, then visibly seemed to relax. "Hugo," he grunted, shaking David's hand.

"Aren't you kind of lost out here?" David asked.

"What do you mean?"

"Well, it's hours since we passed a farm or village. I just wondered how you came to be stuck at the roadside in the middle of nowhere?"

The man's responses closed up as swiftly as they had opened, forming a barrier between them which David sensed.

"I got a lift," he stated. "A farmer. He brought me out from Turbio."

"Sure," David said. "Well, I guess it's none of my business anyhow."

What the hell, he thought, I don't give a damn where he came from or what he's up to. If he wants to be dark and mysterious, that's up to him.

He leaned back in his seat as the bus picked its way across the endless, monotonous landscape, the country unfolding in a sprawl of pancake-flat scrublands broken by water meadows and clusters of leafy timber. He spotted an ostrich-like rhea running for cover, its bunny-white tail feathers fluttering cheekily in the morning sunlight. Two *peons* in ragged ponchos guided a primitive ox-cart along the opposite side of the road. Swarthy and unshaven, they stared at the bus through timeless implacable eyes.

David, twenty-seven, blond, medium-sized, lean and wiry, had left Buenos Aires two days ago, travelling north along the Paraná River, and not once had the levelness of the countryside altered by the slightest degree.

He had the feeling it went on for ever, that if he travelled far enough he might, like the mariners of old, topple over the rim of the world. Just like home, he mused. In Texas, where he had been born and raised, the country was remarkably similar. Drier maybe. A different texture to the topsoil. But basically exactly the same.

Still, it had been a mistake not hiring a car, he realised that now. In Buenos Aires the idea of the bus had seemed appealing. He wasn't the tourist type. He liked to make the most of his travels, enjoyed going his own way, getting close to the country, mingling with the people. But he'd reckoned without this enormous emptiness. The journey seemed to be taking for ever, and he was beginning to wonder if he would ever arrive at his destination.

Beside him, the stranger had recovered his composure and was trying now to hide his tension in a show of normal conversation. David responded willingly, relieved at a chance to break the monotony.

"How long have you been in Argentina?" the man asked.

"Feels like years," David admitted. "These flatlands go on for ever."

"It is a big country," the man agreed, trying to look relaxed, "like the United States. In fact, Argentina is so similar to *Los Estados Unidos* in many ways. The people are the same, a mixture of different races, different cultures, Spanish, Italian, Indian, English."

"English?" David echoed. "Here?"

"Of course. There is a very strong Anglo influence. British immigrants came in the last century to settle the land. They built railways, roads, towns, imported cattle, sheep and horses. Their descendants still remain to this day. Out in *el campo* you will find whole communities where the inhabitants speak not only Spanish, but Welsh and Gaelic too."

"And the gauchos?" David asked.

The man called Hugo smiled thinly. "Everyone wants to know about the gauchos, the true men of the pampa. We seldom call them by such glamorous names any more. They are *peons*, or *campesinos*. The early gauchos were drifters, gypsies who shifted across the country picking up work where they could find it, moving on to the next town, the next village, the next province when they couldn't. Until the war of independence, they were regarded as quarrelsome brawlers, then the gaucho guerrilla armies rose against imperialist Spain, and the gaucho has been an

Argentine hero ever since. He is every schoolboy's dream of
freedom."

The conversation continued, warily at first then, as the
stranger's confidence grew, his air of reserve gradually
diminished and David found him to be an agreeable
companion, intelligent and knowledgeable about his own
country, and surprisingly well informed about the affairs of
the rest of the world. There are fine gradations in events
which change people's lives, subtle nuances and variations
which shape destinies, alter futures. As the bus rattled
drearily northwards, it is unlikely David Ryker would have
chatted with quite such enthusiasm had he known that his
new companion was Colonel Hugo Pinilla, late of the
Second Army Division, special adviser to the commander
of military intelligence, deserter, traitor and, at that
moment, in the eyes of the secret police, the most wanted
man in Argentina.

If he were strictly honest with himself, David Ryker
thought, he scarcely knew what he was doing here. It had
been his father who had talked him into it. One way or
another, everything in his life came back to his father.
Myron "Rusty" Ryker was an American legend. A symbol.
Oil millionaire, cattle baron. Ruthless exploiter to some.
Shining example of dynamic enterprise to others.

David's father was an exasperating bear of a man, a
throwback to the past, a fragment of the American West
that had died with the days of the old pioneers. He had
never accepted the twentieth century, not really, and
believed he could bulldoze all opposition into the ground
by the sheer domineering force of his personality. And
always had, David admitted ruefully. To his recollection,
nobody had stood against Rusty Ryker and survived.

He had made a fortune in the oil business, bringing in
one lucrative well after another, but his real love had always
been ranching. Raising cattle. David had learned the
intricate skills of the cattleman's trade from the earliest age,
herding, branding, lassooing, dehorning, but he had never
cared for it and had wanted from the beginning to build a
future elsewhere. His father, however, had turned a blind
eye to his son's ambitions until David had been obliged to

fight him at every turn, resisting all attempts to force him into a manageable mould and moving, as soon as he was old enough, to an environment far removed from his father's power and influence.

David's stomach still fluttered when he thought of that departure. It hadn't been easy, leaving. It hadn't been easy, standing up to the man he had considered since boyhood as some kind of godlike creature, mystical, immutable, remote. But he'd done it, by God. He had moved eastward to Virginia, largely because he liked the sound of the name. It was different to Texas. Soft and rolling, with pine-studded hills, gentle valleys, rural flatlands. For five years, he had worked for the Fleishman Maritime Institute in Norfolk, specialising in old naval wrecks. He liked the sea, found an aesthetic pleasure in the line and cut of a good ship. The job paid little, but it didn't matter. Happiness was all David cared about. Satisfaction. Fulfillment. The Institute provided him with all three.

The Institute had asked him to travel to the Falkland Islands to investigate the wreck of an old Yankee clipper ship damaged trying to round Cape Horn in the early 1890s. The vessel now lay rotting in Port Stanley harbour and, if she proved seaworthy enough, the idea was to tow her back to Virginia for inclusion in the Institute's Maritime Museum.

When David's father had heard the news, he'd telephoned David immediately.

"You'll have to switch planes in Buenos Aires," he'd said. "I've got an old friend up in Entre Ríos province runs an estancia that makes our own spread look like a damned chicken farm. Why don't you spend a few weeks up there, find out how he harvests that beef?"

David still smiled when he thought of that phone call. Rusty Ryker's diplomacy had all the subtlety of a battering ram. David knew his father was trying to lure him back to the fold. Re-tie the knot. Force him into line. But he'd needed a vacation badly, and the prospect of a pleasant break riding the Argentine pampa had been a tempting one. What the hell, David had thought. The wreck had lain at Port Stanley for nearly a hundred years, a couple more weeks would make little difference. So he'd agreed. A truce. Tentative and shaky, but a truce nevertheless. A man could live his entire life shutting himself off from the things he feared and idolatrised, but until he faced them calmly, honestly, until he satisfied his mind that they intimidated him no longer, he was a prisoner in a cell of his own making. What his father didn't realise—could not possibly understand even if he did—was that he, David Ryker, was about to cut the knot for good.

In the early afternoon David, dozing, felt the bus drawing to a halt. He shook himself and, opening his eyes, peered balefully through the windshield in front. He could see a barrier across the highway, and khaki-clad soldiers waving them down.

A roadblock. He sighed. Argentina was a country of roadblocks. They had passed through several in the lower sections of the province, but he hadn't expected to find one quite so far north. Grimly, he began to fumble in his pocket for his passport and papers. The Argentines were obsessed with bureaucracy, he thought. Even out here on the pampa, the hand of the military was impossible to escape.

Beside him, the man called Hugo stiffened in his seat. His cheeks had paled visibly, and beads of perspiration were trickling down his skin, tracing little channels of moisture through the dust which had caked there during the day.

"I have no identity card," he whispered.

David frowned. "What's that?"

"I lost it. Back . . . back there in Turbio. I was robbed."

"Robbed?"

"My hotel room. Someone broke in during the night."

David felt surprised. The incident hardly seemed serious enough to provoke the kind of consternation the man was clearly experiencing. He peered wonderingly at the shudders of fear rippling through Hugo's emaciated frame.

"Just explain what happened," David said. "I'm sure they'll understand."

"This isn't *Los Estados Unidos*," Hugo insisted. "Without papers, I shall be arrested, interrogated. In Argentina, people who fail to satisfy the secret police become part of the *desaparecidos*, the 'disappeared ones'. They vanish without trace."

David hesitated. He had heard of the "disappeared ones." In *la guerra sucia*, the "dirty war" against the terrorists conducted in the seventies, fifteen thousand were said to have vanished from the streets of Buenos Aires alone.

"Well, I'd help you if I could," David said honestly, "but I don't see what I can do. I'm a stranger here, a foreigner."

"Tell them you are my friend."

"What difference will that make?"

"If you substantiate my story, perhaps they will accept the word of an American."

David felt suddenly uncertain. "Stay out of trouble," his father had warned. And he had travelled enough in the world to understand the perils of interfering in matters affecting the security of the state, particularly in Latin American countries. But Hugo's cheeks were ashen, and the fear in his face was so desperate and intense it made David flinch.

"Please," Hugo whispered, his fingers clutching David's wrist.

David chewed at his lip. Already, two soldiers had entered the bus and were moving along the aisle, checking each of the passengers in turn. They looked absurdly young, like schoolboys decked in grown-up clothing. It was hard to believe their uniformed faces could hold any sense of menace. On the other hand, what Hugo said was true—in Argentina, political dissidents did disappear, the whole world knew that. Could he, in all conscience, ignore a fellow human being in such terrible need?

The soldiers reached their seat and took David's proffered papers, studying them briefly before handing them back. They looked at Hugo. He held his hands palms uppermost to show that they were empty. "I am . . . without identification," he muttered. "I was robbed early this morning. The thieves took my wallet, my money, everything I possessed."

The soldiers glanced at each other. "You reported this?" the corporal grunted.

"I intended to. As soon as I reached my destination."

"But when one is robbed, surely it is policy to notify the authorities at once?"

"I was in a hurry. I had to catch the bus."

The corporal frowned. He was a slender young man with the beginnings of a thin moustache which he kept stroking with his fingertip as if to assure himself it was still there. "If the thieves took your wallet, how were you able to purchase your ticket?"

"I had a few extra bills hidden inside my left shoe. It is a precautionary measure I often adopt whilst travelling."

"What is your name?" the soldier asked.

"Juan Martinez," Hugo said.

David glanced at him, frowning worriedly.

"Can you prove this?"

"My friend here will . . . will confirm my identity."

The soldier's eyes flickered over David. "You are an American, *señor*?"

"That is correct," David replied.

"And you know this man?"

David's mouth felt dry. He peered again at Hugo who was staring fixedly to the front. The Argentine's cheeks were a sickly grey, and David could feel the tension running through his body like a series of small electric shocks. Dimly, he heard himself saying: "I know him well. We left Buenos Aires together yesterday. Last night at the hotel in Turbio, his room was ransacked. He wanted to report it at once, but I insisted on sticking to our schedule."

The corporal hesitated. He looked slightly mollified, but his manner was still cautious. Without a word, he clambered outside and David saw him talking to a man in officer's uniform. The officer climbed on board and moved towards them up the aisle.

"Will you . . . step this way please?" he asked politely.

David heard Hugo suck in his breath. He rose, his fists gripping the seat in front, and David could see his knuckles gleaming white through the skin.

Hugo shuffled past the officer and down the steps to the road beyond.

"Both of you, *señor*, if you would," the officer said.

David felt his heart thumping as he straightened and moved through the door, blinking rapidly in the sunlight. He stood at Hugo's side.

The officer held out his hand. "May I see?" he asked politely.

David fumbled in his pocket and took out his papers for the second time. The officer opened his passport, studying the details. "You are here on business, señor?"

"Partly business, partly pleasure. I'm visiting a friend of my father's who runs an estancia near Las Arenos."

"And how long have you known this man?"

David felt his nerve beginning to fail him. He took a deep breath. "We've been friends for a number of years. We met in Washington back in the seventies."

The officer grunted, glancing over David's shoulder as the bus driver leaned through the doorway to inquire how soon they would be allowed to leave. At that moment, whilst the officer's attention was occupied, the man called Hugo suddenly decided to run. It was a spur-of-the-moment thing, David could tell, an impulse of such idiocy that only an imbecile or a man frantic to the point of madness would have attempted it, for they were completely surrounded by troops and the nearest cover was at least forty yards away.

Under David's astonished gaze, Hugo began to sprint frenziedly toward the barrier, his long limbs moving in an erratic, unwieldy kind of way that was clearly tinged with desperation. Oh Christ, David thought. It was plain to see Hugo could never make it. As David watched, dry-mouthed, he scrambled over the barrier's rim, dropped to the other side and began to race for the nearby trees.

Shouts of alarm burst from the soldiers and David felt himself thrust rudely back as they swung their carbines into position. David's senses seemed mesmerised with shock. It was like watching a film unfolding in slow motion. He saw the barrier, he saw Hugo running, he saw the soldiers, their rifles cradled against their cheeks. Then the shots rang out and he watched Hugo cartwheel into the dust. It was a graceless tumble, a ludicrous flurry of thrashing arms and legs that caused David's stomach to tighten as if the bullet had struck some responsive chord in his own metabolism. Hugo sat up, clutching his thigh, his features twisted with pain and fright. Two of the troops trotted toward him, carbines at the ready.

With a curse, the officer drew his pistol and thrust it under David's chin. His air of politeness had vanished. His eyes were cold and intense, his features taut as stamped steel. David stared at his face and his heart sank.

"You are under arrest, *señor*," the officer declared.

TWO

Ciro Cuellar, major, Third Argentine Army Division, brown-haired, medium-sized, thirty-six years old, parked his car on the front drive of his Buenos Aires home and, after pausing to pick up his mail, let himself in through the front door. He had driven directly from the army base after a week's strenuous manoeuvres near the Chilean border, and for reasons he pushed resolutely out of his mind had refrained from telephoning his wife beforehand.

The house was empty when he entered. He could tell at a glance there was no one at home. The rooms had a certain feel to them, an air of solitude and abandonment. Ciro felt depression descending upon him. He had been away a week. It had been a gruelling slog, the interminable process of attack and counter-attack, leading his men through the crags and gullies of the Andean foothills, and he had longed for this moment, holding it fixedly in his mind as a man lost in the desert might harbour dreams of sparkling cool water, the thought of seeing Tamara again. All through the long flight eastward, his mind had lingered on the memory of her face.

Ciro loved his wife. He had loved her from the first moment he'd set eyes on her at a regimental dinner to celebrate the anniversary of Argentina's independence from imperialist Spain. Her beauty had almost stopped his breath, and he had courted her with all the fervour and gallantry he could muster, marrying her eight months later in an elaborate ceremony which had ended with the two of them escorted from the church beneath an archway of drawn swords.

It had not been a successful marriage. They had quar-
relled almost from the start and, as the years had passed,
their quarrelling had grown more and more bitter. They
were neither emotionally nor intellectually compatible. His
wife enjoyed the gay life—parties, balls, trips to the
theatre, elegant dinners at Tito's bar or Lucs—whereas he,
quiet, introspective, a "gentle" man in every sense, pre-
ferred the peace and solitude of his own home. Tamara
accused him of destroying her youth, of taking the most
precious part of her life and constricting it beyond reason,
and though Ciro tried mightily to fulfil the role she
expected of him, he was too set in his ways to change to any
radical degree.

He loved Tamara, that was his tragedy, loved her to
distraction. He could not bear to imagine life without her,
and clung stubbornly to the belief that one day, by some
miracle, they might find a means of reconciling their
differences.

He moved through the empty rooms, checking them
each in turn. The doors and windows had been individually
locked, the electricity switched off. She had been gone for
several days at least.

Ciro did not like the thoughts which were stirring in his
mind. Despite the shakiness of their relationship, he had
never questioned her fidelity.

The young men who watched her in crowded restau-
rants, slack-mouthed, eyes hollow with yearning, had
never registered in Ciro's head as any kind of potential
threat; but now, for the first time in his life, like the signal of
impending age in a man past his prime, a feeling of
uneasiness moved inside him. Had he been too blind, too
stupid to see the truth?

He left his bags in the hall and went upstairs to their
room. For a long time he sat on the bed, hating himself for
what he intended to do. It was madness, he thought. He
had no proof. She might have gone anywhere. Her
mother's. Her friend Rosa's on the opposite side of the city.
He was turning into a jealous fool, haunted and tormented
by adolescent fantasies. If a man loved his wife then he
must, for the sake of their life together, strengthen that love
with trust, acknowledging his partner's individuality, recog-

nising it, respecting it, in the belief that this acceptance would in turn bring its own reward, if not of endearment, at least of loyalty and allegiance. These thoughts rose in his mind, and though he struggled hard to focus on them, deep down darker thoughts, torturing in their intensity, blundered through his imaginings until at last, unable to help himself, he rose from the bed, crossed the room and began shamefacedly to go through her things. He tore open wardrobes, pulled out drawers, tumbled the contents from cupboards, tossed frilly bits of underwear this way and that until he found what he was looking for. Hidden beneath a stack of blouses was a small photograph. Moving back to the bed, he sat down, studying it intently. The rage within him had given way to a terrible calm.

The face staring up at him was handsome and arrogant, the features clean-cut, even and filled with a curious vitality. There was a mocking glint in the man's brown eyes and laughter lines traced the corners of his mouth.

Ciro recognised the subject instantly. It was Martin Segunda, known as the Gaucho, a noted horse-trainer and rodeo rider. Once, before Ciro had met her, Segunda had been Tamara's fiancé, but the affair had gone wrong and Tamara, though he never allowed himself to ponder on this fact, had turned to Ciro on the rebound.

Pain rose through Ciro, starting at his centre, expanding until it flooded his whole body, and with the pain came a new sensation, a feeling of amazement directed, not at his wife, but at himself. A man could live his whole life and still be astonished in a single moment of ignorance, he thought. Still, it meant nothing. A photograph, that was all. Who could blame a woman for keeping a picture of her ex-lover for sentimentality's sake?

But his brain refused to accept the explanation. Why hide the picture if it meant so little? And Segunda's reputation was legendary. Ciro knew his rodeo image was merely a cover—he worked as an assassin for the government security forces, and rumour had it he was also a notorious womaniser.

Ciro remembered a file he had seen at military headquarters. The words were still etched in his memory: "Informant L-4253, who knew Segunda during his university days, states, quote 'he has one basic weakness, his absorption with the opposite sex. Segunda's physical appetites form the central motivating force for his entire existence' unquote."

Ciro sat for a long time with the photograph clutched in his hand, his anguish almost physical in its intensity. He was still sitting there when he heard the sound of a truck swinging to a halt outside his front door. Footsteps scraped on the gravel drive and the bell rang in the hall. Pulling himself together, Ciro pushed the picture back into the drawer and made his way slowly downstairs.

An army sergeant stood on the threshold. He saluted smartly. "Major Cuellar, sir?"

"That's right."

"You are required at the presidential palace."

Ciro frowned. "But I've just arrived home."

"The order was operation immediate. I'm sorry, sir."

Ciro grunted. He was not accustomed to being summoned in such an unorthodox way. "Who sent you?" he demanded.

"General Ramirez, major."

"Ramirez?"

Ciro's puzzlement grew. General Ramirez belonged to the presidential staff. He was a direct confidant of Galtieri himself, only one step removed from the four-man team who made up the ruling military junta.

"I'd better shave," Ciro said. "Tell the general I'll be there in an hour."

The sergeant looked apologetic. "I'm sorry, major. Our orders were explicit. You are to come at once."

Ciro lifted his eyebrows. "As urgent as that?"

"I'm afraid so, major."

"Very well, I'll leave my car in the drive and ride with you."

The sun was shining brilliantly as they swung into the Plaza de Mayo, a pleasant well-ordered square where tired city-dwellers could watch the changing of the guard across a soothing expanse of manicured lawns. Ahead lay the presidential palace, an impressive and elegant building where much of Argentina's history had been enacted. For generations, crowds had gathered beneath its ornate balconies to roar their approval or fury over a succession of generals, presidents and politicians who had entered office and left it with the regularity of players on a polo team.

The sergeant parked the car at the palace entrance, and after signing Ciro in at the security desk, led him along a series of marbled corridors until they came to a door marked "Ramirez."

"This is it, sir," the sergeant said. "If you go right in, you'll find the general waiting."

Ciro tapped lightly on the door panel and entered. He was in a small outer office with a series of charts on the wall. A young corporal sat typing in front of the window. He stood up smartly when he saw Ciro's rank.

"Major Cuellar?" he inquired.

"That's correct."

"The general will see you immediately, sir. He's been waiting all morning."

Ciro grunted as the corporal ushered him into the inner office. It was much larger than the reception room, with windows along one full wall. Through the polished glass Ciro could see the broad lawns of the Plaza and the Pirámide Memorial at their centre.

General Ramirez was on the telephone when Ciro entered. He glanced up, said something softly into the mouthpiece and put down the receiver. Then he rose to his feet.

He was a tall man with unusually long features. His face seemed distorted, as if the nose and cheeks had been stretched at birth. He smiled at Ciro and held out his hand. "Welcome back," he said. "How did the manoeuvres go?"

Ciro was surprised at the warmth of the general's welcome. He had seen Ramirez only at official military functions, and their relationship was a formal one. He took the hand cautiously. "Exhausting," he muttered. "You must forgive my dishevelled appearance. I'd only just arrived home when your sergeant brought me over here."

"He was acting on my orders," the general confirmed. "I thought you'd want to hear the news as quickly as possible."

"News?" Ciro echoed.

"You have just been promoted. You are now Colonel Cuellar."

Ciro stared at him. "Thank you, sir . . . but isn't this rather sudden?"

"Not at all. We've had our eye on you for quite some time now. Besides, we need you for a very important task. You have been seconded to my department to prepare the way for a major military operation."

"What kind of operation?" Ciro asked.

The general smiled thinly. Without a word, he walked to a walnut cocktail cabinet, opened it and took out two glasses and a bottle of whisky. Carefully he filled each of the glasses and handed one to Ciro. His cheeks looked strangely flushed, as if he could scarcely contain the excitement mounting inside him. He raised his glass in the air. "To the Malvinas Islands," he said.

Ciro felt his senses lurch. In that moment, his thoughts of Tamara were suddenly forgotten as a strange breathless sensation gathered in his chest. He lifted his glass and tapped it gently against the general's own.

"The Malvinas," he whispered softly.

The light blazed fiercely in David's eyes. The room was bare and windowless, the floor uncarpeted, the walls coated with rough plaster. There was no furniture apart from the single hard-backed chair in which he was sitting and the interrogator's desk. An electric fan buzzed on a shelf in the distant corner, but did little to disturb the suffocating atmosphere of humidity and body odour.

They had brought him to the army camp in the scorching heat of the early afternoon, and for nearly two hours he had answered a barrage of questions, terrified out of his wits. His interrogator was a small man in a civilian suit whose sparseness of frame was minimised by the fact that his head seemed abnormally small for his body, giving a misleading bulkiness to the upper portion of his trunk. His features were cadaverous and unhealthy-looking, and there was, David noted, a touch of the actor in him as if, thwarted out of his true vocation, he welcomed any opportunity to indulge in scenarios of his own making. He liked to walk a lot, shifting endlessly around the room. There was a clipped preciseness to the way he moved, and his manner seemed to change with his mood, sometimes threatening, sometimes cajoling.

David's nerves were already at breaking point. He knew the stories, had heard them often enough before—torture sessions, secret trials, clandestine executions. Americans could disappear just as easily as Argentines. He had done precisely what his father had warned him not to do. And now he was scared.

"Let's go over it again," his interrogator said.

"We've done that a thousand times," David protested. "How can I tell you what I don't even know?"

"Your name is David Ryker?"

"Yes," David said wearily, "yes, yes, yes, yes. For the billionth time, yes."

"And you work for the Fleishman Institute at Norfolk, Virginia?"

"That's right."

"Your father is Myron Ryker, the oil millionaire?"

"Look," David said with a sigh, "if you're going to charge me, then for God's sake charge me, but at least stop this ridiculous charade."

"You were on your way to visit Señor Alberto Farrel at the Sacombo estancia?"

"You know all this. If you already know it, why do you keep on asking me over and over again?"

"Señor Farrel is a friend of your father's?"

"Correct. That is correct."

"And how long have you known Colonel Hugo Pinilla?"

"I don't know him. For Christ's sake, why won't you listen? Before this morning, I'd never set eyes on him in my life before."

"Then why did you tell the soldiers he was a personal friend?"

"Because he asked me to," David muttered lamely.

"He asked you?"

The interrogator's eyebrows lifted in the lamplight. Again, there was a note of affectation in his performance, as if he enjoyed the theatricality of the cat-and-mouse game they played.

"Do you always do what total strangers ask you?"

"Look. He said he'd lost his papers in a robbery. He said

if the secret police interrogated him, he was afraid . . ."
David hesitated. "he was afraid he might disappear. I was
doing him a favour. It was a whim, nothing more."

The interrogator placed his fingertips together and
walked across the floor until he reached his desk. He
turned slowly, the lamp between them. Its glow cast slivers
of light beneath his eyes and cheekbones. The rest of his
face was obscured in shadow. "What did you talk about?"

"Nothing important. I've already gone through it item by
item."

"There must have been more."

"There wasn't."

"How long were you together? An hour? Two? There
must have been more."

"Look, what's the point in telling you anything if you take
no notice of what I say?"

"Did you discuss his work in the army?"

"I didn't even know he was in the army."

"He didn't mention it?"

"No."

"Did you tell him you worked for the Fleishman Institute
in Virginia?"

"Yes, I think so."

"Yet you never asked what he did in return?"

"I . . . it never entered my head. It just didn't seem
important, that's all."

"What else did you talk about?"

"I've gone over that till I'm blue in the face. Will you
please, please, listen? I'd never seen Colonel Hugo Pinilla
in my life before this morning. If you want to check my
credentials, get in touch with Señor Farrel."

"We shall," the interrogator promised. "In time. First,
however, you must satisfy us that you are telling the truth."

"What do you want me to do, cut my little finger off?"

The interrogator's face hardened visibly, the muscles
tightening beneath the bland sallow mask so that, though
the surface area remained unchanged, the impression of
anger was unmistakable. It was a delicate manoeuvre which
David suspected had been practised carefully in front of a
mirror.

"Do not imagine, Señor Ryker," he said, "that your

American passport places you above the law. We have no patience with enemies of our country, whether they are our own people or someone else's."

"I'm warning you," David said angrily, "my father is a powerful and influential man."

"Yes, yes, we have heard about your father. In the terrorist war of the seventies, many of those arrested were also the children of powerful men. It did not protect them from the consequences of their actions. In Argentina, there is no crime so indefensible as one against the security of the state."

David slumped dejectedly in his chair. Nothing he said seemed to register with this man. Reason, intelligent debate, they had gone out of the window. Here, he was trapped in a game beyond his understanding, a game with its own rules, its own subtleties of language and communication. Oh Christ, what a fool he had been. A crazy inexcusable fool.

"Please," he said almost tearfully, "contact Señor Farrel. he knows my father, he knows my background. He'll endorse everything I've said."

The interrogator was silent for a moment. He picked up a vacuum flask standing on the desk and carefully unscrewed the lid. Filling the plastic cup with coffee, he raised it to his lips. He seemed to be conducting a ritual in which the timing had to be exactly right. His Adam's apple bobbed as he swallowed, then holding the cup motionless for a moment, he drained it and placed it gently at the corner of his blotting pad.

"Let's go through it again," he said. "Your name is David Ryker?"

David's shoulders drooped and a wave of hopelessness passed through him, as if all his whipped-up courage and defiance had abruptly dispersed, leaving him helpless and alone.

"Your name is David Ryker?" the interrogator repeated in a sharper voice.

David nodded dumbly.

"And you work for the Fleishman Institute in Norfolk, Virginia . . . ?"

* * *

David lay on the bunk in his narrow cell and stared miserably at the ceiling. He had no idea how long he had been here. The interrogation had lasted interminably, and when the nightmare had finally come to an end he had been so tired the guards had almost had to carry him down the steps and along the echoing corridor.

He wondered what would happen now. He had not been fed since his arrival, which he regarded as an ominous sign. After all, there was no point in feeding a prisoner earmarked for execution, it was a question of economics. When they came for him again, would it mean a last step into the gathering darkness, a bullet surreptitiously delivered into the back of his skull?

Of course, there were worse things than dying. They could cripple a man for life with those electric machines of theirs, destroy his sexual capacity, render him useless, functionless, impotent. David remembered photographs he had seen of torture victims in Central America and, in spite of the heat, he felt himself shiver. Pain was a private thing. Some controlled it better than others. When the ordeal started, he had a feeling his last reserves of resistance would finally go.

Footsteps echoed in the corridor outside. There was the sound of a key being turned in the lock, then he door swung inward, flooding the cell with light. David blinked, easing himself up on his elbows. Framed in the doorway was a small, plumpish man in a rumpled grey uniform. Though his face was obscured by the glare, David recognised him as the duty sergeant who had confiscated his effects on arrival. "Come," the man said and, without waiting for David's reaction, began to shuffle back along the corridor.

Blinking, David clambered to his feet. He felt curiously disorientated, as if his body and limbs were out of alignment. A small knot of fear tightened in his stomach as he followed the sergeant to the end of the passageway and up the staircase beyond.

In the central office he spotted his interrogator sitting at a desk reading a sheet of paper clutched between his fingers; his stagy veneer had completely disintegrated and David could tell by the expression on his face that the document's message both angered and exasperated him.

Standing in front of the desk, looking studiously disdainful, was a man in voluminous *bombachos* and an elaborate broad-brimmed Texas-style Stetson. His features were slender, his hair grey and slightly curly, and there were deep lines running beneath his cheekbones, dividing the upper and lower portions of his face into two separate entities. When he saw David, his lips twisted into a tight smile.

"This way," the sergeant said, steering David to a desk at the opposite end of the office. Lying on the blotting pad was David's pocketbook and personal effects. On the floor, he spotted his valise. His heart began to jump.

"You're turning me loose?" he whispered, feeling a faint surge of hope.

"You have been accounted for," the sergeant told him dully, his fat face never changing expression.

"Who by?"

The sergeant shrugged. "That, I cannot say."

He thrust a sheet toward David across the desk and handed him a pen. "Sign at the bottom please, and initial each page on the top left-hand corner."

With his senses reeling, David did as he was instructed. He was trying hard not to lose his composure, but the unexpected switch in his fortunes, coming so sharply after his ordeal, made him feel as if reality had somehow gone askew. A minute ago, he had been convinced beyond any shadow of doubt that his life was approaching a squalid, undignified end. Now suddenly, and without any explanation, he was being released. The adjustment took some getting used to.

When he had finished signing the papers, he handed the pen back to the sergeant. "Is that all?"

The sergeant nodded and pushed his things across the desk toward him. David glanced at his passport, flipped open the pocketbook to check that his credit cards were inside, then thrust them into his jacket.

"You may leave now," the sergeant said.

David hesitated. "What about transport? You can't just turn me loose in the middle of the pampa."

"The señor in the corner will take you where you wish to go."

David stared again at the man in the Stetson hat. Suddenly, he understood.

"Mr. Farrel?" he muttered.

The man smiled. "Got yourself in a spot of trouble, I see," he declared in a perfect English accent. "Lucky these beggars had the good grace to telephone me. Meddling in affairs of the state can be a dodgy business in Argentina."

"Thank God," David breathed.

"Grab your bag. I have a truck waiting at the main gate."

"You mean that's all there is to it?"

"For the moment, at any rate. It'll take us about an hour to drive to the estancia. With luck, you should be in time to bathe before dinner."

Neither David's interrogator nor the sergeant who had released him glanced up as the two men departed through the guardroom door. David waited until they had shown their release permit to the sentry on duty and were driving through the stillness of the empty pampa before he said: "I guess I owe you an explanation, Mr. Farrel."

Farrel grinned. "Forget it. The lieutenant read me the complete report. I assume you were telling the truth. It sounded far too outlandish to be anything else."

"I've been pretty damned stupid," David admitted.

"You'll never know how much. That man you befriended was an extremely dangerous fellow. Substantiating his story was an act of madness on your part. People have been executed for less."

"I'm sorry you've been put to so much trouble."

"No trouble. All part of the service for the son of my old friend Rusty Ryker. But I must tell you that though I enjoy a certain degree of influence in these parts, my word would not, under normal circumstances, have been enough to get you off the hook on a charge as serious as this."

"Then how did you manage it?"

"Well, by a stroke of extraordinary luck, I had an extremely important guest visiting my estancia when the police called. It was his signature which set you free."

"I thought I was on the point of becoming a *desaparacido*."

Farrel's lips twitched. "We're not as bad as you make us sound," he replied. "The secret police don't bother you unless you break the law. And they do have a necessary and unpleasant job to do. You may take my word for it that their methods, extreme though they may seem to an outsider, are infinitely preferable to the wave of terrorism which swept this country back in the seventies. You have no idea what it was like then. There were terrorists everywhere. Right-wing Peronist terrorists, Trotskyite terrorists, army vengeance terrorists, trade-union terrorists, terrorist groups of the Catholic right. The whole country was plunged into a nightmare of anarchy, disorder and fear."

"So now the police reserve the monopoly on violence strictly for themselves," David said dryly.

Farrel smiled. "When you cut out a cancer, it's inevitable you destroy some healthy tissues as well. The authorites had no choice but to use the strongest measures possible to bring the terror to an end. And unpalatable though it may sound to your American ears, the measures worked. The subversive elements were either destroyed or contained. I agree the cure was somewhat extreme, but in my opinion, in this instance at least, the end justified the means."

David rested his elbow through the open window. The warm night air carried an odour of blossoms and lush foliage and he could see the landscape lying flat and heavy on both sides of the road. The stars hung above them in an enormous arched ceiling. He had been so close to disaster, so close to becoming another statistic. A fragmentary footnote in his local newspaper. There would have been questions asked, of course, his father would have seen to that. A few desks banged, a few teeth rattled, but in the end, nothing. One more missing person. One more in fifteen thousand. Within a month, he would have been forgotten.

"I'd be . . . extremely obliged if you didn't tell my father what happened," he muttered.

Farrel looked amused. "You think he might not approve?"

"I know he wouldn't."

"Then he must have changed quite a bit since the old days. Getting mixed up in a jam like this used to be right up Rusty's street."

"You don't understand. My father and I have this certain

relationship. We argue on just about everything under the sun. That's why I moved to Virginia."

Farrel chuckled. "He can be an overbearing beggar, I do remember that."

David peered at him curiously. He knew from his father that Señor Farrel was inordinately wealthy. He had also clearly once been a handsome man, indeed was still handsome if the truth were known, though his face had begun to sag a little with age, and the features, finely pointed and almost delicately proportioned, carried an aura of privilege and indulgence.

"One thing my father didn't prepare me for was you," David said.

"How do you mean?"

"I expected an Argentine, not an Englishman."

"I *am* an Argentine," Farrel grinned. "I was born and raised in this country. I'm one of the Anglos. You'll find us all over Argentina. It amuses us from time to time to indulge in the traditions of our ancestors, particularly the language . . . that is, when we get the opportunity."

"But your accent is impeccable."

"That's funny. The police interrogator said the same thing about your Spanish."

David laughed. He liked Farrel, he decided. The man's openness, his sense of humour, the languid drawl of his English accent were pleasantly appealing. He had a feeling they would get on well together.

An hour later, Farrel swung the truck off the main road, following a narrow track which wound tortuously through the darkness. David glimpsed lights ahead, and the shadows merged as he watched an elaborate building gradually taking shape in front of him. It was constructed hacienda-style, with sloping roofs, gleaming archways and little courtyards decorated with clumps of bougainvillea and blue thunbergia. It carried an air of opulence that even David's father, for all his ostentation, could not have hoped to emulate and, staring at the palatial stateliness of the carefully-ordered pavilions, David realised Señor Farrel's wealth must extend even beyond his first extravagant estimate.

As they swung into the floodlit courtyard and lurched to a

halt, David spotted two helicopters parked on the front lawn. Around them, soldiers with rifles lounged casually in the heat, watching their arrival through dull, incurious eyes.

"What's this?" David grunted. "You've got the place sealed up tighter than Fort Knox."

"Oh, they're not mine," Farrel laughed. "They belong to my dinner guest tonight. They go with his job, you might say."

He clambered out and collected David's suitcase from the rear. "I'll take you to your room. You can bathe and change here. We've still another hour before dinner, so if you fancy a swim, you'll find the pool on the patio at the rear."

David thanked him gratefully and followed Farrel around the side of the house to a line of low outbuildings which bordered a stone patio overlooking the lawns and gardens. Farrel opened one of the doors and stepped aside to let David enter. The room was large and spacious, the floor tiled to emphasise its coolness. Pictures of Paris and Madrid hung from the walls, and the elaborate bedhead was offset by a chintz bedspread in rich royal purple.

After Farrel had gone, David pulled on his bathing trunks and spent the next thirty minutes working the strain and fear from his system by thrashing up and down the swimming pool in the warm, scented night air. It had been quite a day, all things considered. What his father would call "a close shave." Too damned close, David thought. He'd been within a hair's breadth of oblivion. There were no rights in Argentina for political subversives, or for the friends of political subversives. No hope, no future. Only the inevitable end, anonymity, extinction. Thank God for the power of influence, the voice of reason. He resolved not to chance his luck again in such a crazy fashion. From now on, he decided, he would be as good as gold.

By the time he had hauled himself out and wandered back to his room, dripping profusely, he felt considerably better. He showered, shaved, and pulled on his tuxedo, then, feeling pleasantly relaxed, made his way through the maze of elegantly-carpeted corridors to the estancia's library.

He found Señor Farrel standing beneath a portrait of

himself, cradling a glass of whisky and soda. With him was his wife, an attractive woman in her middle forties, and his two teenage daughters, whom Farrel introduced as Pilar and La Perla. A solid, bulky-looking man was lounging comfortably on the sofa. His features carried the thick rubbery resilience of a prizefighter who had gone beyond his prime. His hair was grey and his eyes held a gleam of quiet amusement as he watched David enter.

"Ah, this is the young man I was telling you about, Leo," Farrel said.

The man nodded, his eyes crinkling as his face twisted into a slow grin.

"Come over here, David," Farrel insisted, "I'd like you to meet General Leopoldo Fortunata Galtieri."

David blinked, sucking in his breath. He stared at the man in surprise and confusion. Suddenly he understood why Farrel had managed to secure his release so promptly.

His dinner guest was no less a person than the Argentine president himself.

They ate under the stars, their nostrils filled with the scent of sweet thunbergia. Crickets chirped in the grass and fireflies circled above the candleflames as the dishes were served by dark-eyed señoritas in bright flowery dresses; the meat, an entire carcass of beef, the ribs parted and splayed in the manner of an eagle's wing, was placed in the centre of the table for the guests to carve themselves, and the flagons of red wine were replenished as quickly as they emptied.

Galtieri proved an engaging dinner companion. He talked avidly and with a disarming sense of humour which sometimes bordered on the indiscreet, particularly when commenting on the shortcomings of his fellow members of government. His manners were impeccable, and David noticed he was particularly attentive to the female members of the family. His attitude toward David himself was both considerate and polite. Whatever the subject under discussion, he sought David's viewpoint, listening with an intentness which made David, flushed with wine, feel flattered and grateful.

"The happiest months of my life were spent in the United

States," Galtieri said "I took part in an engineering training course at Fort Belvoir in Virginia. Perhaps you know it?"

"I've driven by there a few times," David admitted.

"The people were so friendly. I shall never forget their warmth and hospitality. Americans in their own country are the most charming race on earth."

"I might say the same about the Argentines," David smiled, "Of course . . ." he paused, and added wickedly, "your secret police aren't so terrific."

Galtieri's features hardened as if David's attempt at levity represented an inelegance which had to be rebuked.

"You were fortunate today," he grunted. "The gentleman you met on the bus was a colonel in the Argentine army who had committed a crime of the gravest nature. If our police were a little rough with you, you will understand why it was necessary."

David felt a sudden flash of annoyance. He had intended the remark as a joke and was surprised at the general's reaction.

"The interrogation I accept," David stated. "I behaved like a fool and I admit it. But speaking as an American and an outsider, I confess to feeling a little concerned about Argentine attitudes to human rights."

"Human rights?" Galtieri echoed.

"I'm talking about the stories of people disappearing."

Across the table, David heard Señor Farrel's sudden intake of breath. In the candlelight he glimpsed his host's features, pale as alabaster, the deep lines under his cheekbones emphasised by the flickering yellow glow. Alarm showed clearly in Farrel's eyes.

For Christ's sake, David thought, I'm not one of the general's sycophantic creeps. I say what I like, and to whom I like.

Galtieri's own face looked puffy and uneven, and the bulbousness of his nose was highlighted by the tightness of his lips.

"Señor," Galtieri said seriously, "In *la guerra sucia*, the campaign against the terrorists, we were fighting a war, and in any war, people disappear. It is unavoidable. We are not proud of what happened, but it was our duty to destroy the forces of terrorism, to establish order instead of chaos, humanity instead of fear. We did not shrink from our duty. In that at least, we may take comfort."

"What about me? Would I have disappeared too?"

Galtieri's eyes were sombre. "Let me put it this way. You may regard it as a piece of the most remarkable good fortune that I was not only in the process of visiting my old friend and comrade Alberto here, but that I had also heard of your father's reputation."

"My father?" David echoed.

"Of course. His political views and attitudes are well-documented. It was that fact which convinced me the affair was an unfortunate mistake."

David felt a momentary disappointment. He had lived so long in the shadow of his father, had struggled so hard to establish his independence that any evidence of that all-embracing paternal influence still depressed him, even when helping to save his skin.

"Your father is an oil man, is he not?" Galtieri said.

"That's correct. But ranching is the thing he really cares about. In some respects, general, my father is an incurable romantic. I guess he was born about a hundred years too late. He still longs for the days of the old pioneers. He finds something intrinsically American in punching cattle."

"I understand that," Galtieri nodded. "Here in Argentina, cattle have provided a major source of our livelihood for generations. And not only cattle. Oil, coal, rich farmland, tin. It may surprise you to know, señor, that toward the end of the 1800s, experts predicted the two most important nations of the twentieth century would be the United States and Argentina. However . . ." Galtieri shrugged his shoulders expansively, "we are mercurial people in many ways. We carry our emotions out here." He waved his hand in front of his face. "You must remember this is the country which invented *machismo*. The Argentine male likes to prove his manliness, it is part of his nature, part of the essence bred within him. With the aid of the guachos, he rose against the Spanish oppressor, defeated the British at Buenos Aires, subdued the indians in a series of savage wars which would make your Wild West look like child's play. If only he had been able to sort out his politics also, who knows where Argentina might be today?"

David was silent for a moment, toying with his wine glass. One of the señoritas, smiling, tried to refill it, but he shook his head, covering the top with his hand. Galtieri reached across and helped himself to another portion of beef, expertly carving the rib from the carcass with his razor-sharp knife. He was a hard man to figure, David thought. Charming and amusing one minute, cold and authoritive the next, clearly quick to anger, intolerant of attitudes which did not match his own.

"I understand you specialise in old maritime wrecks," Galtieri muttered.

"That's right. As a matter of fact, I'm on my way now to the Falkland Islands to check out an old Yankee clipper for the Fleishman Institute in Virginia."

Galtieri looked at him sharply. "You mean the Malvinas," he murmured.

"Oh sure, I forgot. I guess that's sort of a sensitive subject from your point of view."

"It is a matter of national honour, Señor Ryker. The Malvinas belong to Argentina. They were taken from us by force. Though we have tried endlessly to establish our rightful sovereignty, the British refuse to give them up."

Again, David felt an upsurge of annoyance, a sense of indignation at the general's placid assumption that he alone possessed some kind of divine power which made him unarguably and indisputably right. Damn the man, was he the only one allowed to express an opinion?

"I guess that's because the British don't see the situation in quite the same way," David said, glimpsing out of the corner of his eye the features freezing again on Señor Farrel's face.

Galtieri paused in the process of cutting up his meat and stared at David, frowning, the candlelight catching a solitary pimple on the left-hand side of his cheek. "Señor Ryker, what we are discussing here is a matter of history. The British took those islands unlawfully. You must understand the emotive nature of this issue. We are a strange people, we Argentines. We squabble among ourselves, we rail against authority, but one thing we are all agreed on. The Malvinas are Argentine."

"But the British have lived there for a hundred and fifty years."

"Possession does not constitute legal or rightful ownership. The British government wants nothing to do with the islands. It finds them an embarrassment. They are expensive to administrate and impossible to justify such an immense distance from London. In a hundred and fifty years of British rule, there is still only one road. It runs from the airstrip to the Royal Marine camp, a total distance of seven miles. The only hospital was built in the 1930s and doubles as an old-people's home. The island schools are small and primitive, and their methods are so archaic that many islanders choose to send their children to schools in Buenos Aires. It was Argentina which built the airport at Port Stanley. It is Argentina which carries supplies to the island's inhabitants. Without Argentina, those poor people would still be living in the Middle Ages."

David shifted uncomfortably in his chair. The conversation had entered a new plane, one on which he felt too ignorant to argue. He could see the anxious expressions on the faces of Señor Farrel and his wife and regretted his momentary boorishness. For Christ's sake, he thought, I'm supposed to be a guest here.

With a conciliatory shrug, he muttered: "Well, I guess if you look at the map, it's hard to argue with the fact that the islands are pretty damned close to the Argentine coastline."

Galtieri was silent as he went on carving his meat into small portions. He laid his knife by the side of his plate, and spearing one of the pieces with his fork, popped it into his mouth, chewing methodically. The anger had faded from his eyes, and now David could see a new look settling there, one he could not immediately identify.

"I understand your father is a friend of the American president," Galtieri grunted.

"That's right," David admitted.

"You know the gentleman personally?"

"Mr. Reagan? No sir, we've never met."

"But your father must have talked about him?"

"Yes, from time to time."

"Let me put to you a hypothetical question. What would you imagine would be President Reagan's reaction to an armed takeover of the Malvinas?"

David stared at him in disbelief. "You mean an invasion?"

"Hardly. Invasion implies an assault upon someone else's territory. I am talking about the liberating of our own sovereign soil."

"You wouldn't," David breathed.

"Of course we wouldn't. You must not take this in such a literal sense. We are speaking . . . how shall we say? . . . for argument's sake. Let us assume that Britain continues to refute our claim. Let us assume that with our honour at stake, our *national* honour, Señor Ryker, *machismo* at last replaces our sorely-tried patience."

"Well," David said slowly, "the kind of action you've just described would present the United States with a difficult dilemma. Our government might well be sympathetic to the Argentine viewpoint, but I'm sure it could never countenance deliberate armed aggression against one of its major allies. On the other hand, I'm equally sure it would never become militarily involved, in view of its commitments in Latin America."

Galtieri smiled. He seemed pleased with the response, as if David had confirmed some deeply-held personal conviction, giving it credence, substance. The tension at the table seemed to waver somewhat and, glimpsing the relief on the faces of the Farrels, David realised with a sense of guilt that the chill in the atmosphere had been largely his fault. He had allowed pique and vexation to cloud his judgement and challenge the most powerful man in Argentina. He didn't give a damn about the Falkland Islands, or the disappearance of Argentine dissidents, or any other damn thing which didn't directly concern his life and work in Norfolk, Virginia. Galtieri was the Farrels' honoured and respected friend and he, David Ryker, had acted like a prize jerk, repaying the kindness of these people with discourtesy and impertinence. It was unforgivable.

He spent the rest of the meal trying to make amends, regaling the dinner guests with stories of his youth on his father's ranch in Texas. Galtieri and the Farrels laughed appreciatively and David felt reassured as the mood swiftly lightened.

It was two o'clock in the morning when Galtieri made his

departure. The entire family walked with him to the
helicopters. When the soldiers saw him coming, they
sprang to attention. There was a low droning as the pilots
started the massive rotor blades, and the general turned to
look at David, his eyes wrinkling.

"You must visit our naval academy when you return to
Buenos Aires," he said. "It has one of the finest collections
of maritime wrecks in the world. As an expert, I'm sure you
would find it interesting."

"Thank you, I'd enjoy that," David said, nodding his
head.

"Contact me on your way to the Malvinas. I shall arrange
it," Galtieri promised.

He said goodbye to the Farrels, kissing the wife and
daughters ceremoniously on both cheeks and, twenty
minutes later, they watched him waving from the window
as the helicopters, with a thunderous roar, rose slowly from
the courtyard and clattered away into the night.

As he undressed for bed, David reflected on the start to
his visit. He had been arrested, interrogated, released. He
had gotten into an argument with the country's president,
and had been invited by that same president to pay a visit
to the nation's premier naval academy. No one could say he
hadn't made his presence felt. Even his father, for all his
ebullience and vitality, could hardly have done better than
that.

Grinning, he turned off the light and crawled into bed.

Colonel Hugo Pinilla lay on his bunk staring into the
darkness. The room was long and narrow, the floor made
from what seemed to be some kind of corrugated cement,
its surface coated with a thin wet slime. There was no light,
and his body twitched and jerked convulsively.

His thigh still ached where they had dug out the bullet.
The operation had been conducted without anaesthetic and
in a manner clearly designed to intensify his pain. After the
surgery he had been taken, hooded, from the operating
theatre and carried in darkness to a place of interrogation.
There, strapped to some kind of wooden frame, electric
wires had been attached to his genitals and anus. The
actions of his torturers had been delicate, almost con-

siderate as if, realising the enormity of the pain he would have to endure, they had been anxious not to minimise its impact by unnecessary rough-handling. When the current started, Pinilla had lost all sense of reality. His spine had arched, his muscles tightened, his mouth, still muffled inside the hood, had bellowed an endless string of obscenities. There had been no way to visualise that pain, no way to describe it afterwards, even to himself. His anguish had been a blind fragmented torment in which his brain had hallucinated feverishly, struggling to escape. They had kept up the treatment for hours, and in the end he had told them everything. Only when they were satisfied he had held nothing back had his suffering come to a close.

Now, trapped in the confines of the tiny room, his body was still reacting to its dreadful ordeal. Stale vomit crusted his chin and throat and his eyes, blank with shock, peered uncomprehendingly into the curtain of blackness.

He heard the sound of footsteps outside and the door was roughly opened, shooting a beam of light into the narrow cell.

"On your feet," a voice snapped harshly.

As he lay there quivering, two soldiers entered and dragged him bodily from the floor. Whimpering with pain, he felt them haul him from the room and through a doorway at the building's rear. The army camp was shrouded in darkness. Rows of silent huts stood bathed in the eerie starlight, and he saw a group of four soldiers, rifles slung across their shoulders, waiting in the bushes at the far end of the neatly-trimmed lawn. A fifth stood relieving himself against a nearby tree. They watched in silence as the two guards dragged Hugo toward them, and when he reached the bare soil, one of the soldiers thrust a shovel blade-first into the loose, crumbling earth.

"Make it deep," he ordered. "We don't want the rats digging you up for breakfast."

In a daze, his movements awkward and erratic, Pinilla began to scoop out a narrow grave. Shivering engulfed him each time he jabbed the shovel into the soil, and he tried not to think, tried to focus his mind on the simple methodical process of clawing out the dirt, depositing it in neat little mounds around the mouth of the yawning hole.

Several times he toppled over, to the immense amusement of his waiting executioners, but at last they were satisfied with the length and depth of the hole he had dug, and unslinging their rifles, ordered him to cast aside the shovel and stand facing them with his hands on his head, the grave at his rear.

Dumbly he watched the soldiers cock their carbines and take careful aim. He felt no fear, that was the strangest thing. Pain had taken it out of him. Pain, anguish and despair. In silence, he waited for the rifles to crack. The soldier's fingers tightened on the triggers. Click-click, the rifle bolts rattled on empty chambers. Pinilla blinked.

The troops lowered their weapons and burst out laughing. All the soldiers were laughing, including the two prison guards. Pinilla felt a wave of nausea sweeping upwards from his stomach and, unable to help himself, doubled forward, vomiting on to the ground.

The laughter faded. "Look at the dirty bastard," one of the soldiers muttered. "He's spewing like a pig."

"Get him out of here," another snapped. "I don't want to spend my morning cleaning up his stinking mess."

Pinilla felt himself being dragged across the empty lawn. He saw a truck parked in the darkness, its camouflaged markings almost indiscernible. He was hurled bodily into the vehicle's rear, and two of the soldiers clambered over the tailboard, handcuffing his wrists to the metal framework. In a daze, he heard the engine start.

Then, with the soldiers still guarding him, the truck eased between the silent rows of huts, turned through the gate on to the gravel-strewn highway and rattled off slowly into the night.

FROM: Colonel Ernesto Camero, Army Security Division, February 5th 1982. Classified Secret. Not to be opened without C/2 authority or above.
SUBJECT: Colonel Hugo Pinilla.
In view of the subject's contact with American tourist David Ryker, whose father is a friend and confidant of US President, Mr. Ronald Reagan, it is recommended no action to be taken against Pinilla at the present time.

Instead, he is to be removed to a place of maximum security and held in reserve until it is deemed safe to proceed against him in the customary manner.

Letter from unspecified operative to Charles Winward, Director of South American Division, CIA, Washington DC:
GF/42100, an informant who has proved reliable in the past states that heavy mobilisation has been taking place among army and naval reservists in the Argentine provinces of Cordoba, Santa Fé, Corrientes and Entre Ríos. He suggests this indicates an expectation of civil disobedience and unrest in the face of Argentina's rising inflation rate. However, the possibility cannot be ruled out that these troop movements have a more sinister meaning.

THREE

Ciro Cuellar sat outside the Polo Lounge of the Leandro Hotel and watched General Ramirez slowly finish his meal. The general was a methodical eater who chewed every mouthful at least thirty-two times, a procedure which prolonged the luncheon process by more than an hour. Ciro had finished his own meal twenty minutes earlier and had sat staring patiently across the manicured lawns of the Plaza San Martin and the canopied branches of the giant rubber tree where lovers dallied in the shade.

A great deal had happened to Ciro in the few days he had been seconded to the general's department. In the first place, he had been worked to a standstill, studying the plans for the forthcoming military operation in which he was soon to take part. In the second, his wife Tamara had at last come home. There was little doubt in Ciro's mind she had been surprised to find him there. In fact, she'd openly admitted as much. "I'd expected you'd be gone for at least another week," she'd said, with no remorse on her features, no sign of contrition or repentance. Tamara wasn't like that. She never made excuses.

Her story had been weak and unconvincing. She had been to her sister's in Necochea, he could telephone if he wanted to check. Such a phone call, Ciro knew, would be pointless. Tamara's sister would back her story to the hilt. So he'd stifled the impulse to question her, had said nothing about the photograph he'd found in her drawer, and had shrewdly kept his own counsel. Lovers who believed they were safe, he'd reasoned, often made mistakes. He would simply watch and wait.

In the meantime, there was his new assignment to consider—a momentous assignment, he realised, one which would not only aid his career, but would imbue his whole life with a purpose he had never before experienced. That was, if Ramirez ever finished his infernal meal. When it came to eating, the man had the patience of the devil, devoting his entire attention to each mouthful as if nothing else in the world existed. At last, the general put down his fork, dabbed lightly at his lips with the paper napkin and took a sip of wine.

"You must forgive me," he apologised. "I have trouble with my digestion. If I do not chew my food thoroughly, I suffer for hours afterwards."

"Do not trouble yourself," Ciro assured him politely, "I have nowhere in particular to go. My afternoon is entirely at your disposal."

"Coffee, señor?" the waiter asked, gathering up their empty plates.

The general nodded. "And two brandies," he said, "doubles."

He glanced at Ciro inquiringly. "Would you care for a cigar?"

Ciro shook his head. The general took out a packet of cigarillos, put one in his mouth and lit it carefully. He leaned back in his chair, turning his face to the February sunshine. Smoke curled from his lips in a lazy column. He waited until the waiter had moved out of earshot, then he said: "Have you studied the files?"

Ciro nodded.

"Tell me your impressions."

"A highly complex operation, general. Rather like using a mallet to crush a grape. According to our intelligence reports, there are barely sixty British marines stationed on the Malvinas. I wonder if it's necessary to attack the islands in such force?"

"We could do it with less," the general admitted, "but by cutting our numbers, we increase the possibility of casualties on both sides. One thing we must avoid at all costs is civilian dead. Our position with the United Nations will be delicate enough without complicating it further."

"What about British reaction?" Ciro wondered.

"Our intelligence services have been monitoring British responses for some time now. According to their assessments, and to certain reliable informants, the general feeling is that the British will rant and rave a bit for appearance's sake, but secretly, they'll be relieved to have the islands taken off their hands. Our primary objective is to make sure the occupation is sharp, effective and successful."

He paused for a moment, taking the cigar from his lips and studying it thoughtfully. "There is, however," he said, "another problem to consider. We know the location and strength of the British land forces. But a much more dangerous threat is the Royal Navy's ice patrol ship."

"HMS *Endurance*?"

"You know her, of course."

Ciro nodded. "She was originally the Danish vessel *Anita Dan*, converted by the British for operation in Antarctic waters in 1968. She has a displacement of four thousand tons and carries a crew of 137. She represents the British naval presence in the South Atlantic."

"Correct. From our point of view, she also represents the one factor we are unable to make allowances for."

"In what sense?"

"She's mobile. That means she can hit us from any angle. Oh, she's no match for our fleet once it gets under way, of course. But as long as the *Endurance* remains in Falkland waters, she has the capacity to wreak havoc with our operation."

"Her firepower is extremely limited," Ciro pointed out.

"But not without bite. She carries two Wasp helicopters with heat-seeking missiles. Bear in mind we'll be in an extremely vulnerable position, especially during troop landings. If she took us by surprise, she could inflict a crippling degree of damage."

"Where is she at the moment?"

"Out of harm's way, happily, but according to our intelligence sources she's due to return to Port Stanley just before our fleet sets sail."

Ciro grunted. "Well, if we postpone the invasion for a month or two, the *Endurance* will be out of our hair completely. She's being withdrawn in April as part of the British defence cuts."

"We can't postpone the invasion," the general told him flatly. "If we leave it any longer, winter will be here. You know what those South Atlantic storms are like. A major assault would be unthinkable. We have to strike before the weather changes. Besides . . ." He hesitated. "There are certain . . . political considerations involved."

He paused as the waiter arrived with the coffee and brandies, and sat silently contemplating his cigar until the man had withdrawn from hearing range, then he said gently: "I'm sorry, Ciro, but I'm afraid that's your job."

Ciro frowned. "The *Endurance*, sir?"

"She has to be destroyed."

Ciro felt his stomach muscles tightening. He stared at Ramirez, his face expressionless. "You can't be serious," he whispered.

The general continued to study his cigar tip, avoiding Ciro's eyes. "Deadly serious, I'm afraid."

"But barely a minute ago you were talking about keeping casualties to a minimum. Now you want to eliminate an entire shipload of men."

"There's no other way," the general sighed.

"May I remind you, general, we are not yet at war with Britain? If we sink the *Endurance*, how is it going to look to the rest of the world?"

"We can't do it openly, of course. But the *Endurance* is at present patrolling the Atlantic Peninsula. If she were to vanish beneath the Antarctic icecap—vanish without trace before the invasion takes place—Argentine involvement could never be actually proved."

Ciro felt physically sick. The calm, almost detached way in which the general discussed the act dismayed him. He thought of the *Endurance* steaming through the Antarctic channels, blissfully unaware of the plans for her proposed destruction.

"General Ramirez, I cannot do this," he whispered.

"Why not?"

"The *Endurance* captain, Nicholas Barker, is a personal friend of mine. When the vessel calls at Buenos Aires, he is a frequent visitor to my home. In fact, I am acquainted with most of the *Endurance*'s senior officers."

"Which is precisely why you have been chosen," the general told him flatly. "Know your enemy, a cardinal rule in any man's war. You understand how Captain Barker thinks, how he's likely to react under stress. I'm afraid that makes you the perfect man for the job."

His face softened, and he looked at Ciro with an expression of sympathy and concern. "I know how you feel, my friend," he said. "I too have met Captain Barker on a number of occasions and find him to be a most likeable man. The thought of sending 137 British sailors to the bottom of the Antarctic Ocean is deeply repugnant to me both as a man and as a Catholic. I want you to understand that if there were any alternative—any other way at all—we would not hesitate to take it. But there's too much at stake. We can't risk the future of our country on the fate of a single vessel. The order is reluctant but unretractable. HMS *Endurance* must be destroyed."

David steered his little *criollo* pony along the riverbed, guiding it through the boulder-strewn shallows and around the narrow fissures which indicated patches of loose, crumbling ground. His padded sheepskin saddle had neither horn nor cantle, but he felt surprisingly secure as he sensed the pony responding with an almost uncanny instinct to the subtle movements of his body and limbs.

Behind him, the gauchos in their flat-brimmed sombreros were steering the cattle away from the water's edge. Their cries rose on the air in a series of harsh, mewing sounds.

The gauchos had greeted David warily at first, but David's adeptness in the saddle, a skill the gauchos recognised more than any other, and the adroit way he had brought down a maverick steer, roping its ankle at full gallop, had wrung roars of approval from their throats. "*Acriollado*," they had yelled.

"What are they saying?" David had asked Farrel.

"That you are one of us," Farrel had smiled. "A true son of the Argentine plain."

David had almost forgotten his experience on the bus,

his interrogation at the army camp, and even his imprudent confrontation with the president, General Galtieri. He had apologised to his host the following morning, but Farrel, with the wry humour that seemed to characterise everything he did, had laughed and slapped him affectionately on the shoulder. "Where do you think you are?" he had said. "This is not Russia under Stalin. Here a man may say what he likes, even to *el presidente* himself. Of course . . . ." his eyes twinkled, ". . . he may only get to say it once."

David was delighted to discover that his first impressions of Farrel had been correct. The man was gentle, kind, and filled with an irrepressible sense of humour. He laughed at everything, a full-bodied, deep-throated laugh that seemed to echo around the entire estancia. David could see at a glance that Farrel's wife and daughters adored him and the gauchos, the lean, leathery men of the pampa who occupied the line of ramshackle houses at the edge of the paddock, regarded Farrel with a touching warmth and respect.

The gauchos were quite unlike the Argentines David had seen in Buenos Aires. Small men for the most part, their limbs were thin and wiry, their features jagged and fierce, their skins smooth and brown as old leather. They wore battered sombreros, fringed ponchos, baggy *bombachos* and wide belts studded with silver coins. Each man carried, thrust into the belt at the base of his spine, a huge *facón*, or knife, with a fourteen-inch blade. The *facón* was the gaucho's only true companion, Farrel explained. He used it for everything that mattered in life, eating, working, fighting. A gaucho's *facón* was as sacred as a priest's crucifix. No man would have the temerity to handle the knife of another. And if any did, retribution would be swift and bloody.

"Surely they can't kill each other?" David asked. "Even out here on the pampa, there's still the law."

"Well, most fights these days stop short of murder. Like German duellists, they try to slash each other's faces. But mistakes do happen. Only last month a man was disembowelled in Tostado."

"What about the police?"

"Oh, they'll take action if they can find a witness. But it's amazing how little anyone sees when a fight of honour takes place."

"They're a remarkable people," David said, shaking his head.

"Yes, violence is in their nature. Inbred, so to speak. Their ancestors were outcasts, driven by the law from Buenos Aires and the coastal settlements. They mingled with the indians, hunting wild cattle, breaking the horses left behind by the Spanish conquistadores in the sixteenth century. It was only when Argentina rose against Spain and the gauchos of the pampa mobilised into a unified guerrilla army that their image sank so deeply into the Argentine consciousness. Now of course, we Argentines see the gaucho as a symbol of freedom and manly conduct."

David watched the horsemen waving their sombreros as they steered the cattle through a line of prickly thorn trees, their fierce moustaches rippling in the wind. They looked like remnants from a distant age, he thought.

One of the men reined in his mount and stood upright in his stirrups, his elaborate spurs with their massive rowels arching weirdly from his heels. He turned and shouted something in Farrel's direction. Farrel frowned.

"What's up?" David asked.

"Smoke on the horizon. Somebody trespassing."

Farrel bellowed an order and three of the riders broke away from the herd, following in Farrel and David's wake as, their bodies moving with the loose loping motion of the gallop, they steered their mounts through the thorny scrub towards the smoke on the skyline. Drawing closer, David's nostrils caught the odour of cooked meat.

The scrub gave way, and the five horsemen emerged on an area of open grassland dotted with clumps of spindly trees. At the centre of this clearing a man knelt over an open fire. He was tall, sturdily-built and dressed in pampa clothing, sombrero, poncho and knee-length calf-hide boots. Above the fire a side of beef was gently sizzling, and several feet away David glimpsed the rest of the animal, freshly-skinned and butchered, scattered bloodily across the ground. The intruder's horse, a massive bay, stood hitched under a tree in the shade.

David frowned as he nudged his *criollo* alongside Farrel. "Looks like our friend here slaughtered one of your strays."

Farrel said nothing. His face looked dark and wary, and David detected a deepening in the lines beneath his cheekbones and sensed the tension lying within him. Behind, the three gauchos were muttering uneasily.

"What are they saying?" David asked.

Farrel slowed his pony to a walk. "They recognise this man," he said. "His name is Martin Segunda, known as the Gaucho. He works for the government in Buenos Aires. He is under their protection."

David frowned. "Protection?"

"It means we would be unwise to challenge his presence here."

"But Señor Farrel, he's just butchered one of your cattle."

Farrel shrugged. "We have a saying on the pampa, 'Meat is what remains when nothing else is left.' Every gaucho knows he is welcome to beef if he truly needs it. Besides, Segunda would be a dangerous man to rebuke. He is a professional assassin. His reputation with a *facón* is legendary."

The horsemen reined in their mounts and stood in line, peering down at the man kneeling over the cooked fire. Now that he was closer, David saw that the intruder had an agreeable face, with merry eyes which betrayed a distinct inclination to laughter. He was chewing on a ribbone, and in his free hand he held a *maté* gourd, a small coconut-shaped bowl filled with a bitter herb tea which formed the gauchos' staple drink.

Rising to his feet, Segunda strolled toward them, moving with a curious fluid grace that reminded David of a snake preparing to strike. He was grinning, and there was a tricky little gleam in his eyes that made David feel uneasy.

"Good morning, señor," he said, sucking through the traditional straw from his *maté* gourd and offering it in a gesture of welcome to the first of the gauchos. The man took it from his hand, sipped from the straw in turn and passed it to his nearest companion.

"Señor Segunda," Farrel said in a cool voice, "I am surprised to find you so far from Buenos Aires. I thought the diversions of the city occupied most of your time these days."

Segunda grinned, spreading his hands. "City life amuses me, but only for a time. You forget, this is where I was born. Like Martin Fierro, our great Argentine hero, I must return to the open plain and live as free as the bird that cleaves the sky."

"You surprise me, señor," Farrel said dryly, "I did not take you for an admirer of poetry."

Segunda laughed. "But the ballad of Martin Fierro is an epic, señor. An inspiration to us all."

The *maté* bowl was pushed into David's hand and, blinking quickly, he took a sip through the narrow straw. The liquid tasted hot and bitter. Twisting his face, he offered it to Farrel who silently refused, shaking his head.

David leaned forward in his saddle and handed the gourd back to Segunda. Segunda had noticed Farrel's gesture, but he was still smiling affably. "I butchered one of your steers," he said. "The animal was lame, too badly injured to keep up with the rest of the herd. Killing it was an act of mercy."

"In that case, I am indebted for your thoughtfulness."

Segunda's grin broadened, enjoying the exchange. "You have a visitor, I see."

"That is correct," Farrel said. "This is Señor David Ryker, an American."

Segunda removed his sombrero politely. His dark hair tumbled over his forehead. "You are the *hombre* who befriended the fugitive on the bus last week?"

David was startled. He had thought the incident already forgotten.

Glimpsing his discomfort, Segunda smiled. "News travels fast on the pampa, my friend. One *campesino* tells another. Pretty soon, it is known everywhere."

"It was . . . a simple mistake," David explained, feeling uncomfortable.

"A dangerous mistake, Señor Ryker. Mistakes like that can have a terminal effect."

Segunda used his sombrero to gently fan his cheeks. There was a curious animal quality to the man, a sense of physical presence difficult to ignore and yet, in a strange, almost paradoxical way, it seemed minimised to some extent by his natural elegance, as if Segunda had at some point in his past suffered a split in identity, becoming two distinct individuals, each separate and opposed to the other.

"How long do you expect to remain in Argentina?" he inquired.

"No more than a week or two. I'm sort of in transit," David explained.

"Going where?"

"The Falkland Islands."

"You mean the Malvinas, señor."

"Of course. The Malvinas."

"Then you grace our country with your presence."

"Thank you, you're very kind."

Segunda's smile broadened, his eyes still fixed on David's face. "May you become familiar to us, like an old friend," he added.

"And you, señor," Farrel put in, as if he was trying to divert the man's attention, "how long do you expect to remain on my land?"

Segunda shrugged. "Until tomorrow," he said. "I am taking part in the *jineatada*."

He grinned up at David, his eyes still twinkling. "You know the *jineatada*, señor? It is what you Americans call the rodeo. You must come and watch me ride. I am the finest horseman in Argentina."

"Thank you. I'd like that."

"You too, Señor Farrel. You must bring your charming ladies also. You are all welcome as Segunda's honoured guests."

Farrel bowed his head gravely. "And you in turn are welcome on my land," he said. "Camp as long as you wish, or stay in the gauchos' quarters at the estancia. We wish you luck at the *jineatada*."

"My thanks, señor. May your fortune be as eternal as the sun, and your name be sacred always."

With his face still frozen, Farrel gestured to his gauchos and wheeled his mount, riding off stiffly in the saddle. David glanced once at Segunda who continued to smile affably, the *maté* gourd clutched in his fist, then, twisting his hips, David steered the *criollo* in Farrel's wake, driving his heels into the animal's flanks until he was trotting alongside. Farrel's natural charm had completely vanished and in its place there was an expression of vivid distaste.

"I take it you don't like him very much," David said quietly.

"It is what he represents that I do not like. He is a psychopath. He kills without feeling. During the war against the terrorists, he is said to have murdered many innocent people. He is also said to work for the KGB."

"And yet he seems such a personable man."

Farrel glanced at him coldly. "Do not let his laughter fool you. Segunda laughs because he is crazy. He laughs at everything, even death."

He hesitated a moment, then added: "He is also blessed with exorbitant appetites."

"You mean . . . physical appetites?"

"Yes, he likes the ladies. Considers himself a great lover. But beneath it all, he is a dangerous man, a dangerous *hombre*. I shall be glad when he has left my estancia."

David stared at Farrel wonderingly, surprised at the force of his host's reaction. Ruthless Segunda might be, but it was hard to believe he was a killer. He just didn't seem the type somehow. Too merry, too irreverent. Men with murder on their conscience rarely laughed so easily. Still, there was no mistaking Señor Farrel's feelings and David decided to be prudent, reserving his judgement as they rode the rest of the way back to the cattle in silence.

It was dark when David returned to the estancia. The windows of the massive house were blazing with light and in their glow he glimpsed a car parked on the cindered forecourt, its bodywork thickly coated with dust.

He dismounted and led his pony into the stables, his muscles protesting from the long day's ride. In the darkness of the stalls, he peeled off the layer of sheepskin fleece which coated the saddle-top, the two bars of leather called *bastos* which made up the central frame and the piece of cowhide, the *corona*, which protected the animal's back.

He groomed and fed his *criollo* then, aching with weariness, left the stables and crossed the paddock to the estancia door. He was making his way to the privacy of his room when Farrel's wife, Rosa, called him into the library. She was sitting on the sofa smiling, and David felt his breath catch in his throat as he glimpsed, perched at her side, dressed in a silk shantung suit and cradling a glass of white wine in long, slender fingers, a girl somewhere around his own age with a supple figure, blonde hair held in place by a carelessly-tied scarf and blue mischievous eyes.

"Sorry," he said, "I didn't realise you had company."

"Come in, David," Rosa said cheerfully, "I want you to meet our visitor. This is Miss Anne Danby. She's from the same part of the world you're going to."

The girl grinned. "That's right, I'm a kelper."

"Kelper?" David's lips moved in bewilderment.

"A Falkland Islander," the girl laughed.

"Oh," David replied.

"She's broken down in her automobile," Rosa explained. "Two of our men found her on the highway and towed her back to the estancia. I've tried to persuade her to stay for the night, but she insists on going to the hotel in the village."

"I have to," the girl told him amiably. "It's the only place I can pick up another car. I've been in Corrientes visiting my uncle, but I must be back in the capital by tomorrow. I'm due to return to Port Stanley on Thursday morning."

David was silent, studying her. Beneath the folds of her scarf her blonde hair fell in a luxurious tangle, ending just above her shoulders and her eyes, startlingly blue, formed the focal point for her entire face. Beneath their humour, David detected something he couldn't quite decipher, a hint of promise, of physical awareness which he felt himself responding to.

"I've called the hotel and they've agreed to keep her a room," Rosa put in, "but I'm insisting she stays for dinner. I won't hear of her dining alone in that miserable mausoleum."

"Rosa's right," David said to the girl. "It's a pretty beatup kind of place. Rumour is, the bedbugs gobbled the last three guests whole."

The girl laughed. "You should see some of the places I've slept in. Believe me, when you travel about as much as I do, you can't afford to be choosy."

"Help yourself to a drink, David," Rosa invited, waving toward the cocktail cabinet.

He shook his head, backing toward the door. "I guess I'd better go bathe first. I'm not fit for civilised company, dressed like this. Keep the wine cool for me, I'll be back in twenty minutes."

He glanced at the girl as he ducked from the room, his eyes noting the almost pristine cleanness of her features, the delicate elegance of the cheekbones, the classical curve of chin and throat. How confident she looked, how remarkably assured—not a girl who'd had to struggle in life, you could see that at a glance. Her face carried a kind of poise, of practical containment, as if nothing in the world could possibly surprise her.

If he were honest about it, he thought as he stripped off his clothes in his room and stepped under the shower, totally and resolutely honest, she was probably just about the most exquisite creature he had seen in his entire life. And she was going to the Falklands. Coincidence? Hardly. More like an omen, he told himself, a twist of fate.

David had to admit his experiences with the opposite sex had not been altogether happy ones. He was too damned impetuous, that was his trouble, always had been where women were concerned. That Marti Culpepper from Cincinnati, it had taken him months to get over her. And Elsa Hazelhoff from New York—bad memories, both of them. But neither had invoked such an immediate response, such a direct and unmistakable attraction as the girl now sitting in Farrel's library.

He studied her all through dinner, feeling a host of unfamiliar emotions stirring inside him. For some reason, he seemed incapable of gathering his thoughts, his pathetic attempts to attract her interest floundering into silence almost as soon as they had begun, and he was grateful for Farrel and Rosa who kept the conversation flowing rapidly as one course followed another.

The girl herself seemed oblivious to David's discomfort and chatted away with a complete lack of self-consciousness and an almost artless sincerity David found enchanting. She had been born and raised on Pebble Island, she explained, but her father had sent her at an early age to live with relatives in England where she had spent her formative years. Now she worked as a personal secretary to one of the richest men in the world, Magnus D. Stone.

"The Antarctic naturalist?" David echoed.

The girl peered at him with surprise. "You've heard of him?"

"Well, only through my father. They were in the same business for a while. Oil."

"Yes," the girl agreed. "That's where Magnus made the bulk of his money. Now though he spends his time doing pretty much as he likes. At the moment, he's studying the penguin populations on East and West Falkland."

"Do you travel with him everywhere?" David asked.

"Just about. Sometimes he leaves me behind in London, but not very often."

"It must get terribly wearing, moving around all the time," Rosa suggested.

"Not for me. I love travelling. I suppose it has something to do with being born on an island. I still think of the Falklands as my home, you understand, but they do tend to imbue one with a certain restlessness."

"Have you been in the United States?" David asked.

"Only Manhattan. Magnus has business interests there. He keeps an office on Fifth Avenue. We don't visit it terribly often, but every once in a while some crisis crops up and Magnus has to stop everything and hightail it to New York."

"He's a lucky fellow, your employer," Farrel said. "Not many men can indulge themselves so completely in their private pleasures and interests."

"Well, Magnus has a simple philosophy in life. Enjoy it while you can, he says. And he does have a remarkable capacity for enjoyment. You know, most people, particularly business people, seem to regard him as some kind of snarling ogre, but he's a darling really. He's terribly kind, and very thougtful, and he does have this extraordinary appetite for living."

"Does he take you to the Antarctic?" David inquired.

"Sometimes. I've spent three seasons there. It's a marvellous corner of the world. So beautiful and so empty. It's

Magnus's idea of paradise. He's convinced it's where everyone goes when they die."

She smiled brightly. "I think he regards it as some kind of personal sanctuary. There are no telephones in the Antarctic. No business luncheons either. He's a very important man, you know, on first-name terms with most of the British Cabinet. But that kind of eminence can sometimes be a terrible drag."

David nodded understandingly and lapsed into silence, conscious again of the inexplicable sense of restraint her presence seemed to impose on him, as if her vitality, her verve, touched some chord deep in his psyche, rendering him helpless and inept.

When the meal was over Farrel glanced at his watch and rang the bell.

"I'll get Ramon to run you to the hotel," he said to Anne.

"Don't," David put in hurriedly, blushing when they turned to look at him. "What I mean is . . . I'll be happy to drive Miss Danby to the village. There's no need to trouble Ramon."

Farrel's eyes twinkled. "Why not?" he replied. "Ramon's probably in bed by now anyhow. Take the saloon parked in front of the house. We'll arrange for the local garage to pick up Miss Danby's car in the morning."

The girl thanked the Farrels profusely, scribbling down their address and promising to write. Then she and David walked to the sleek-lined limousine standing on the cindered forecourt.

Driving toward the hotel, he felt his uneasiness at last beginning to fade. The girl's perfume hung in his nostrils.

"You know," he said, "it was quite a coincidence you arriving tonight."

"How's that?"

"Did you know we had Galtieri here last week?"

"The president?"

"He's a personal friend of Señor Farrel's, can you beat that?"

"I had no idea."

David grinned. "He gets kind of uptight when you mention the Falklands."

"You discussed it with him?"

He nodded. "We had sort of a rough-house over who is the rightful owner. Funny thing, at the end of the evening, he invited me to visit the Argentine naval academy on my way back through Buenos Aires."

Her eyes regarded him soberly. "Are you going?"

"Why not? They've got a selection of old maritime wrecks there. Sounds right up my street." He glanced at her. "How long do you expect to stay in Port Stanley?"

"Another month or two at least. Until the weather breaks."

"Maybe we'll see each other then."

"I should think that's inevitable. Port Stanley is a very small place."

"You must find it strange after living in London."

"The Falklands are in my blood," she said simply. "I'm a kelper born, and I'll be a kelper when I die."

"I guess it must be kind of difficult though, with the Argentines wanting to take the islands over."

Her face was a pale blob reflecting the headlamps' glow, her lips slightly parted, revealing the gleam of her teeth through the darkness. He sensed the emotion within her, recognised it for what it was and stayed silent, conscious now of a certain intimacy between them, a kind of tension, honed by their differences.

"Let me tell you something," she answered quietly. "The island where I was born has nothing but sheep. We ranch sheep the way you Americans ranch cattle. The settlement is hardly what you could call a settlement at all, just a few huts, a company store, a schoolhouse which doubles as a games-hall and social-centre. There are no roads, no movie houses, no public transport system. My father has spent his entire life on that island. He's never been to a city, or watched a television set, or glimpsed traffic on a crowded highway, or encountered more than a dozen human beings at one time. But when he talks about 'home' he means a country eight thousand miles to the north, a country he's never seen and probably never will."

"That's remarkable," David agreed.

"He can tell you the name of every player in every British football team, and where that team stands in the British league. He can tell you how they did last season and

what their chances are for the coming year. He can tell you
which shows are playing in London's West End, what the
winter temperatures are, and how the farmers are manag-
ing in the Highlands of Scotland. He can tell you which
programmes are popular on British TV, and where Prince
Andrew spent last summer, and what the price of meat is. It
may sound quaint and silly to an outsider. Illogical, even.
But that's what being British means to the Falkland
kelpers."

"But looking at it reasonably," David insisted, "I mean,
the damned Falklands are practically on the Argentine
coastline."

"That's not true," she hissed. "There are three hundred
miles between them. And don't believe all that flannel
about the British grabbing them by force. We were the
ones who settled there first. We've occupied those islands
for a hundred-and-fifty years."

David was startled by her vehemence. He kept his eyes
on the road ahead, watching the headlamps carve cones of
light through the misty darkness. Christ, he thought, why
do I keep getting caught up in this damned stupid
argument?

"Let me ask you a question," she said. "Where is it you
come from, Texas isn't it?"

"That's right."

"Wasn't Texas once part of Mexico?"

"Lot of Mexicans seem to think it still is."

"Well, try to imagine how you would feel if one day you
woke up and heard on the radio that the United States had
decided to hand you back."

"I guess it would take a bit of getting used to," David
admitted.

He saw the village looming up and felt a sense of relief.
He didn't want to alienate her, so was holding back his
natural responses, hoping they could find some unanimity,
some common bond to build on.

Lights gleamed across the unpaved street from the
windows of the miserable shacks and dowdy rough-walled
ranchos as he slid to a halt in front of the hotel, a sombre
building, grey-concrete and cheerless.

He hesitated. "You know what day it is tomorrow?"

"Tuesday."

"It's the *jineatada*, the rodeo. The whole village closes down. Your chances of picking up a fresh car are practically zero."

"Damn," she whispered, compressing her lips.

"Why don't you stay over one more night? Let me take you to the festival."

"I can't. I have to catch the plane on Thursday."

"What the hell, you'll probably miss it anyhow. It's a good day-and-a-half's drive to Buenos Aires."

She studied him in silence, her lips relaxing into a gentle smile. "You're a very persuasive man," she said.

"I have to be. You're getting away."

She chuckled. "Very well. One more day. I'll telephone Magnus in the morning."

He felt his spirits rise, as if he had surmounted some difficult obstacle with unexpected ease. "I'll pick you up at noon," he said.

She stopped him reaching into the back for her suitcase. "Don't bother. I can manage perfectly well from here."

He watched as she clambered from the car and began to walk toward the hotel entrance, her movements fluid and graceful beneath the swish of her short silk skirt. Halfway there, she stopped and put down her bag. Puzzled, he watched her turn back, strolling toward him with an enigmatic smile on her face. Opening the door, she leaned in, her features lost in the shadows, the fragrance of her perfume lingering tantalisingly in his nostrils as her fingers, light and delicate, held his chin. Then to his utter astonishment, her lips fastened on his, kissing him firmly, expressively, opening moist and receptive against him until his body throbbed. He was panting when she let him go.

"Tomorrow," she whispered, her face obscured by darkness.

Startled, he stared at her in silence, unable to speak. Then the car door slammed and she was gone.

David undressed for bed, his mind in turmoil. Something had happened to him he couldn't quite put a name to, a kind of lightness, of transcendence, of things changed in some indefinable but impossible-to-ignore way, and he was conscious of the change fermenting within him, affecting his emotions, the thought-processes of a lifetime. He must be losing his wits, he decided. The girl was exquisite, no question about it. She excited him more than any girl he had ever known. And the way she had kissed him back there, without any warning. Just came back and did it, and like she really meant it, too. But it was crazy losing his head over this. They had only just met. He had to keep a sense of perspective.

He slept badly, despite the arduousness of the day. There was a warm insistent sensation in the region of his loins, and the memory of the girl's face, the fragrance of her perfume, the touch of her mouth against his kept intruding on his senses.

Sometime in the early hours, he woke with a start to hear men shouting in the darkness outside. Puzzled, he threw back the sheets and reached for his pants. Barefooted, he padded over the cool tiled floor, opened the door and peered across the shadowy lawn. Lights flickered among the gaucho quarters, and dimly through the darkness he could see figures moving about.

A flashlight beam slid along the estancia wall and he saw Miguel, the ranch foreman, coming toward him, a *facón* in his hand. Miguel was dressed in *bombachos* and boots, but he was naked from the waist upwards.

"What the hell is going on?" David demanded.

"Do not trouble yourself, señor," Miguel mumbled apologetically, lowering the flashlight. "One of the hands discovered a stranger lying with his wife. The man escaped into the darkness. It is a matter for the *campesinos* alone and does not concern you."

David hesitated. Miguel's face was impassive behind his fierce moustache, but David sensed the outrage in the man, part of a universal anger against the profaning of things which, in the gauchos' world, should have remained inviolate. David knew that if the transgressor were caught, his punishment would be swift and brutal. He nodded thoughtfully and, stepping back, closed the door and returned to bed. In many ways the Argentines were like children, he decided. In Buenos Aires they had seemed so worldly and sophisticated. But here on the pampa they settled every issue, every dispute, in the most direct and physical way.

He lay for a while with his eyes closed, listening to the commotion outside. The voices sounded harsh and discordant, calling to each other through the darkness. He was on the point of nodding off when he heard someone tapping lightly on the door. Puzzled, he crossed the floor for a second time and drew back the bolt. Then he blinked in surprise. Framed against the starlight stood Martin Segunda, totally naked from head to foot. His dark hair looked wild and dishevelled and he was laughing silently, his teeth gleaming in the fractured light.

"What the hell?" David began.

"I am sorry to trouble you, *camarada*, but if these vulgar fellows catch me, they might take it into their heads to cut off my *cojones*. Think what a waste that would be for a handsome stallion like myself. I take it you are suitably neutral in this matter?"

"Come on in," David grunted, moving back.

Segunda slipped swiftly into the bedroom and David locked the door. He checked to see that the curtains were drawn, then switched on the bedside lamp. Segunda was leaning against the dressing-table, his shoulders shaking with suppressed mirth. His body was strong-muscled and powerfully proportioned, the skin hairless except for a coating of dark curls just above the breastbone. The darkness of its hue emphasised the sinews rippling across his chest and shoulders. An ancient scar ran from his ribcage ending just above the naval. Seeing the man in such a predicament it was harder than ever to believe Farrel's story that he was a trained assassin.

"How did you know this was my room?" David demanded.

"I saw you talking to Miguel, the foreman."

"Are you the one who seduced the ranch-hand's wife?"

Segunda shrugged cheerily. "Some women are just too beautiful, *amigo*. It would be a crime against nature if a man did not bow to his baser instincts."

"That's why you came then, to meet this woman?"

"Not at all. I told you this morning, I am taking part in

the *jineatada*. But it is the first duty of every *domador* to
see that his mare is properly serviced."

David grunted and sat on the bed. Segunda's hilarity was
probably a madness of sorts, a self-induced mania wrought
by the danger of the moment. It seemed strange to find the
man in such close and unexpected proximity. A curious
calmness settled over David. Unlike that afternoon when
he had been caught offguard and thrown into a flurry of
confusion, he now felt he had a certain advantage. "What
do you want from me?" he asked.

"Well, if you'd let me remain in your room for an hour or
two, I would be most grateful. Just until the commotion
dies down. And then . . ." Segunda grinned apologetically, "if you could give me something to cover myself? It is
so undignified hopping around without one's pants on."

"You can use my work jeans," David said, "but they
might be a tight fit. I'm pretty skinny."

Segunda picked up the dusty garment and began to pull
it on. He managed to tug up the zip, but was unable to
fasten the front button across his muscular waist. He had
stopped laughing, but his eyes were still dancing as he
moved back toward the chest of drawers.

"I don't suppose you have a cigar in the place?" he asked,
"I'd give my right arm for a smoke at this moment."

"Cigarettes only, if they're any good."

"Well, they're better than nothing."

"Second drawer. You'll find a pack tucked down the side
of my things. Toss me one too, will you?"

Segunda rummaged about until he found the cigarettes.
He took one out, placed it between his lips and threw the
packet toward the bed. David caught it, lit a cigarette with
the lighter on the bedside table. Then he tossed the lighter
to Segunda.

"I saw you with the girl tonight," Segunda said. "The one
with the golden hair."

David was startled. "You were watching?"

"Of course." Segunda shrugged. "It was necessary. I had
to ensure that the coast was clear."

He paused for a moment, then he said: "You like her, this
girl?"

"Sure, I like her."

"But she makes you a little unsure of yourself, hey?"

"Christ, did it show that much?"

"Not to every observer perhaps, but I am an expert in these matters. I see you are . . . how shall we say? . . . hooked. And why not? What man would not be struck speechless in the presence of such beauty? She has the face of an angel, the body of a goddess. Listen to me, *camarada*, I can help you."

"How?"

"I am a man of the world, a lifelong student of the feminine sex. A few words of wisdom from my lips and your problems will be over."

David sighed. "No thanks," he said. "If I have to play your kind of game, my relationship with this girl isn't going to be worth a damn."

"Ah *compañero*," Segunda said earnestly, "you are really serious about this one."

"Don't be ridiculous. I never set eyes on her before tonight."

"No, no, you are serious, I can tell. This is more than a matter of the *cojones*. It is an affair of the heart."

"Listen, just forget it, okay," David told him wearily.

He leaned back against the pillow, conscious as he did so that despite the bizarre nature of the circumstances, it was no accident that Segunda had chosen his door out of all the others. The Gaucho had come for a purpose, David felt certain—he was standing now returning David's scrutiny with his own, his thin lips twisted into their crooked, inevitable grin, his eyes shrewd, appraising, calculating.

"You really believe in pushing things to the limit, don't you?" David said.

"What other way is a man to live?" Segunda asked innocently.

"Have you never heard of moderation?"

Segunda chuckled. "I hate doing things in moderation. Takes all the fun out of life." He paused, inhaling slowly and letting the smoke curl from his nostrils, than he added: "In any event, you believe in pushing things pretty close to the edge yourself, *compañero*."

"How's that?"

"That business with the fugitive last week, what was his name? Hugo Pinilla?"

Suddenly, everything clicked into place. Of course, David thought. Pinilla. Segunda worked for the security forces. The woman had been a diversion, nothing more. He had come because it was his job to come. He had come to see David.

"Don't look so surprised *camarada*," Segunda said, "The whole pampa knows what happened. You're a celebrity. Not many men can claim to be the companion of such a notorious traitor and still be around to talk about it afterwards."

He grinned, peering down at his cigarette, his eyes focusing intently on the fiery tip as if somewhere in its crimson glow he might glimpse the secret of the universe. "That is what I would like you to do," he whispered. "Talk about it. I would like you to tell me everything you can remember, everything you discussed during your conversation that day."

"Why should I?" David demanded.

"Because I am a student of human nature. Because I would find it fascinating to hear what Colonel Pinilla had to say about our wonderful country. And because, since circumstances have forced us together *camarada*, we have precious little else to do."

David was quiet for a moment. There was no denying the man had charm, but he had something else besides—a streak of ruthlessness David could feel right down to his toes. And against such a powerful physique, he knew his own lean frame would stand little chance if it came to a rough-house.

"You're some kind of government agent, aren't you?"

"Farrel told you that?"

David nodded.

"Well," Segunda sighed, "I could tell at once the man disliked me. I thought I was such a engaging fellow too."

"He said the security forces used you to eliminate undesirables."

Segunda laughed out loud. "Ah, we are such a romantic race, we Argentines," he declared. "We cannot accept reality without a little embellishment. I confess I do work in a small way for the security services. I am not, however, an assassin, as you call it. Do I look like a murderer, *compañero?*"

"I don't know," David admitted honestly. "I haven't known too many murderers in my lifetime."

"But look at the character in these features," Segunda stated, peering at himself in the mirror. "Look at the symmetry, the nobility. How can you believe such stories about a face like that?"

David grunted. Beneath Segunda's frivolous manner, he glimpsed an air of resolution, a totality of purpose that refused to be impeded.

Leaning forward, David gently tapped the ash from his cigarette. "Is that the real reason you came here tonight, to question me?"

"Let's say one of the reasons. I like to mix business with pleasure."

"In that case, you're wasting your time. I already told everything I know to the authorities. You'll find it all on the file."

"But this man Pinilla, he said nothing about his job?"

"Not a thing. In fact, he spoke very little about himself. Mostly he asked questions about America."

"Did he tell you what he was doing in the army?"

"I didn't even know he was in the army until the soldiers grabbed me."

Segunda smiled. "Nevertheless, just for me, would you mind going through it once again?"

David hesitated. He did not feel angry, that was the surprising thing. There was a charm to Segunda he found vaguely disconcerting, and though he recognised it for what it was, he still could not help liking the man.

He's got one hell of a nerve, David thought. On the other hand, he himself had nothing to hide. And if the authorities were unhappy with his story, he might be well-advised to try and convince Segunda at least that he'd been telling the truth. It was one thing standing on dignity, but dignity wouldn't help much after he left Farrel's protection. It was two days' drive to Buenos Aires, another day before he picked up the flight to the Falkland Islands. Plenty of time for a man to disappear . . . a roadblock; a knock on his hotel door in the middle of the night; whisked away in an unidentifed car, no word, no trace, no witness . . . Better to co-operate while he still could, he thought, and sighing, he sat forward on the bed, crossed his legs and began to speak in low methodical tones, outlining everything he could recall of his journey with Hugo Pinilla.

Segunda listened in silence, his face impassive. When David had finished, he began to ask questions and David answered as best he could, shaking his head when Segunda pushed too persistently. By the time their conversation had ended and Segunda was finally satisfied, the noise from the gauchos' quarters had faded into silence. David drew back the curtains, surprised to see that dawn was already breaking. "You'd better get out of here," he said. "Another half-hour and it'll be daylight."

"I can never thank you enough for the gift of the trousers," Segunda told him. "It is so unseemly to be seen wandering along the road with one's private parts jangling."

"Just remember to stay out of ladies' bedrooms. Especially the married ones."

"It is a cross I have to bear," Segunda told him seriously. "Wherever I go, women adore me, and I am bound by destiny to satisfy their lascivious natures."

"Well, everybody's got a problem," David said. "I guess that's yours."

He opened the door and Segunda eased into the gathering dawn. He paused for a moment, peering around, then with a quick backward wave slipped cautiously along the side of the estancia.

David walked back to the bed and lay down, tugging the sheet around his neck. It was five-thirty in the morning. Another six hours before he saw Anne again. The anticipation made his spirits lift.

Closing his eyes, he slept.

FOUR

The throb of guitars was like a hypnotic chant on the hot afternoon air. Tents had been erected across the massive field, and people wandered among them, peering at the displays of baubles, brooches, jewel-encrusted *facóns* and hand-woven lariats laid out for their approval, their voices mingling with the music to create a constant babble of indecipherable sound. At the far end where the tents finished, an enormous arena had been carefully fenced off, and here gauchos in gaily-coloured costumes entertained the spectators with daring displays of horsemanship, mounting and dismounting at the gallop, standing upright in their saddles or hanging beneath their animals' bellies.

David was filled with a sense of excitement heightened by the hubbub of the shuffling throng. His night-time encounter with Segunda was forgotten. In the pristine brilliance of the afternoon, it seemed like a vague dream he wasn't even sure had actually happened. Wearing his best jeans and sports shirt, he had picked up Anne at twelve o'clock, his heart thumping wildly as she'd walked into the hotel lobby looking fantastic in a pair of hip-hugging denim pants and a fringed cowboy jacket that did little to tone down the lines of her lithe figure.

Now, walking beside her through the crowd, he was conscious again of that curious intimacy between them, a feeling born not so much out of personal contact but from a kind of mutual awareness that was largely instinctive. He felt elated, as if something had started inside him he couldn't control.

They stopped at a makeshift stage on which dancers in

71

scarlet tunics or flowing white robes were stamping their
feet to the frenetic rhythm of the guitars.

"They're re-enacting Argentina's war of independence,"
Anne explained. "The dancers in red are meant to represent imperialist Spain. The white robes stand for the purity
of freedom."

He smiled. "How come you know so much about the
Argentines?"

"I've spent a lot of time here over the years. Don't forget
it's a staging post between Britain and my homeland. I like
the Argentines, they're wonderful people."

"I like them too," David admitted.

A group of gauchos sat gambling in the shade, their
swarthy faces deeply sombre in the seriousness of the
moment as they passed a *maté* bowl from one to the other,
taking it in turns to sip through the narrow straw. Children
watched them with solemn eyes.

"I'm so glad you brought me here," Anne said. "I'd hate
to have missed it."

"Well, to tell the truth, it wasn't an entirely unselfish
gesture. I was kind of hoping you might return the
compliment."

"How's that?"

"In a week's time, when I come down to the Falklands, I
thought if you're still at Port Stanley you might show me
around."

She laughed. "That won't take long. You could lose the
whole of Port Stanley in Times Square."

"Just the same, you can fill me in on the local colour. You
know . . . which bars to drink in, which women to avoid,
that sort of thing."

She chuckled. "You have a very romantic idea of where
you're going," she said. "I hope it doesn't come as too much
of a let-down."

Casually, he took her hand, feeling her fingers interlace
in his. The touch of her skin sent a thrill up his forearm.
"Want something to eat?" he asked.

She nodded. "I'm ravenous."

They found a food van and David ordered two kebab
slivers and a couple of bottles of beer. As they chewed
hungrily, standing together in the sunshine, they heard a

series of roars from the direction of the arena. "Looks like the bronco-busting's started," David said.

"Oh, don't let's miss it."

"Plenty of time. It'll go on well into the evening."

He watched her eating wolfishly, wondering at his reaction to her, aware that he was probably behaving like a fool yet somehow unable to help himself. Oh, she was a delectable creature all right, and there was a curious vitality in her face, a kind of electric magnetism that was impossible to ignore. He knew beyond any shadow of doubt that he wanted her, not just physically, but mentally and emotionally too.

"What are you looking at?" she asked, her eyes crinkling at the corners.

"Just you."

"Well, I hope you're satisfied."

"If you want to know the truth, I was thinking how beautiful you are."

"How very American."

"It's American to think you're beautiful?"

"It's American to say so. An Englishman would be far too reserved. Well, I think you're beautiful too. Much too good-looking for comfort, in fact."

He laughed. "Enough to fall for me?"

"I might. If the circumstances were right."

"What about now?"

"Too early to say. I'd have to know you better first."

"Well, that's exactly what I had in mind."

She smiled at him roguishly, her eyes twinkling. "I know what you had in mind. It shows all over your face."

"Am I that easy to read?"

"Men. You're all the same. Like an open book."

He grinned. "Biology, I think they call it."

"I've heard it called a few other things too."

He took a sip of beer, feeling the cool liquid spreading through his stomach and when he looked at her again, her smile was gone. She was watching him soberly, her face deadly serious.

"What's wrong?" he asked.

"I was wondering if you would tell me something."

"Try asking."

"You remember last week, when you were on your way to visit Señor Farrel?"

"Sure."

"You sat on the bus next to a man called Hugo Pinilla."

David felt a cold pall gathering in his chest, a kind of sick feeling starting deep in the pit of his stomach and funnelling upwards. The magic of the moment vanished abruptly. "How do you know about Hugo Pinilla?" he breathed.

"It doesn't matter how I know. All that matters is . . ." She broke off and sighed, shrugging her shoulders. "You've got to tell me everything he said to you during that bus ride."

"For Christ's sake, what the hell is this? I hold a brief conversation with a total stranger and everywhere I go, people want to know exactly what we talked about."

"Please, David. It's important, really."

He glared at her. "That's why you stayed today, isn't it? It had nothing to do with the *jineatada*. It was Hugo Pinilla you cared about. When you broke down outside Señor Farrel's estancia, it was no accident."

She sighed. "You're right. The breakdown was a put-up job. I had to find some way of getting to you."

"Well, forget it, lady, you're wasting your time. Everything I know is already on the interrogator's report. You can tell your intelligence friends you've drawn a big fat zero."

He stormed into the crowd, to control the anger rising inside him. God, what a fool he had been. She had played him like a salmon on a line, using every miserable trick she knew, every subtle nuance of expression, every glance, every sly little lift of the eyebrow.

She hurried after him, her cheeks bright with concern. "Don't get upset," she pleaded. "You're right, I did lie in the beginning. But I swear I'm not a government agent."

"Who are you then?"

"Let me talk, please. It's terribly important."

"Okay, go ahead and talk."

"Not like this. At least slow down a bit. You're too angry to listen."

He slackened his pace, turning back toward her, ignoring the jostling throng who lurched against him from behind. "I warn you," he grunted, "it'd better be good. I don't like being treated like a fool."

She brushed back a curl that had fallen over her face, and he detected in her eyes a sudden gleam of anxiety as if she half-feared the truth might constitute a betrayal of sorts. "I wasn't lying about my background," she said. "I really am personal secretary to Magnus D. Stone. But Magnus is more than just a wildlife enthusiast. He's the only man in England who knows what's going on down there."

"Antarctica."

"The South Atlantic."

"You'd better explain that. I'm kind of slow on the uptake."

She sighed. "At the end of the month, British and Argentine delegates are meeting in New York to discuss the future of the Falkland Islands."

"So?"

"What the British Foreign Office doesn't know is that Argentina has already drawn up plans for a full-scale invasion."

David snorted. "You're nuts."

"I'm telling you the truth. Colonel Pinilla was in charge of security, he knows the full details. Magnus . . . that is, my employer persuaded him through an intermediary to inform the British Embassy in Buenos Aires. Unfortunately, the secret police placed the building under heavy guard."

"You're saying that this Hugo Pinilla, this senior Argentine officer, was prepared to reveal everything?"

"I know how unlikely it sounds. But you have to consider one very important thing. In 1978, Colonel Pinilla's only daughter disappeared off the streets of Buenos Aires. She was picked up during a terrorist purge and taken to the notorious naval academy. There she was raped, sodomised, and subjected to several days of intensive torture. Such things were common place in Argentina during the dirty war of the seventies. Pinilla realised what had happened, of course. He used his influence to discover her whereabouts, not an easy task in those days when the secret police were virtually a law unto themselves. He managed to trace her eventually, but by then he was already too late. She'd been shot and buried in an unmarked grave deep in the pampa.

Pinilla almost went insane. He'd doted on that girl, and
when the truth gradually materialised, he had to be placed
in hospital for a while. By the time he came out, he had one
aim in mind. The overthrow of the Argentine government.
Pinilla isn't pro-British by any means, he wants the
Falklands to be Argentine too, but he's willing to postpone
that event for a chance to usurp the military junta. He
believes the man who approached him, Magnus Stone's
agent, was a member of the Montenero guerrilla movement. When Pinilla failed to break through to the British
Embassy, he took refuge in La Boca, the old waterfront
district, with his bodyguard Luis Masetti. The police
discovered them there, and Masetti was killed. Pinilla
managed to escape in the confusion. He was heading for the
border when his bus was halted at an army roadblock. You
know the rest."

David was silent for a moment. He began to walk again,
thrusting his hands into his trouser pockets. Anne followed
at his side.

"How does your employer come into this?" David
demanded.

"He's been travelling to the Falklands for years. He loves
those islands as much as I do. He's done his damndest to
make the British Foreign Office aware of what's going on,
but they simply won't listen. Colonel Hugo Pinilla is the
only physical proof we have that Argentina intends to go to
war."

Pursing his lips, David watched the crowds in front. At
last the puzzle was beginning to make sense. The police
interrogation. Segunda's visit. Even Galtieri's remarks at
the dinner table. Suddenly, he knew the girl was speaking
the truth.

"What do you want from me?" he asked.

She hesitated. "We want you to find out what happened
to Hugo Pinilla."

"You're kidding."

"You are our only source. It's possible they've killed him,
of course. But it's equally possible he's still alive, hidden
away somewhere in custody."

"But why me?"

"Galtieri invited you to the naval academy, didn't he?

That's where they interrogate their political prisoners. Somebody down there must know something. Scout around, ask a few questions."

"Aren't you forgetting something? I'm a neutral, remember?"

"Too neutral to avert a war?"

"You really think Hugo Pinilla can do that?"

"If we can find him, if we can present him to the British Foreign Office, they'll be forced to sit up and take notice."

David filled his lungs with air, his fury settling. A strange emptiness had gathered in his stomach, but with it he sensed another emotion, a feeling of relief, of thankfulness that at long last the puzzle was a puzzle no longer. Now he knew what everyone was getting so excited about, and with the knowledge came a new awareness. What the hell, there was no harm done. His pride had been a little dented, he'd been made to look like a fool, but it wasn't the first time and he reckoned it wouldn't be the last. The girl had tricked him expertly, had laid her trap, baiting it with the oldest lure in the world, but already his resentment had given way to a feeling of wry amusement. It was impossible to remain angry with this girl. Segunda was right. She had him hooked.

He was asking for trouble, of course, getting involved again. He'd sworn he wouldn't do that. But he couldn't turn her down, not really. And after all, where could the harm lie? A few innocent queries. A word dropped in the right ear. Nothing subversive, nothing sinister. They all knew he had met Pinilla. A discreet inquiry about his whereabouts could hardly be construed as a crime against the state.

He nodded slowly. "Okay," he agreed. "I'll see what I can do."

"You won't regret it," she whispered, her smile brightening. "Do me this one favour and I promise you a look at the Falklands you'll never forget."

"Just one thing I want you to promise. Don't ever lie to me again. No matter how difficult it might seem, I want you always to tell me the truth."

"I give you my word," she breathed.

A sudden roaring noise came from the crowd in the arena. It rose on the air, swelling into a mighty crescendo.

Through the clamour, David heard the voices merging into an obsessive chant, one name repeated over and over again: "Segunda, Segunda, Segunda, Segunda, Segunda . . ."

"What's wrong?" Anne asked, scanning his face.

"Come on," he snapped, grabbing her arm. "I've got to see this."

They hurried down to the arena, squeezing through the jostling crowd. Near the fence-rail, a small group of *campesinos* stood around a horse tethered to a solitary post. The animal's head was covered by a blanket, a padded skeepskin strapped to its spine. From the direction of the competitors' tent a man was walking toward the middle of the ring dressed flamboyantly in sequined jacket, baggy *bombachos* and calf-hide riding boots. From his wrist dangled a short *rebenque*, a leather quirt. He moved with a delicate grace that belied his powerful musculature and, as he strode into the centre, the voices of the crowd swelled to a deafening intensity: "Segunda, Segunda, Segunda, Segunda, Segunda . . ."

For a moment, the figure stood quite still, then he threw back his head and hurled both arms dramatically into the air. The crowd went wild and David smiled to himself. My God, how the man loved to show off.

When he had finished acknowledging the applause, Segunda turned and strolled toward the blanketed horse tethered at the ring-side. The small group of *campesinos* watched him approach through implacable eyes. Reaching the twitching animal, Segunda eased his *facón* out of the sash at his waist and handed it gravely to the leading *campesino* then, without a moment's pause, he leapt lightly into the makeshift saddle, gathering the reins in his left hand.

He nodded to the men beneath him, and in one swift motion the horse was untied from the hitching post, the blanket whipped from its head. For almost a full second it stood there, legs trembling, nostrils quivering, ears laid back along the line of its mane. Then in one spectactular motion it arched upwards, its head corkscrewing in a vicious curl. Miraculously, Segunda remained aloft. The animal twisted into a series of violent shuddering lunges designed to unseat the strange creature clinging to its back, but Segunda hung stubbornly on. He seemed almost a part of the horse itself, his left hand gripping the reins, his right flung outward to maintain his balance, the *rebenque* flapping furiously from his wrist. His body swayed and dipped with a graceful fluidity as the mount hurtled around the arena in a frenzied effort to dislodge him. David whistled in admiration.

At last the signal bell rang and, without waiting for the relief riders, Segunda leapt lightly from the saddle, leaving the horse to go bucking crazily toward the opposite side of the arena. As the crowd roared its approval, he strode majestically to the centre and stood once more with his arms outspread, his nostrils flared, his lips drawn back in a grin of pure ecstasy.

David shook his head in wonder. Segunda might be a raving egomaniac and an extrovert of the worst order. He might be a Casanova and libertine who seduced other men's wives without a trace of moral conscience. He might even be, as Farrel claimed, a vicious assassin who murdered with neither fear nor favour. But one thing nobody could argue with.

The man could ride.

The rain hit them as they were driving home in the early evening. There was no warning. David noticed a strange whirlwind kicking up the dust on the unpaved roadway then, as he was in the process of running his hand across the windshield, the downpour came in the blinding deluge that almost stopped their vehicle in its tracks. Never in his life had David seen a thunderstorm like it. The heavens seemed to descend and wrap themselves around the earth. Startled, he struggled to see through the glistening windshield. The wipers were having no effect at all. "God, will you look at this," he croaked.

A flash of lightning split the air, then another, and suddenly the whole pampa was resounding in a reverberating explosion of sound.

"It's like the end of the world," Anne exclaimed, her face pale and breathless. "Ought we to stop for a while?"

David had already decided it was the only possible course. It was pointless driving when he couldn't see an inch in front of his nose. The rain was pounding the Jeep so hard he was afraid it might tear the canvas covering from the roof. He swung the wheel to the right, desperately peering through the blinding sheets of moisture for the roadside. Suddenly, he felt the vehicle lurch. "Christ," he gasped, "the rain's churning the dust into a sea of mud. We're stuck."

Anne was peering out at the adjacent ditch. "Look at that," she whispered.

Leaning across, David squinted through the side window. He could see water swirling by in a furious torrent, boiling into a frothing maelstrom which filled the slender channel almost to the rim. They were perched above it, sagging precariously.

"We can't stay here," David said. "If the jeep turns over, we'll probably drown."

"There's a light ahead," Anne said, peering through the windshield.

David followed her gaze. Dimly, through the water-logged glass, he could see an orange glow rippling and undulating in the distance. "Probably a rancho," he decided. "Can't be far. Twenty or thirty yards maybe. We're going to get drenched, I'm afraid."

"Better drenched than drowned."

"Okay, when I open the door, run like hell."

He reached across, pressed down the handle, and watched Anne tumble into the downpour. He followed her in an instant, gasping instinctively as his feet slithered in the ankle-deep mud. Water surged around his lower calves frothing against the vehicle's wheels. The road had turned into a seething river. In front, Anne was battling against the torrential waves of rain driving savagely into her face, her shirt and jacket moulded to her frame. He saw her stumble and, reaching down, dragged her to her feet, mud coating the front of her upper jeans.

The rain seemed like a solid wall. It was almost impossible to breathe for whichever way David turned his head, the watery pellets drove remorselessly into his nostrils.

Gripping Anne's arm, he struggled toward the glimmer of light, his clothes already sodden. Through the curtain of grey, he watched the building gradually take shape, not a rancho as he had supposed, but a wooden two-storey chalet with a wide verandah and a painted sign outside. A *boliche*, he thought, a grocery store-cum-tavern.

They stumbled up the steps and through the open doorway into the bar. The room was deserted, its bare wood floor scattered with empty tables and chairs. Bottles lined the polished gilt mirror on the rear wall and the lamps were blazing, though each time the lightning flashed they flickered alarmingly, and the noise of the rain on the metal roof sounded like a continuous fusilade of machine-gun fire.

"Anybody home?" David bellowed.

There was no answer. Water oozed from their clothing and spread around their feet. He looked at Anne, blowing moisture drops from the tip of his nose. Her blonde curls were hanging down both sides of her face in soggy strands. Impulsively she giggled.

"Hello," David shouted again, "is anybody here?"

Feet scuffled in the passageway outside and the *boliche* owner came through the door in the rear. He was a big man, fleshily built, with a large hanging belly and a drooping moustache. He wore a checked shirt, dark pants, and a grey bartender's apron. His eyes peered at David and Anne inquiringly, noting their bedraggled condition. "Señor?"

"Our car's stuck down the road a-piece," David said. "It looks as if we'll have to remain until the storm is over. Any place we can dry ourselves?"

The *boliche* owner studied them silently for a moment. "I can rent you a room," he offered. "It is not very special, but it has its own bath. You can bathe in there, and I will hang your things in the kitchen by the stove. They should be dry by the time you are ready to leave."

David hesitated, glancing at Anne. She made no attempt to protest.

"Good," he said, shaking the drops from his hair. "That sounds just fine."

The room was small and primitively-furnished, but the bath, ancient though it looked, was blessed with an endless supply of hot water.

"I will get you my son's robe," the *boliche* owner promised, "and one for the lady also."

"Thank you," said David. "You're very kind."

When he had gone, they looked at each other and started to laugh. Anne sat on the solitary bedside stool, her shoulders shaking uncontrollably. The sound of the plumbing made weird wailing noises which echoed through the building, mingling eerily with the thunder of rain on the roof above. "Not exactly the Ritz," David said.

"Better than that infernal Jeep. Who's first in the tub?"

"Flip you for it."

"Okay."

Grinning, he took out a coin and tossed it into the air. "Heads or tails?"

"Tails," she called.

He shrugged ruefully. "You win. I'll wait for the robes to arrive."

He heard her singing in the bath as he sat by the window peering into the storm. She did not sing very well. It had been a funny sort of day, he thought. A lot had happened in a surprisingly short time, enough to shake a man out of his peace of mind, make him wonder if there was anything in the world he could truly rely on. The business of Hugo Pinilla, he should have seen that coming, should have realised from the beginning the girl was just playing him along. Still was, when you came right down to it, only now he didn't care any more, now he wanted to be manipulated, enjoyed the sensation, revelled in it.

Then there was the rain, and this decrepit old hotel room. A compromising situation, in the happy Victorian phrase. Or might have been, if it hadn't been so damned funny. That was the story of his life. Whenever he steered a girl into the vicinity of a bedroom, they ended up laughing. Every time.

There was a knock on the door. It was the *boliche* owner's wife. "I hope these will do, señor," she smiled, pushing the robes into David's hand. "My son is rather a large man, but if you pull the belt very tight, perhaps you will not, after all, look like a sack of potatoes."

"They'll do just fine," David grinned. "We'll send our damp clothes down later."

He tapped lightly on the bathroom door and easing it ajar, pushed the two robes through the narrow opening. Ten minutes later, Anne came out smiling, drying her hair with the towel. She was wearing the *boliche* owner's housecoat which was clearly at least three sizes too big for her, but in spite of that, she still looked delectable, David thought, the voluminous folds fluttering tantalisingly around the curves of her firm round figure.

"Your turn," she said. "Water's running."

"I hope it's still hot."

"Well, there've been no complaints yet."

In the bathroom, David stripped off his wet clothes and, sighing contentedly, eased himself into the tub. He closed his eyes and lay back soaking his limbs, listening to the frenetic drumming noises on the roof above. Why, he wondered, couldn't he have been more seductive? Cool and smooth and devastating. Not that women were a problem in his life. He'd always had plenty of lady friends, but in the platonic rather than the sensual sense. That was the tragedy of it. In terms of relationships, girls seemed to view him as the brotherly type, which was all very pleasant and flattering but didn't do a hell of a lot for his ego, or his physical urges.

He dozed for a while until the water began to cool, then he hauled himself out, dried his skin briskly with the faded bathtowel, and pulled on the borrowed robe. Moving through the door, he suddenly stopped in the surprise. Anne's housecoat was draped across the foot of the bed. She herself was lying on the mattress, the sheet drawn up to her chin. Its folds had gathered around the contours of her body, and he could see her nipples pushing out against the flimsy fabric. She propped herself up on one elbow, the sheet falling from her shoulders, revealing the swell of her naked breasts, smiling as she caught his quick intake of breath. When she spoke, her voice sounded deep and husky. "I thought since we'd paid for the room," she said, "we might as well use the bed."

When David woke up, the storm had slackened. It was still raining, but not quite so fiercely. He peered at his watch in the glow of the bedside lamp. It was almost midnight and his stomach was aching with hunger. They had not eaten since early afternoon.

He turned to look at Anne sleeping by his side, her hair spread across the pillow. The sheet had fallen from her shoulders and he could see the line across her chest where the suntan ended and the creamy flesh of her breasts began. He could still recall with a startling clarity the burning coolness of her limbs against his, the all-enveloping warmth as he'd driven himself inside her, the soft mewing sounds which issued from her lips as she'd clung to him, furiously impaled. Watching her now, still sleeping, he experienced a sudden stirring of desire and contemplated waking her up, but decided against it for the moment. Instead, he would try and order some food, and perhaps a flagon of wine. He hoped it wasn't too late.

Easing back the sheet, he slipped from the bed and pulled on his borrowed houserobe. Then, moving as quietly as he could, he left the room and tiptoed along the passage for a moment, peering down. Sitting at one of the tables was a small party of gauchos, steam rising from their saturated clothing. They were talking in low guttural tones to a member of their group, a thick-set, swarthy man with a bristling moustache who was staring beligerently at the wall. The *boliche* owner was wiping down the counter with a damp cloth. His thick face looked bland and unconcerned, but David noticed that his eyes were wary, his movements unusually precise. There was an air of tension in the room that seemed to crackle like an electric charge.

Frowning, David walked slowly down the steps, trying to determine the reason for the strained atmosphere. The *boliche* keeper's wife met him at the foot of the staircase. Her face looked pale, and in her eyes he detected a faint glimmer of fear. "It is better if you remain in your room, señor," she whispered. "There is going to be trouble here."

David looked at her. "What kind of trouble?"

"The *campesino* in the corner, the one who stares so savagely at the wall, he is waiting for the man who has been lying with his wife."

David glanced again at the tiny group at the nearby table. "How does he know the man will come?"

"He knows. A message has been sent. The man will not refuse."

"And when he gets here?"

"Why, then they will fight, señor. The *compesino* must vindicate his honour. That is the gaucho way."

Christ, David thought, we're only two day's drive from one of the most modern cities in the world, and it's like watching a scene from *High Noon*. He was perceptive enough to recognise that as an outsider nothing he could say or do would alter the inexorable nature of the events about to follow, but a feeling of distaste filled him. It seemed grotesque, the idea of two grown men ready to carve each other to bits out of some grisly and exaggerated sense of masculinity. The old *machismo* thing again. He shuddered.

"You must return to your room, señor," the woman urged. "It is not good to witness these things. You are not one of us."

"You're right," David agreed. "But we haven't eaten since early afternoon. I wonder if it might be possible to order some food?"

"Naturally, señor. I will show you a list of what we have."

The woman ducked through the open door at the rear and David heard her rummaging about in the kitchen. The *campesinos* were watching him balefully, their eyes curiously distant, the handles of their *facóns* sticking out beneath their soaked ponchos. The silent one, the enraged husband, went on staring at the wall, his features solid and immobile.

David heard the winny of a horse and footsteps clattering on the verandah outside. Instantly, the party at the table tensed. David glanced at the *boliche* owner. "Can't you call the police?" he whispered.

The man shook his head. "Impossible. The storms have brought down the telephone wires. Whenever it rains in Entre Ríos, the phone system distintegrates."

The footsteps drew closer and David felt his stomach tightening. A board creaked on the porch-front and the footsteps stopped. Then a man appeared in the doorway, his massive frame filling the entire space. Water dripped from

his sombrero, running in a steady trickle to the floor at his
feet. Segunda, David thought.

The Gaucho did not look at him. He was staring at the
party grouped around the table, a crooked smile on his lips
as if he found the situation macabrely amusing. For a
moment, he stood on the threshold, then, still smiling,
moved through the doorway into the bar. Instantly, the men
at the table rose from their chairs and spread out around
the walls. The *campesino* whose wife had been seduced
alone remained seated. He was no longer staring at the wall
but peering at Segunda, his body shaking violently. Moving
with agonising slowness, he pushed back his chair and
straightened to his feet, edging sideways to the centre of
the floor. Neither man said anything, but for a full ten
seconds they stood facing each other, Segunda mocking and
defiant, the *campesino* trembling with rage. David wanted
to cry out, but fear of being drawn unwillingly into the
vortex of violence caused the words to lodge in his throat
and the only noise was the rattle of the rain and the steady
drip from Segunda's sombrero.

Segunda was still smiling, that was the remarkable thing.
He was watching his adversary like a snake, cool, calm,
infinitely dangerous. Suddenly, he laughed. The noise was
quite distinct, and as David stared dry-mouthed, he turned
deliberately and began to walk toward the counter. The
campesino glowered at his retreating back, his eyes filled
with a kind of bleary amazement as if he could not believe
Segunda would do something so fundamentally foolish,
then moving with an almost comic deliberation, he
dropped to a crouch, his hand darting to the handle of his
facón, drawing the blade free in one smooth notion. As the
savage steel glinted in the lamplight, David stared with a
sickly fascination at the scene being enacted in front of him.

Segunda was still strolling easily, the smile on his lips a
little tighter now, his eyes dancing but not with merri-
ment—he seemed instead filled with an almost deadly
awareness, as if every fibre and nerve-end in his body was
stretched to breaking point, honed into a complex alarm
system which surrounded him like a physical force. The
campesino lunged forward, jabbing his blade spear-fashion,
and Segunda moved with a swiftness that was almost a blur.

Without stopping, almost without pausing, his body twisted to the left, turning, his right arm streaking behind him to the small of his back, drawing his weapon in one incredibly fluid motion that was so fast David blinked, not glimpsing the *facón* clearly, seeing only the flash of the blade as it swung upwards, curving in the light, Segunda's body swaying in unison, the whole movement supple and precise like a deadly ballet routine practised over and over again. Something clattered across the ground and a hoarse cry emerged from the *campesino's* throat as he stared in horrified amazement at the stump of his arm, still extended, spouting blood in a grotesque fountain where the hand had been amputated cleanly just above the wrist.

As David sucked in his breath in shock, Segunda, moving with a reflex action that was almost too quick to follow, turned his body toward his opponent, scything his *facón* in a vicious uphand curve that caught the man just above the crotch and opened up his belly almost to the ribcage. The *campesino* hit the floor like a fallen tree, struggling to cram back his protruding entrails with his one free hand. For several moments he lay wheezing desperately, as a terrible shuddering racked his frame. Then, caught in a rapidly widening pool of blood, his body seemed to relax and his features settled into the unmistakable rigidity of death.

A stunned silence filled the room and David felt nausea rippling upwards from his stomach, choking his throat with bile. He wanted desperately to be sick, and his legs seemed to buckle under him like indiarubber.

Segunda alone seemed unaffected by it all. He was whistling a pleasant tune and, almost as if the sound had been a signal, two policemen appeared in the doorway. They stared at the scene with neither surprise nor alarm, and David realised they had been there all along, hiding furtively on the verandah.

"What is happening here?" one of the policemen demanded in an uncurious voice. He was tall with a pock-marked skin.

Segunda shrugged. "I was on my way to the bar for a glass of wine," he said, "when this scoundrel attacked me wickedly from behind. He was probably after the money I won at the *jineatada*. In the interests of self-preservation, I was obliged to defend myself."

The policeman's expression was bland. "You have witnesses to substantiate this?"

Segunda smiled, waving his *facón* at David. "The señor here saw it all."

The horror of the moment had left David dazed and breathless. Still struggling to control his emotions, he glared at Segunda angrily as the policeman's eyes fixed on his. "Is this true?" the man demanded.

David nodded, his features tight with disgust. "It's true he was attacked from behind," he agreed.

Segunda seemed unmoved by David's hostility. He took off his sombrero and laid it on the bar, running his fingers through his thick dark hair. His smile broadened and his eyes danced merrily. "What an astonishing fellow you are, *compañero*," he said. "Wherever I go, I find you there. First you lend me your pants, now you corroborate my story. One way or another, I seem to spend my entire life thanking you."

Letter to Director, South American Division, CIA:
Dear Miles,
    The President is becoming concerned about the proposed naval manoeuvres by Argentina. First reports suggest unusual consignments of weapons and equipment are being assembled at Argentine ports. Also, heavy accumulation of troops and large cargoes of canvas tents. He wants to know if Admiral Isaac is on the level. Can we check? Soonest.

                                        Bill Richter,
                                        Special Assistant

Excerpt from diary of Private Julio Ospina, Second Argentine Army Corps:
Our furlough has been cancelled. We are being transferred to Rosario. It is scarcely possible to think for the clatter of helicopters ferrying guns, vehicles and missile batteries across the water to the ships moored in the harbour. We have been forbidden to telephone our

wives. Manoeuvres, the order sheet says, but nobody believes it. Our sergeant reckons something is in the wind.

The engines changed rhythm as the plane prepared to land. Hugo Pinilla leaned against the hull, his ears adjusting to the faintly increased roar. He was strapped into a bucket seat in line with eight other prisoners, their ankles shackled together by a length of chain secured at each end with massive padlocks. Armed guards squatted along the aircraft's deck, their faces impassive beneath their khaki helmets. At the opposite end of the cabin, slightly removed from both guards and convicts alike, sat three pregnant women, their seat harnesses carefully adjusted to avoid constriction to their swollen bellies. No one had explained what the women were doing here, or why they had chosen to make the trip in such unsavoury company.

Pinilla did not trouble himself with unnecessary questions. His weeks in hospital, locked in a tiny room fifteen feet by ten, his only human contact an occasional nurse or the daily visit by the doctor, had caused him to sink into an habitual introspection. He had lost the ability to communicate, they had driven it out of him, forcing him back into the dim recesses of his own mind.

The wound in his thigh was healing cleanly, though he still walked with a distinct limp. But the scars which would never heal were the ones on his psyche, the lurid memory of the anguished hours he had spent strapped to that terrible torture machine. Now he knew what his daughter Amparo had suffered. The destruction of will. The annihilation of identity. The emergence of a nightmare world where only the pain was real.

Pinilla had thought often of his daughter throughout his weeks of captivity. In the beginning, during the immediate aftermath of her death, he had forced such thoughts from his head, seeing in them the path where madness lay, but trapped like an animal, obliged to fall back on his own fragmented past, he had dwelled longingly on the memory of her face. She had been a beautiful girl, slender and petite, with long hair which she'd worn coiled across her shoulder. Smiling, she was like a child, mischievous and appealing. In repose, she'd assumed the stature of a grown woman. Her entire life had lain before her, and they had destroyed it, senselessly, pointlessly, in a single act of refined violence. Something new had been born in Pinilla the day he'd learned about her death. Hate. It was the system he'd hated, the system which had shattered his life, the centre of his universe. He had tried to fight it, tried to hit back at the faceless creatures who committed such unspeakable acts in the name of society. But he knew now he had failed. The system would destroy him just as it had destroyed Amparo. Trapped in his hospital cell, his mind had sunk into a tortured reverie, filled with remorse at the waste and emptiness of his remaining years.

They had taken him from the hospital at last, and after two days in solitary confinement had loaded him with other convicts on this decrepit old aircraft. He had no idea where he was going, but twice they had put down to refuel and each time the prisoners had been forced to remain in position under the watchful eyes of the guards. The pregnant women had joined the aircraft at the final fuel stop. Unlike the other passengers, they had come aboard without escort, and now sat huddled at the opposite end of the cabin, ignoring the line of wretched men.

The aircraft shuddered as the wheels touched down and Pinilla heard the engines change rhythm again as the pilot taxied in a slow half-circle, bringing the massive machine to a halt. One of the guards unlocked the door and a blast of icy air reached them through the open hatchway. The women were the first to disembark. The prisoners waited in silence, blinking owlishly at the flurries of snow which came dancing through the opening like carelessly-tossed confetti. At last one of the guards unlocked the padlocks on their ankles and the massive chain was drawn free.

At a command, the men rose, unsteady after so many hours in cramped confinement. They moved in line towards the hatch, the chill air scouring their faces. They had been issued with padded jackets and overtrousers for the flight but, in spite of his winter clothing, Pinilla felt the cold biting deep into his vitals. He blinked again as they moved into the open air. Jagged snow-covered mountains surrounded them on all sides. A line of oil-drums marked the route of the narrow runway, and in the foreground Pinilla could see a series of strange towers, their frames criss-crossed with metal girders. Convicts in padded jackets worked under the eyes of armed guards. In the distance, on a saucer of crusted snow, he spotted a massive enclosure surrounded by barbed-wire fences. Watchtowers marked the fences at intervals, and inside the compound sprawled rows of squat wooden huts.

The prisoners were shepherded into line, and with the soldiers flanking them on each side, they began to march toward the waiting encampment.

"Where the hell do you reckon we are?" hissed the man stumbling along at Pinilla's side. Like Pinilla, his hair had been shaved close to his skull.

Pinilla's feet slithered in the snow and he leaned down, gently rubbing his wound with his fingertips. "Hard to say," he grunted. "Somewhere in the Andes probably, judging by those mountain tops."

"That means we must be close to the Chilean border."

"I imagine so."

The man glanced at him eagerly. "If we knew the right direction, we could lose ourselves easily in those peaks."

"You mean . . . escape?"

"I don't reckon on spending the rest of my life in this miserable place; what about you?"

Pinilla stared at the desolate expanse of ice and snow. He had to admit the very sight of such austerity was enough to chill a man's blood. Escape would be something to hold to. An element of hope, sustaining, supporting.

"You're right," he muttered. "It's our only chance."

As they drew level with the metal towers, the soldiers brought the column to a halt, exchanging pleasantries with the workparty guards. The nearmost convict was less than eight yards away, leaning over a pipeline, adjusting one of its connections.

"Hey," Pinilla hissed, "where is this place?"

The man peered up at him, his features broad, Jewish-looking, clumps of white hair sprouting incongruously under the folds of his forage cap. "Camp Digepol," he said.

"How far to the Chilean border?"

The man spat on the ground. Moisture from his breath

had frozen to his beard stubble, turning his face grey from
the nostrils downwards. "Chile hell," he snapped, "you're
in Antarctica."

Pinilla blinked with surprise. Antarctica, he thought
dully. As the column started to move again, his flush of
optimism faded. There was no need to hope, no need to
plan. Even if they eluded the guards, where could they run
to? They were surrounded by cold and emptiness. Escape
was out of the question. They were trapped here until they
died.

The truck rattled through the pampa night. Sitting in the
rear, Ciro Cuellar stared over the driver's head at the
headlamps picking out the road ahead. They had been
travelling for several hours and Ciro was feeling decidedly
tired. He was also feeling depressed. Ever since General
Ramirez had ordered him to destroy HMS *Endurance*, he
had been filled with an air of profound foreboding which
stubbornly refused to be shaken.

The general was sitting beside him now, smoking one of
his inevitable cigarillos. The general reeked of tobacco, day
and night, and it was a wonder to Ciro how he didn't smoke
himself completely to a frazzle, the number of cheroots he
went through.

Perched in the front alongside the driver was a young
man Ciro knew only vaguely. His name was Lieutenant
Ramon Trujillo and he was a pilot in the Argentine air force.
They had picked him up on the outskirts of Buenos Aires
just as day had been fading, and for the past three hours he
had sat staring into the darkness without uttering a single
word.

Ciro did not care for Trujillo. There was a curious
coldness to the man, a haughty disregard for the feelings of
other people. Ciro wished it had not been necessary to
involve someone so demonstrably limited in human emotion in an affair which he himself already regarded with the
deepest misgivings.

Ciro hated the thought of what he was being called upon
to do. Invading the Malvinas, that he understood. Like all
Argentines, he felt that the British occupation of the islands
was a stain on his national pride, but the cold-blooded

extermination of an entire ship's crew, the obliterating of an unsuspecting vessel in the solitary expanses of the Antarctic Ocean, was a different thing entirely. He knew Ramirez felt no better about the affair than he did. He was not an uncompassionate man, he understood the consequences of what they were planning and the knowledge disturbed him deeply but, unlike Ciro, he was, above all else, a realist. For complete success, the Malvinas operation had to be undertaken without interference. The *Endurance* was a threat. She had to be eliminated. There was no other way.

Their truck slowed, and through the darkness Ciro glimpsed lights off to the left. They turned in at a wide gate where MPs in air-force uniform silently checked their papers. Stepping back, they saluted smartly, and the truck rumbled on toward the floodlit area ahead. In the orange glare, Ciro saw lines of aircraft drawn up in orderly rows. Mechanics sat on the wings or crouched beneath the fuselages, servicing the engine interiors.

Their driver swung to a halt on the narrow apron and a man strolled toward them wearing blue dungarees and a pair of heavy workboots. General Ramirez peered at him through the open window. "M'sieur Le Gras?" he inquired politely.

The man nodded and Ramirez clambered from the truck, waving at Ciro and Trujillo to follow. Ciro was glad of the chance to stretch his legs. He inhaled deeply, the odor of diesel fumes lingering in his nostrils.

Ramirez introduced the man in dungarees as Emile Le Gras, a French engineer and missile expert. Clutching a clipboard under his arm, he led them across the runway and into a nearby hangar. Perched among the shadows, Ciro glimpsed the fuselage of a shiny jet fighter.

"Do you know what this is?" the Frenchman asked.

Ciro shook his head. Trujillo, the pilot, stared at the plane impassively.

"It's a Dassault-Breguet Super Etendard," he muttered.

The Frenchman looked pleased, as if Trujillo had just passed some complicated intelligence test. "Good," he muttered, then said it again. "Good."

He led them beneath the aircraft's fuselage. Mounted under the starboard wing, Ciro saw a torpedo-shaped object with a series of sharklike tail fins. Its bodywork had been painted white to contrast with the silver superstructure above it. In the humid atmostphere, beads of moisture coated its metal hull.

"This is it?" General Ramirez inquired with a disappointed tone.

The Frenchman patted the object affectionately. "Do not be misled by its modest size, gentlemen. What you are looking at is the deadliest weapon of its kind in the world. It will revolutionise sea warfare."

"It must be swift," Ramirez warned him, "and above all, silent. At least until the last possible moment."

"Do not worry. This is the perfect instrument for the job you have in mind."

Ciro blinked at the object poised above them. "Will someone please explain what it is we are talking about?" he said.

The Frenchmen smiled. "This is an Aerospatiale Exocet AM 39 anti ship missile," he declared. "It operates at a maximum range of forty-five miles, and is capable of destroying the largest warship from at least thirty miles away. We call it Exocet because it skims the waves like a flying fish, making it difficult to detect and impossible to escape. It carries its own tracking radar and guidance command computer. The steering mechanism is in the rear, the rocket fuel in the mid-section and the explosive warhead just behind the nose. It's what we term a 'fire and forget' missile, which means that once the pilot locks on to his desired objective, the rocket's guidance system will carry it at practically the speed of sound to home in on its target with devastating accuracy."

Ciro stared at General Ramirez, a tight constricting sensation in his throat. "This is what you intend to use against the *Endurance*?"

The general's face was dark and sombre. "We have no choice," he stated. "The attack must be swift and sudden. By the time Exocet appears on the vessel's radar screen, she will have less than one minute to decide what she is looking at. The chances of getting a radio message out in that time are infinitesimal."

"General," Ciro pleaded, "there must be another way. An

act of sabotage perhaps. Just enough to disable the *Endurance* and delay her return to the islands."

The general sighed. Rubbing his nose with his fingertips, he draped one arm around Ciro's shoulders like a friendly uncle or understanding schoolmaster.

"Ciro," he said gently, "please believe me when I tell you we have gone into this a thousand times over. We have exhausted every possibility, every alternative. If there was any way to avert the deaths of these poor men, we would take it without hesitation. But the sabotage idea is simply too risky. Send a commando team into the Antarctic, and they would stand out in that emptiness like a sore thumb. If anything went wrong, the British would know at once who was responsible. The *Endurance* must vanish without trace."

Ciro did not answer. He felt the general's fingers massaging the base of his neck. "Trujillo here will fly the aircraft," Ramirez said. "He is one of our most experienced pilots and is fully trained in the use of Exocets. He will be under your personal command. Since there are no airstrips large enough to accommodate a Super Etendard on the Antarctic Peninsula, Lieutenant Trujillo will have to take off from our air base at Rio Gallegos. That means he will be able to carry just enough fuel for one direct sortie, but with the accuracy of the Exocet, that should be sufficient. The important thing is to establish the exact location of his target and that, Ciro, will be your job. You will fly to our base at Camp Digepol and keep Trujillo informed of the *Endurance*'s position by radio."

Ciro was silent for a moment, staring at the lethal cigar-like cylinder hovering above him. It looked so small and innocent it seemed hard to believe it was capable of destroying an entire ship while the pilot who fired it was still out of vision range. He shuddered instinctively. Even for a man in his profession, the capability of modern weapons seemed terrifying.

"Are there any questions?" the general asked.

Trujillo shook his head. He looked bored with the whole thing. Ciro did not answer. He felt sick and miserable. This wasn't the way to fight a war. The British didn't even realise they were coming. There would be no warning, no declaration of hostilities. Only the missile, abrupt and final. It would be nothing more than coldblooded murder.

Glimpsing the expression on Ciro's face, General Ramirez sighed wearily and turned toward the hangar door, rubbing his hands together. "Let's go to the mess," he said. "Long drives always make me thirsty. I don't know about you two, but I think I can use a drink."

Inside the building's lobby, Ciro excused himself and stepped into the public phone booth. He dialled the number of his home in Buenos Aires and waited, his heart beating wildly, for his wife Tamara to answer. There was no reply. For several minutes he stood listening to the ringing on the far end of the line. Then he replaced the receiver. She had distinctly said she was not going out tonight, he thought. Of course something might have come up. A forgotten appointment. An emergency. Perhaps she'd gone to La Cora's, her friend's? She sometimes did that when she was feeling lonely. Tamara was not the type to sit around alone. She liked people, conviviality . . .

On an impulse, he lifted the receiver and dialled La Cora's number. Her voice came on the line, faint and distorted. "Hello?"

"La Cora?"

"Who is this?"

"It's Ciro. Ciro Cuellar."

"Ciro?" Her tone sounded theatrically bright. "This is a surprise. Where are you speaking from? You sound terribly faint."

"I'm . . . out on the pampa. I just wondered, is Tamara with you by any chance?"

"Tamara? No Ciro, should she be?"

"Oh no, it's just that I couldn't get an answer at home, and . . ."

"She's not at home, Ciro?" La Cora's voice was archly innocent.

Damn the bitch, she's laughing at me, he thought. "No," he said miserably, "she doesn't appear to be there."

"Well, she isn't here, Ciro."

"I see. Well, thanks anyhow."

"If I see her, I'll tell her you've been calling."

"No, don't worry. I . . . I'll phone her myself tomorrow."

"Whatever you say, Ciro. Goodbye."

"Goodbye," he said, and hung up.

He stepped from the booth, feeling angry with himself. What a damn fool he had been. It was just the kind of situation La Cora loved. By this time tomorrow, all her friends would know.

A flash of pain shot through Ciro as he thought of his wife and Segunda. He felt so helpless and ineffectual. If only he didn't love her so much. If only he could throw her out on her ear, tell the two of them to go to hell. But he couldn't. He just couldn't. The very thought of losing her made him almost demented. What a joke life was. You could plan out your future to the most fractional degree, but fate, with a single throw of its dice, could blast your perspective into little pieces.

Sighing, he loosened his tie and strolled through the lobby to the mess beyond.

FIVE

The sun was shining as David came out of his hotel and stood on the steps breathing in the warm scented air. Across the street, he could see the extravagant opera house, the Teatro Colón, the pride of Buenos Aires. Traffic thundered by, modern cars and vintage automobiles mingling with the *collectivos*, the multi-coloured service buses which soothed their passengers with a constant flow of taped tango music. People thronged the sidewalks hurrying to and from the shopping precincts of Florida, Maipu, Esmeralda and the stately Avenue Cordoba. It was an elegant city, Buenos Aires, David thought, a wonderful mixture of European and Latin cultures, with gracious buildings, leafy boulevards, friendly cafés—a remarkable contrast to the emptiness of the Argentine pampa.

He walked down the steps to the massive limousine parked at the kerbside. It carried no numberplates, and a solitary flag danced from its hood. A few passers-by cast curious glances as the uniformed driver saluted smartly and opened the rear door for David to get in. Settling himself comfortably in the seat cushions, he reflected that knowing the right people certainly had its advantages, for scarcely had he made his phone call to Galtieri's office than the car had been sent on the direct orders of *el presidente* himself. Now he was on his way to visit the famous Argentine naval academy and, in an oblique sense, to uncover for Anne's sake whatever information he could on the whereabouts of Colonel Hugo Pinilla.

Three weeks had gone by since Anne's return to the Falkland Islands. Three weeks, David thought. Almost a lifetime. He was already counting the hours till they met again. Bad policy, he knew, wearing his heart on his sleeve. Not the way to operate at all. If he had any sense, he'd keep himself aloof, take things in his stride. Letting a girl know how crazy you were about her made her lose interest, that was the way it went with women. But he couldn't hide his feelings, he wasn't the type. And he couldn't wait for the following morning when he would be flying south to meet her again. He sat back in his seat, watching the driver speed confidently through the mid-morning traffic, enjoying the sunshine, letting his mind linger tantalisingly on the prospect of meeting Anne next day.

Twenty minutes' later, the car drew to a halt outside a massive pink-stoned building which reminded David of the Casa Rosada, the presidential palace. Waiting for him at the top of the steps was a young commander with sallow cheeks and a carefully-trimmed sailor's beard. He smiled as David approached, and held out his hand. "Señor Ryker?"

"That's correct."

"Welcome to the academy. Commander Lavalle at your service. I've been asked to look after you. You'll be glad to know I speak English very well."

"Great," David grinned, "but language is really no problem. I'm lucky enough to be bilingual."

"I understand it's our maritime collection you are anxious to see."

"That's right. According to your president, it's not to be missed."

"Yes, we have quite an assortment of old ships stored at our museum in the academy grounds. If you like, I will sign you in at the security desk and we can make our way directly there."

The formalities were conducted in a massive lobby where statues of Argentine military heroes lined the walls in marbled splendour, then, their footsteps echoing beneath the vaulted ceiling, Commander Lavalle led David along a corridor at the rear and through a pair of swing-doors to the gardens beyond.

The area bordering the building itself had been laid out in the style of a municipal park, with cindered footpaths, elegantly-trimmed lawns and flowerbeds, but beyond the first hundred yards or so the land lay wild and untended, studded with woodland and clumps of tangled underbrush. The lower portion of the grounds, the commander explained, was used for military training purposes, and as if to confirm this a series of explosions rang out and the trees suddenly parted to reveal a cluster of long wooden huts with a large hangar-type building in front of them. Smoke drifted over the sloping rooftops, and as David watched a party of troops, their faces blackened, their frames bulky with weapons, rose from a ditch at the side and hurled themselves through the doorways. The sound of machine-gun fire rattled from inside. The commander grinned at David.

"The *Buzo Tactico*," he said. "These men are the equivalent of the British SAS, commando troops who specialise in anti-terrorist techniques. You are very privileged to watch them in action."

Inside the huts, the rattle of machine-gun fire continued unabated. Smoke was now pouring profusely through the open windows. A shout reached them on the bright morning air, and David spotted an officer in a goldbraided uniform waving angrily from the cover of the bushes. "He doesn't look too happy to see us," David said.

Commander Lavalle pulled a face. "They're a sensitive bunch, these *Buzo Tactico*; they like to keep all their operations secret, even when it's only make-believe. Come, we must move at once to the museum. This is a prohibited area."

In the farmost corner of the estate, set in the open air but surrounded on all sides by large girder support-posts over which tarpaulins could be drawn in bad weather, stood an artificial harbour, specially constructed for the academy's purposes and bristling with ships of every size and description. There were stately coasters which had ridden the straits around Tierra del Fuego, freighters which had ploughed the waters between Uruguay and Brazil, paddle-steamers which had butted upriver carrying food and supplies to the settlers of Chaco and Córdoba, all lovingly preserved and moored along the narrow quay in fascinating array. David's eyes gleamed, and for the next two hours he completely forgot his escort as he wandered from deck to deck, examining fittings, accoutrements, superstructures, emitting murmurs of envious amazement, oblivious to the passage of time.

It was close to twelve when at last the commander glanced at his watch and said: "It will soon be time for lunch. There is someone I would like you to meet."

David looked at him, bringing his mind back to the present with an effort.

"Who's that?" he murmured.

"Our chief intelligence officer. He asked if he might have a word with you."

Wonderingly, David followed the commander back to the academy building where they took the elevator to the third floor. His brain was suddenly sharp and alert. He realised now Galtieri's invitation had not been an entirely hospitable one after all. There had been a deeper, more complicated reason behind it, and he was about to discover what it was.

The intelligence officer turned out to be older than David expected—at least sixty, he estimated, and his air of calm assurance suggested considerable seniority, though it was impossible to determine his rank since he was dressed in civilian clothing. As he welcomed David into his private office, he introduced himself simply as Gonzalo Uceda.

"Please sit down, Señor Ryker," he said, as the commander diplomatically excused himself. "I'm glad to have this little opportunity for a chat before you leave us for the chilly climes of the South Atlantic. They tell me that even when the sun shines down there, the Antarctic winds almost flay the skin from your bones."

David settled himself in the chair and crossed his legs. A new wariness had entered him now. The relics in the museum were almost forgotten. Who else would be more qualified to tell him the truth about Colonel Hugo Pinilla than the man now sitting in front of him?

Gonzalo Uceda leaned back behind his desk, eyeing David pleasantly.

"I trust you had an instructive morning?"

"Exhilarating," David agreed. "Some of those old ships out there would make my employers' mouths water."

Uceda chuckled. "Speaking for myself, I would be delighted to allow your institute to take its pick as a personal gift, but alas, they are not mine alone. They are part of our national heritage."

"I understand that," David said.

Uceda's features grew more serious as he leaned forward and, picking up his pen from the blotting paper, began to play with it absently. His face in repose looked markedly older. "How long do you expect to be in the Malvinas, Señor Ryker?" he asked.

"Hard to tell. It depends on the state of the wreck I'm going to investigate. If it's seaworthy, probably no more than a week. On the other hand, if it needs patching up, I could run into quite an extended stay."

Uceda nodded. "You know, of course, that Argentina has been trying for many years to establish her rightful sovereignty over the islands?"

"I believe I discussed that very point with your president, General Galtieri."

"So I understand. But what about you yourself Señor Ryker? Where do your own sympathies lie?"

"My sympathies?" David echoed with surprise. "I have none. I'm American, a neutral."

"Good." Uceda nodded thoughtfully, tapping the pen against his finger. "Good," he said again. "In Argentina, it is wise to remain aloof from such emotive issues."

"Señor Uceda," David said bluntly, "why have you brought me here?"

Uceda dropped the pen and leaned back in his chair, shrugging lightly.

"It is nothing of importance," he insisted. "It simply occurred to us that since you are visiting the Malvinas, and since you are something of an expert in maritime matters, you might be the perfect man to supply us with certain details, certain pieces of specialist information we require on what is going on down there."

David frowned. "You'd better explain that, señor."

"As you know," Uceda said, "we are at the moment negotiating with the British government on a peaceful solution to the islands' future. However, when one approaches the negotiating table, it is always prudent to have a comprehensive knowledge of the issue under discussion, to be aware of the strengths and weaknesses of one's rival, the strategies likely to be employed, the implications involved."

"You want me to become a spy?"

Uceda laughed out loud. "My dear señor, such a thought never entered my mind. I merely meant that in the interests of international co-operation, you might be prepared to drop me a note from time to time on the number of vessels which visit Port Stanley harbour, their classes and tonnage, their reasons for being there, and—in the case of military warships—the strength and range of their firepower."

My God, the man has gall, David thought, but he was careful to allow no flicker of emotion to cross his face, for though he had not the slightest intention of acting as an informer for Uceda or anyone else for that matter, he realised that if he handled this right, he might uncover the answers he was seeking.

"May I speak frankly, señor?" he asked.

"Please do," the Argentine smiled.

"I understand your concern, but you, in turn, must understand my hesitation."

"I take it you are afraid of upsetting your new hosts, the British?"

"It's more than that," David admitted. "To be blunt, Señor Uceda, your country has an unenviable record in the field of human rights. Even in the United States, we have heard of the *desaparecidos*."

Uceda shrugged impatiently. "You must not believe such rumours. They are perpetrated by enemies of the state in an attempt to discredit our country's government."

"I myself witnessed the arrest of a gentleman who fell foul of your security police. To my knowledge, he has not been seen again." David paused. "You understand it is not easy to ally myself with a country in which people can disappear so readily?"

Uceda smiled. "I assume you are referring to Colonel Hugo Pinilla?"

David nodded.

"But Colonel Pinilla has not disappeared. He is merely being held in custody until the prosecution case can be

completed. As a matter of fact, I had his file delivered to my
office only this morning."

He rose to his feet, and opening the metal cabinet
behind him, began to rummage in the drawer. David
watched him silently. He knew it was no accident that
Señor Uceda had Pinilla's dossier ready to hand. His query
had been anticipated.

Withdrawing a cardboard folder, Uceda placed it on the
desk and leafed through the opening papers. Unclipping a
sheet, he passed it across to David, together with two
photographs. His heart thumping wildly, David took the
proferred document and read it, frowning. It stated in
terse, unelaborated sentences that Colonel Hugo Pinilla
had been transferred to the high security wing at Camp
Digepol prison to await subsequent court martial. The
pictures showed the man David had met on the bus
standing inside a barbed-wire stockade. He looked leaner
than David remembered, and his hair had been shaved to
the skull. He was dressed in padded overclothing, and
beyond him David could see a line of snowcapped mountains etched against the sky. He struggled to keep the flush
of triumph off his face as he placed the papers back on the
desk. He hadn't realised discovering Pinilla's whereabouts
would prove so easy.

"Satisfied?" Uceda murmured.

David nodded. Uceda gathered the documents together
and slipped them into their folder. "You must not believe
the stories you hear," he chided. "It is true that during the
war against the terrorists, many bad things were done, but
that period is over now. We are a civilised nation, Señor
Ryker, and dedicated to the same principles of peace,
equality and freedom as the United States."

He sat staring at David quietly for a moment, then he
reached for a pad on his desk. "I am going to give you an
address," he stated, scribbling briskly. "It is my own
address, and I would like you to drop me a note whenever a
new vessel arrives in Port Stanley harbour. There will be no
need to sign the note. Simply draw a tiny square on the top
left-hand corner of the envelope, and I shall know the
message is from you."

He wrinkled his forehead. "Incidentally, it is not only

shipping we are interested in. Anything at all you think might be important . . . the attitude of the people, strangers who suddenly appear in the capital, unexplained changes in island routine . . . it's remarkable how much you can learn from the smallest details viewed in their proper perspective."

David regarded him soberly. "I'll think it over," he promised.

Next day, David flew down to Comodoro Rivadavia. He had slept badly, his brain unsettled by the memory of Uceda's tactless approach, and by the exciting prospect of seeing Anne again.

The airport at Comodoro was part of a military encampment, the terminal bare and functional, its windows peering across the empty runway to a line of barren grey hills. The sun was shining and the air warm, but it was distinctly cooler than Buenos Aires.

For three hours, David fidgeted restlessly in the coffee lounge until at last the flight to Port Stanley was announced over the crackling intercom. The three-hundred-mile shuttle service between the mainland and the islands was conducted by the Argentine air force on an old-fashioned propellor craft into which the passengers, Falkland Islanders for the most part returning from holidays abroad and a party of sailors rejoining their ship at Port Stanley, squeezed with their baggage and belongings. They took off, circling once above Comodoro's shoreline oil-rigs, then the pilot set a course south-southeast and David watched the Argentine coastline fading rapidly behind.

It was late afternoon when he caught his first glimpse of the islands. They looked stark and inhospitable, their rugged inlets drained of density by the altitude. The plane circled over the narrow harbour, and David spotted a starburst of tiny clapboard dwelling-houses below. Port Stanley, he thought.

The pilot landed, taxiing slowly to a halt. Unclipping his seatbelt, David joined the line of passengers waiting to disembark, the cold air hitting him like a blow in the face as he moved down the steps to the runway. It was hard to believe he had left Argentina's sunny clime barely two hours before. This place was like a different continent. To the west, he could see a pair of twin peaks etched against the sky, their crests trimmed with outcrops of rock. The wind pounded his cheeks, stinging his skin with its icy blast, and he shivered as he crossed the tarmac toward the terminal building. The customs officials were studiously polite and quaintly English. They seemed to double as baggage handlers, currency changers and even policemen, shepherding the arriving passengers through the immigration department to a line of Land Rovers waiting on the forecourt outside.

David spotted Anne standing in the wintry sunshine, her trim figure muffled inside a bulky anorak. He dropped his suitcase and ran toward her, seizing her in his arms and kissing her wildly on the mouth. Laughing, she eased herself free. "Don't make a spectacle of yourself. People know me here, remember. What are you doing to my reputation?"

"To hell with your reputation. I've waited too long to care about proprieties."

"Well, you'll just have to wait a little longer," she told him, moving around to open her Land Rover door. "You're in the Falklands now, my lad. We don't go in for all that dissolute living over here. Toss your suitcase into the back and I'll drive you into town."

The road was narrow and badly maintained. Anne explained it was the only one on the islands and ran for seven miles to the Royal Marine base at Moody Brook. As they curved across the purple moorland, David spotted a bespectacled figure in blue dungarees digging up the turf at the side of the track. "Who's that?" he grunted.

"It's the Chancellor of the Exchequer collecting peat for his kitchen stove."

David shook his head wonderingly. "It's like *Gulliver's Travels* and *Alice in Wonderland* rolled into one," he whispered.

The road steepened, climbing past a cluster of tall radio masts, and David glimpsed to the right the waters of a narrow inlet and the rusting hull of an old three-masted sailing vessel jammed among the rocks. "My God, will you look at that? Is she my clipper?"

Anne shook her head, smiling. "That's the *Lady Elizabeth*, abandoned in 1913," she said. "Your ship's down in the harbour, and in a far more pathetic state, I'm afraid. Wood's at a premium on these islands. There are no trees apart from the ones the settlers have planted in their gardens, so you can hardly blame them for grabbing any timber they can get their hands on. Over the past hundred years, your Yankee clipper has helped to shore up half the housefronts in Stanley."

"Christ," David sighed.

They were coming into town now. The houses looked little more than prefabricated shacks, neatly arranged in rectangular rows, their clapboard walls brightly-painted, adorned in places with glass porches and conservatories, their tin roofs bristling with chimneys and occasional attic windows. He spotted a sign on a gatepost which said: "Half a sheep today, please."

"That's a message for the delivery man," Anne explained. "He brings the meat every morning. Mutton's the staple diet, the cheapest food in town. We've so many sheep here, there's nothing else to do with their dead carcasses. Twenty thousand get tossed over the cliffs every year."

"What a waste," he said.

She nodded in agreement. "For years, the people in London have been talking about building a freezer plant so that our meat can be exported. But like everything else to do with the islands' future, all anyone ever does is talk."

She swung to the right, guiding the Land Rover down a steep hill towards the harbour. He glimpsed the wooden jetty below, and the waters of the inlet sparkling in the afternoon sunshine. "You've just passed the pub on your right," she said. "There are only three in town, and I must warn you they keep strict British licensing rules."

As they swung along the waterfront, David spotted a solid, much more permanent-looking building with a red roof and impressive belltower. The jawbone of a whale decorated its garden like a grotesque arch. Port Stanley cathedral, he realised.

The housefronts bristled with patriotic posters. "God Bless Our Gracious Queen." "Don't Cry For Us, Argentina." "The Falklands are Beautiful—And British."

"They sure don't believe in leaving anyone in doubt," he grunted. "I mean, where their sympathies lie."

"I told you. These people are more British than the British themselves. They'd rather die than accept Argentine sovereignty. If only the government in Westminster could understand that."

They drew to a halt outside a large house with a glassed-in verandah. Trim lawns sloped down to a narrow hedge lining the roadway.

"The only hotel in town is booked solid," Anne explained, "so I had to put you up at the Malvinas Guest House. You'll have to share a room, I'm afraid, with a scientist from the British Antarctic Survey team, but don't worry, this place serves the best food in the Falklands."

"When do I get to see you?"

"Tonight," she grinned. "That's my employer's cruiser in the harbour. You've been invited to dinner."

David stared at a sleek, beautifully-painted vessel moored in the centre of the inlet. He recognised it as a two-hundred footer of the Badger/Aquarius class, with an overall weight of six hundred tons and a maximum speed of eighty knots. It looked almost the size of a passenger liner with its command bridge a good thirty feet above the waterline, and David could see quite plainly the blue rectangle of a swimming pool centred on its foredeck, and white-clad sailors moving around the focsle. "My God, he must be wealthier than Croesus, your employer," he exclaimed.

"Didn't you know? He *is* Croesus," Anne laughed, leaning across to open the door for him. "We eat at eight, drinks at seven-thirty. There'll be a boat waiting to ferry you out from the dock. Oh, and incidentally, the governor and his wife are invited, so don't forget to dress."

He clambered from the cab, wincing as the wind's blast caught him in the face, then Anne swung the Land Rover into a sharp U-turn and, tossing her curls, rattled back the way she had come. Clutching his suitcase, David stared after her moodily. Their reunion had not been the romantic one he'd expected. He was halfway to the front door when he realised she hadn't even asked about Hugo Pinilla.

* * *

At seven-thirty that evening, David was ferried out to the yacht by two sailors in heavy wool jerseys. There was a sharp wind blowing from the west, and flecks of seaspray whipped up from the narrow inlet, peppering his cheeks and throat. As he clambered on board, he heard the soft murmur of taped dance music drifting up from the cabins below. The decks were ablaze with light, and an officer in white uniform saluted him smartly. "Mr. David Ryker?" he inquired.

"That's right."

As David entered the main saloon, his ears caught the low drone of conversation. A group of men and women stood sipping cocktails in front of the teak service bar, talking very brightly. David paused in mid-step. He had not expected such a large number of people and the sight of them made him feel hesitant and uneasy. He was relieved to see Anne moving toward him clutching a glass in her hand and looking magnificent in an organza halternecked dress with a white piqué jacket that contrasted perfectly with her healthy tan. Her blonde curls had been gathered into a coil on top of her head, and she exuded an air of warmth and vitality, a welcome respite from the chill winds sweeping the upper deck.

"Now that's what I call teutonic timekeeping," she smiled.

"Is all this because of me?"

"Of course not. Magnus likes to entertain. It's one of his great passions in life."

"What about his other passions?" David demanded balefully. "Do they include you?"

"Be quiet. Don't you realise you're practically the guest of honour? Come on over and meet some of the local hierarchy, beginning with the governor and his wife, Mavis."

The governor was a small man, well-dressed and incredibly neat, who told David he had been airlifted out of Saigon during the final days of the Vietnam war. He had a pleasant habit of smiling as he talked which David found vaguely reassuring. His wife was lively and extrovert, and David warmed to them both immediately.

They were joined after a short while by a group of executives from the firm which owned most of the sheep farms in the area, the Falkland Islands Company. Almost at once, the topic of conversation switched to the subject of island sovereignty.

"I hate to admit it," one of the executives said, "but administration here has been one long story of neglect. They've taken everything they can out of these islands and put damned little back. Damned little. When the company decided to axe the monthly supply ship, it was the Argies who started flying stuff in. You could hardly blame these people if they decided to look to Buenos Aires for their future welfare, but they insist till they're blue in the face that they're British and intend to remain that way for ever."

David did not bother commenting. The debate seemed to ebb and flow around him as if he had somehow drawn apart from his immediate surroundings and was standing, physically visible, but beyond the level of response. He was too preoccupied with Anne to care about political assessments of the Falkland Islands. She had changed, there was no point ignoring the fact any longer. It was nothing he could put his finger on, just a slight, almost imperceptible withdrawal, a kind of aloofness as if she regretted her indiscretion in Argentina and was delicately trying to re-align their relationship. He had dreamed so long of this meeting that her manner troubled and confused him.

Anne herself seemed oblivious to David's discomfort as, still smiling brightly, she steered him across the crowded cabin. "It's time you met my employer," she said. "He's heard so much about you, I know he'll be annoyed if he doesn't get a chance to chat to you before dinner."

At first glance, Magnus D. Stone looked like someone who had managed to escape the passage of time, for despite his years his face was smooth and unexpectedly youthful, but after closer scrutiny, David decided the reason for this was the curious force which seemed to emanate from within the man, a powerful vitality that somehow matched Anne's own. He was, David estimated, about sixty years old, extremely slim and elegantly dressed in a suit that looked beautifully tailored and unarguably expensive. His hair was almost pure white, brushed back strongly from the fore--

head, and his face was tanned and fit. His features were sharply chiselled, the nose pronounced, almost elongated, the cheeks slightly hollow, with the skin stretched taut across the frontal bone structure conveying an air of poise and breeding. Behind this carefully refined manner, however, there was an underlying impression of toughness. He looked like a man who knew how to make trouble, how to get what he wanted, and how to impose his will upon others.

"David Ryker," he declared. "I knew your father, did Anne tell you that? We used to meet at those infernal oil conferences in Fort Worth. I was the only foreigner he never managed to drink under the table."

"My father's mentioned you a couple of times," David admitted.

"Has he, by God? You must give him my warmest regards next time you write. I always admired his rapacious appetite for living."

David hesitated. "I write to my father extremely rarely," he said honestly. "If you want to know the truth, we don't get on too well at all."

"I'm sorry to hear that, but not overly surprised. He had an appalling habit of throwing his weight around as I remember. Still, I always felt his heart was in the right place. We were the same kind of animal, he and I."

David studied Stone coolly, trying to assess whether the man represented a threat in his relationship with Anne. He was not at all the way David had expected. Not like his father, for instance, although they were both about the same age. There was no bloated look to Magnus Stone, no sign of excess or indulgence. He looked upsettingly healthy, and despite his white hair, a good twenty years younger than he ought to.

In Buenos Aires, David had done a little research into his host's background. Stone, he'd discovered, had been famous in his youth as a sportsman. He had played cricket for Harrow, had rowed and fenced for Oxford and had won the British amateur punting championship. In his business dealings, he had displayed an instinctive flair for financial double-dealing beginning at twenty-one when he had formed a company in Switzerland called Fips Fledocher and sold them a block of flats in Bayswater, London for five hundred thousand pounds. Fips Fledocher had renovated the flats and resold them for three million pounds, and since Stone had been liable for tax on the first deal only, the Inland Revenue had been unable to touch his massive profit of two-and-a-half million pounds. Stone had then moved his money around the globe, investing in the oilfields of the Persian Gulf, North Africa, Texas and Mexico, and now, semi-retired, he was reputed to be the fourth richest man in the world.

"You've left the oil business now, I hear," David said.

"Not entirely. Still have my interests there—investments, that sort of thing. Most of the time, however, I concentrate on the things I like best. A little cruising, a little wildlife filming. I go down to the ice as often as I can."

"The ice?"

"Antarctica. The most beautiful continent in the world. People simply have no idea. They imagine it as an empty wilderness of ice and snow. I tell you, my friend, nothing quite prepares you for the staggering beauty of an Antarctic summer. No corner of the globe offers such breathtaking landscapes, such purity of vision. It's the last great continent, yet it's been visited by virtually only a handful of human beings."

"Obviously you love it," David observed, watching him closely.

Stone nodded. "Antarctica's my bolthole, the perfect escape from life's tensions. I had my cruiser reinforced to handle the icepacks. Oh, she's no icebreaker, not in the true sense, but she can handle a limited thickness. There's a strange sense of calm, you know, when you approach the end of the world. Even the seas feel it. Their waves smooth out and steady, their rollers flatten. That's the first sign that the icepack is approaching. And when you set foot on the mainland, it's impossible not to be aware of the fact that you're at some extreme corner of the universe. It may sound childish and absurd, but there's something inexplicably satisfying in being able to say to oneself: I am the first man to stand on this spot since the beginning of time."

He smiled. "Don't let me bore you. I'll happily rhapsodise about Antarctica until the cows come home, but I do realise not everyone shares my enthusiasm."

David was scarcely listening. He was watching the way Stone's eyes lit up, the way exuberance flowed out of him in an irresistible flood. Magnus Stone was not an easy man to ignore, and David had the uncomfortable impression that despite his age, he would be uncommonly attractive to women.

At dinner, David did little more than pick at his food. He was growing more and more certain that his suspicions were correct. Anne herself scarcely looked at him. They had placed her at the far end of the table with Governor Hunt and his wife, and throughout the meal she ignored David completely. David felt his misery deepening, and found it increasingly difficult to keep up with the conversation which, naturally enough, centred on the dispute with Argentina.

"We have to face the fact that our lifestyle is dangerously threatened," a man said. "In the eyes of the UN, the villain of the peace is definitely Britain."

"Speaking personally," another man grunted, "I think Britain's deliberately allowing the Falklands to run down so the conflict can be resolved without too much fuss and bother. I mean, let's face it, they're nothing but an embarrassment to the government in Westminster. Everywhere you look, there are opportunities for expansion—oceans teeming with fish, coastlines crammed with kelp, even oil—yet nothing's done to exploit them."

"Come off it, Roderick," a woman put in, "the oil's pure guesswork, and you know it."

"Well, all the indications suggest that it's there. The Argentines already have oil wells reaching far out into the Atlantic. Who knows, the Falklands could be the Shetlands of the future, and if we're not bloody careful, the Argies'll grab it all."

"I doubt that," one of the company executives said. "The British government has promised there'll be no agreement without the islanders' full approval, and the Argentines would never be foolish enough to actually invade."

"Why not? They've done it before."

"When?"

"Back in 1966. A group of Argentines hijacked an aircraft out of Buenos Aires and landed on Port Stanley race-course."

"You're joking."

"It's true. The locals thought the plane had crashed. When they went running up to help, they found themselves confronted by armed men who announced they'd come to liberate the islands from the yoke of British oppression. It was rather embarrassing really. Nobody could speak Spanish. The Argentines gave themselves up in the end, of course, but it does underline the vulnerability of our position here. Britain is eight thousand miles away, Argentina barely three hundred. If they do decide to attack, there's precious little we could do to stop it."

"What's the American view?" a man asked, peering across the tabletop at David.

David shifted uncomfortably on his chair, forcing his mind onto the issue at hand. He could see the faces staring back at him, polite, intent, genuinely interested in his attitude. He coughed in embarrassment, and choosing his words with care, said: "It seems to me the Argentines do have proximity on their side. What about the leaseback proposal? In other words, recognise Argentine ownership and rent the islands from them for an agreed period of time?"

The man shook his head. "Wouldn't work. The islanders regard any question of leaseback as tantamount to a sellout."

"But sooner or later, Argentine patience is bound to run out," David insisted.

"I know it and you know it, but try telling that to the British in Westminster. Expediency's the only thing they care about, with all due respect to the governor here."

David sighed and let the matter drop. There was an element of unreality in the atmosphere, a feeling that for some reason, everything had been arranged for his benefit. He scarcely gave a damn one way or the other, anyhow. His main concern was the change which had taken place in Anne. We've got to thrash it out, he thought. She owes me an explanation, for Christ's sake. Something at least.

He did not get a chance to speak to her again until the

meal was over. Then, as guests gathered in the adjoining saloon for coffee, she gently squeezed his shoulder. "Magnus would like to see you in the master stateroom," she whispered. "We'll sneak off while the others aren't watching."

Wonderingly, he followed her along the companionway. Stone was sitting at his chart-table, cradling a glass of brandy in his palm. His face looked uncommonly serious, and shadows lay in the hollows of his cheeks.

"Come in David," he said. "Please close the door behind you."

David did as he was ordered.

"Sit down." Stone indicated to a chair.

David sat opposite him while Anne moved over and stood at Stone's side.

"Drink?" Stone asked.

David shook his head. "I think I've had enough tonight."

"Very well."

Stone's manner had completely altered. Gone was the ebullience David had witnessed earlier. In its place, he detected a kind of measured caution. Stone's face had settled into a sober mask in which the vitality, the curious inexplicable force of the man, had somehow receded. Now, moody and reflective, he regarded David quietly. "You do know what I wish to ask you about?"

"I imagine it's Hugo Pinilla."

Stone nodded. "Were you successful in uncovering any information on the man?"

"Maybe," David stated.

He crossed his legs, conscious of a certain unwillingness to deliver his news, a feeling born partly out of pique that Anne was treating him in such a cursory manner, and partly out of an instinctive wariness. "First you have to tell me why you're doing this," he said. "Are you working for British intelligence, or what?"

"Nothing quite so glamorous, I'm afraid. This is purely an independent operation. I've tried for months to make the Foreign Office grasp the seriousness of things out here, but they simply won't listen. They regard me as a crank, a scaremonger. Besides, if they could quietly negotiate the islands away, it would make things a damn sight easier all round from their point of view. Less espensive, too."

"So what's your personal interest?"

"Patriotism, mainly. Plus a touch of nostalgia. I've been sailing to the Falklands for a great many years on my way to Antarctica. There are eighteen hundred people here. British people. They want to remain that way. I believe we have no right to abandon them."

David considered for a moment. "What makes you so damn sure the Argentines will attack?"

Stone peered down at his brandy glass, gently rocking the liquid with his palm. Deep lines had formed across his forehead and around his mouth. "If I tell you, I must have your assurance that it will go no further than this stateroom," he replied.

David nodded slowly. "Agreed."

"Some months ago, I was approached by a certain representative of the Argentine junta to carry out an assessment of the British government's reaction in the event of a Falklands takeover. My reward was to be the sole exploitation rights on the oilfields beneath the Falkland seas."

David stared at him. "Are you serious?"

"Absolutely."

"What made them come to you?"

"I'm a frequent visitor to Buenos Aires and a personal friend of the president himself. I'm also the perfect man for the job since I have a number of associates on the British Cabinet."

"Did you do it?"

"Of course not."

"Did you inform your friends in England?"

"They wouldn't believe me. They said I'd cried wolf once too often."

He paused and sipped delicately from his glass, his brow creasing in thought as if he felt reluctant to take the matter further. David waited, conscious that the Englishman was weighing in his mind whether or not to trust him. At last Stone said: "The real issue, however, is not the Falklands at all. They're only part of a much more complex and elaborate takeover plan. This is where the real conquest lies." Leaning back in his chair, he slapped the wall chart behind him. "Antarctica."

David frowned. "I don't understand."

"The Antarctic Peninsula is claimed jointly by both Britain and Argentina. At the moment, all territorial rights have been suspended under the terms of the Antarctic Treaty which expires in 1991. The treaty states that no weapons or armies are to be deployed, and that only scientific research work is allowed to take place. The Argentines are flouting that rule on two counts. First, they have troops stationed at each of their principal bases. Second, they're carrying out drilling operations aimed specifically at exploiting Antarctica's mineral resources. They're also flying in pregnant women to have their babies on Antarctic soil. They believe that when the treaty comes up for renewal, Argentina will strengthen its claim by pointing out that it has colonised the area."

"But why should they do that?" David asked, puzzled.

"Oil," Stone said simply. "Enough oil to float the whole of Saudi Arabia. If the seismograph readings prove correct, the Antarctic Peninsula could be the world's last big oil bonanza. At the moment, it's not worth touching. Getting it out under such harsh climactic conditions, transporting it back across the Cape Horn waters would be a monumental operation. But by the turn of the century, when technology will have progressed to a much more efficient level, when the industrial nations may be facing energy starvation, our entire future may depend upon what lies beneath Antarctica. The Argentines intend to grab it for themselves."

David sat staring at him in silence for a moment. There was no expression on Stone's face. He was gazing back at David impassively, his brandy glass still clutched in his slender fingers.

"Is your government aware of this?" David asked.

"Oh, they're aware of it all right. They're refusing to acknowledge it, that's all."

"And what part do the Falklands play?"

Stone leaned forward to place his glass on the table. "Argentina has always wanted the Falklands," he stated, "but why do you imagine they've suddenly extended that claim to include South Georgia, a rocky outcrop more than

a thousand miles away in the middle of nowhere? I'll tell
you why. Because they know that if they can remove the
last British presence in the South Atlantic, not only will the
British claims in Antarctica lose substance, but British
naval forces will have no deep-water ports from which to
mount an offensive if the Argentines carry out a future
Antarctic takeover."

David sat back in his chair, visibly shaken. For the first
time, he was beginning to believe in the possibility of war.

"And Hugo Pinilla?" he whispered.

"The Falkland Islands must remain under British juris-
diction. It's the only way British interests on the Antarctic
Peninsula can be safeguarded. If I can produce a high-
ranking Argentine officer who will publicly admit that his
country intends to mount a Falklands invasion, if he can
announce details of those invasion plans, perhaps I can
force my government to sit up and take notice. At the
moment, they refuse to take me seriously on anything at all
connected with the South Atlantic."

David drummed his fingers lightly on the tabletop. He
realised his own knowledge was too important to keep
secret any longer.

"Okay," he admitted, "Colonel Pinilla's still alive. He's
being kept under high security in a prison called Camp
Digepol until the authorities can finalise their case against
him, then they plan to put him on trial."

Briefly, David filled in the details of his meeting with
Señor Uceda the previous day. When he reached the part
where the Argentine had asked him to supply details of
Port Stanley shipping, Stone shook his head wonderingly.

"One thing about their intelligence service," he muttered, "you could never accuse them of subtlety or finesse."

"What about Camp Digepol?" David asked. "Have you
ever heard of it?"

"I've heard of it all right. It stands on the Antarctic
Peninsula, about twelve miles inland between the Bellings-
hausen and Weddell Seas. Clever place to stick high-
security prisoners when you think. Even if they manage to
escape, they simply die in the snow. I imagine the
authorities have little trouble with absconders."

"What will you do?"

Stone shook his head moodily. He looked crestfallen. "God knows. It appears as though Pinilla is beyond our reach. What we need is a new strategy, a new approach. I'll have to give the matter some analytical thought."

Absently, Stone reached up, ruffling Anne's hair, and watching, David felt his stomach contract. The gesture had been artless, natural, unobtrusive, but it indicated a level of familiarity, of human contact, of fleshly love. A profound misery took hold of David, blinding in its intensity. In that one simple movement, he felt his worst fears had just been confirmed.

SIX

Next morning, David left the guest house early and walked down the road in the blustery wind. It was a chilly day and waves lapped the surface of the narrow inlet, hurling pellets of icy spray into his face and throat. He found the wreck jammed against the rocks at the water's edge, a pitiful hulk of age-blackened timber. Its hull had deteriorated to such an extent it was scarcely recognisable as a ship, and he felt his spirits sink as he stood in the wind and silently contemplated the vessel's remains. She would need an awful lot of work if they planned on towing her back to Virginia, he decided.

Taking out his pocketknife, he began to examine the timber, digging his blade deep into its waterlogged surface. He was trying hard not to think about Anne. He had thought about her all through the night, tossing and turning restlessly on his narrow bed, but now, in the pale light of morning, he had resolved to get his thoughts in order. He was convinced Anne was Magnus Stone's lover. Though the man was old enough to be her father, David could see at a glance he would exude an animal-like fascination for women. He was flamboyant, assured, inherently graceful. He was also rich. Qualities enough to turn a young girl's head.

What the hell, David thought, that brief episode on the Argentine pampa had been an interlude, nothing more, a welcome diversion from the evening storm. He didn't own the woman, after all. What was he getting uptight about?

He was bending forward, scraping at the blackened hull, when a vehicle hooted on the road above and glancing up he saw a Land Rover parked on the gravel track. Sitting behind the wheel was Anne. The window was open and her blonde curls were dancing in the wind.

"Come on," she shouted, "we're going to be late."

Frowning, he slipped the pocketknife inside his jacket and scrambled up the grassy bank. "Late for what?" he grunted.

"The plane. It leaves at eight-thirty. Didn't you listen to the radio this morning? Your name was called on the passenger list."

David looked confused. "I don't understand."

"I managed to get us two seats on the first flight to Pebble Island. We can have lunch there and catch the return plane to Stanley in time for tea. After all, I did promise to show you the Falklands, didn't I, and you can't spend your entire stay mooching around the capital. You ought to find out what life is like 'in camp', in other words, the outback. Now hop in, for pete's sake, and be quick. The pilot won't wait for ever."

Bewildered, David scurried around to the opposite side and clambered into the passenger seat. Without waiting for the door to close, Anne stabbed her foot on the accelerator and they hurtled along the narrow roadway, leaving the shacks behind and following the ragged shore of the windswept inlet. David saw a hangar looming up ahead and, moored to the seashore, a tiny seaplane, its wings and fuselage painted a brilliant red.

"That's our transport," Anne declared. "The only way of getting around, unless you plan to travel by sea, and that can take ages. The Falklands cover an area roughly the size of Wales."

She parked the vehicle and they hurried along the wooden jetty to where the pilot was waving urgently for them to board. Still confused, David balanced on the aircraft float and helped Anne to clamber through the open hatchway, then he followed quickly, locking the door behind him and strapping himself into a tiny bucket seat beside her. The cabin was crowded. Passengers huddled shoulder to shoulder in the tightly-confined space and strapped in the rear David glimpsed boxes of provisions scheduled for delivery to the outlying islands.

The pilot cast off and taxied his flimsy craft into the centre of the inlet. The wind was growing stronger every minute, and David peered anxiously through the porthole window at the white-spumed wave crests dancing across the narrow harbour. The engines roared as the pilot commenced his take-off. They sped across the water's surface, their twin floats kicking up feathery curtains of spray, then slowly, gently, they banked skyward, skimming over Port Stanley's rooftops and turning in a steep arc over the rocky summits of the adjacent hills.

For more than an hour, David peered down at the rugged country unfolding steadily beneath him. The roar of the engines made conversation impossible, so he had little alternative but to watch the desolate landscape spreading below. He saw scarce evidence of human habitation. Occasionally, they passed a cluster of white-painted huts, but his overall impression was one of utter emptiness.

Just after ten, the pilot signalled they were coming in to land. David spotted a settlement cluttering the adjacent shoreline. The houses looked small and flimsy, with white tails and metal roofs. The pilot circled once, then they were skimming across the water of the massive bay.

The pilot slowed his speed and taxied the aircraft in a narrow arc. David saw a wooden jetty probing into the turbulent water, and by its side two Land Rovers, the drivers huddled against the blustery wind.

David disembarked first, balancing precariously on the narrow float as he helped Anne climb down behind him. She ran along the jetty, throwing her arms excitedly around the first of the Land Rover drivers, a tall raw-boned man with a lantern jaw and wind-reddened cheeks whose head was almost completely obscured beneath a fur-lined cap with the flaps pulled down to cover his ears.

"Daddy," she cried, "you get younger every time I see you."

The man grinned happily, his grey moustache stirring in the wind. "We heard on the radio you were coming," he said. "I said to your mum, I can't let my little girl walk from the landing stage. Who knows, after all that soft living in London, she might catch cold."

Anne introduced David to her father who shook his hand welcomingly, then they scrambled into the Land Rover and set off across the lee of the nearby hillside. David could see the settlement three hundred yards ahead, its buildings tracing the opposite shoreline. They looked primitive and functional, but their gaily-painted exteriors seemed bright and cheery in contrast to the stark grandeur of the surrounding countryside.

Anne's father took David first to the company manager's house, the largest building on the island. The interior had been decorated lovingly with furniture imported from England and Europe, and though the walls were clapboard and scarcely adequate for the savage Antarctic winds, the peat-turf stoves pervaded the house with a glow of warmth and comfort.

The manager himself was a thick-set man in his late fifties, who had the power, Anne said, to hire and fire on the company's behalf, distribute food, try criminals and conduct marriages. His position was as near to that of a feudal overlord as it was possible to get in the twentieth century.

"You've heard that the Argies are trying to take us over?" he said as they sat drinking beer at his kitchen table.

"You can hardly miss it," David admitted. "It's the only damn thing anybody talks about."

"They're crazy. We'd rather be dead than Argentine."

"That's something I can't understand. I mean, what the hell has Britain done for you anyhow?"

"Nothing. Not a damn thing. In fact, most of the people here believe the British are trying to sell us down the river. But it makes little difference. British is what we are, and British is what we'll stay."

"And if the Westminster government reaches a settlement with the Argentines?"

"Then we'll pull out. Every last family will move to Scotland or New Zealand. The Falklands will become nothing more than a collection of ghost settlements."

David shook his head. "Sounds crazy to me," he grunted.

Later, Anne took him out to meet some of the neighbouring shepherds. The sheep-shearing was in progress, and they stood for almost an hour watching the men strip the wool from their helpless animals with electric clippers run by an ancient home-operated generator. The people were almost embarrassingly friendly, and talked in totally unselfconscious terms about their loyalty to the British Crown. It was the one topic of conversation which arose spontaneously wherever David went.

At noon, they moved to Anne's parents' house where her mother, a large homely woman with blonde hair heavily streaked with grey, had prepared lunch, the usual fare of soup, mutton and potatoes. Her father joined them at the table, his cheeks redder than ever in the muggy warmth of the peat-fire stove. David was amazed at the matter-of-fact way in which the Danbys regarded this unexpected visit by their only daughter. They were stolid people, ruled by the seasons, their daily rhythms simple and uncluttered. It was clear to see they loved Anne deeply, yet they seemed to regard her comings and goings with an air of stoic resignation that characterised everything they did.

There was nothing resigned however, about their attitude toward Argentina.

"I don't trust them Argies as far as I can spit," her father told David. "Tell you what they want these islands for. A penal colony, that's what. If they move in, they'll destroy our whole way of life."

"But they've treated you with the greatest consideration so far," David protested.

"That's how clever they are. They try to win us over by kindness, but as soon as we let our defences down, the bastards'll be in like a bunch of bloody locusts. We don't even understand why Britain's negotiating with the Argies in the first place. This is our land, we was born and raised here. The Argies don't belong. Why doesn't the Foreign Office tell them to go to hell and be done with it?"

David gave up in the end. It was clear that no amount of argument could persuade any of the islanders to change their opinions, so he eventually stopped trying and steered the conversation along less emotional lines.

It was late afternoon when they said goodbye to Anne's parents who kissed and hugged their daughter affectionately. Then they drove to the jetty and waited for the seaplane to pick them up on its return journey. All through the long flight back they sat in silence, their voices stilled by the constant roar of the engines. As they disembarked at Port

Stanley, David caught Anne's elbow. "Don't let's go to the Land Rover yet," he said. "It's still early. I feel like a walk."

She looked at him. "If you like."

They strolled along the narrow roadway, the town at their back, the craggy outline of Tumbledown Mountain rising up in front. The wind battered their faces, scattering their hair in blasts of icy salt spray. David's senses were taut. He knew he had to get this settled once and for all. Solve and forget it, that was the only way.

"Well, what did you think of Pebble Island?" Anne asked.

"I thought you made your point very well," he said.

"How do you mean?"

"That was why you took me there, wasn't it? To show me how passionately the islanders care about their future?"

She was silent for a moment. "Perhaps," she admitted.

"Did your boss tell you to do that?"

She didn't answer. He kicked at a pebble, sending it skimming across the water's surface. "What exactly is he to you anyhow?" he said.

She peered at him sharply. "In what sense?"

"I mean what is he? Employer? Friend? Lover? What?"

Her lips tightened and he saw her cheeks grow slightly paler. "You have no right to ask that question."

"I have every right in the world. Back in Argentina, you led me to believe . . . that is . . ." he hesitated. "I got the impression that you cared for me."

"Oh David, don't be so damned childish. I like you, of course I like you. You're a very attractive man. What happened in Argentina was a whim of the moment, nothing more. It's over now, we're ourselves again. The *jineatada*, the storm, they're all gone. We're back to reality."

"That night at the *boliche*, are you saying it was just a sham?"

She sighed. "I'm saying it's a question of keeping things in perspective, that's all."

"Great. That's great. Supposing I say I've fallen in love with you?"

"David, don't be ridiculous. It was great fun and we both enjoyed ourselves, but for God's sake don't try to build it into something it never was."

"So you belong to Stone, is that it?"

She was silent for a moment. Her hair fluttered in the wind, covering her face. "He needs me," she said simply.

David felt his stomach tighten and a wave of weariness engulfed him. There was no longer any need to plague his mind with vague uncertainties. He knew the truth at last.

"I was right then?"

She nodded.

"For Christ's sake, Anne, the man's old enough to be your father."

"What has that to do with it?"

"I don't like to see you throw your life away, that's all."

"It's my life, my decision. For all his outward show of confidence, Magnus Stone is a very lonely man."

"What about me, don't I get lonely too?"

"Yours is a different kind of loneliness, David. You're a loner by nature. You don't need anyone, not really."

"How the hell do you know what I need? You've never taken the trouble to find out."

She turned her head into the wind. "I don't blame you for being angry, but I wish you'd try to understand. What happened in Argentina was one of my happiest memories. Please don't spoil it."

David thrust his hand into his anorak pockets, watching the road curve, tracing the edge of the narrow inlet. Beyond it rose the hills, grey and tawny under the swirling sky. "What do you see in Stone?" he growled. "Is it his gentlemanly charm, or is there another, more pertinent reason? I know how you feel about these islands. I know that it looks as though the British government's planning to hand them over to Argentina. I also know your Magnus Stone is doing his damnedest to stop that happening. And a man as rich as he is is bound to wield a good deal of power and influence."

"Are you suggesting I'm using him?" she asked coldly.

"Not 'using'," he corrected. "Just keeping your finger on the pulse, so to speak. Making sure his interest doesn't flag. Spurring him on when you figure he needs it."

"That's utter nonsense and you know it."

"Then why are you looking so angry?"

"Because you've made me angry, that's why. I'm not your property, I never was. What I do with my life is my own affair. Nobody asked you to poke your nose in, and nobody asked you to psycho-analyse me either. I've been as honest with you as I know how. At least have the grace to accept the situation intelligently, instead of flying off the handle like a callow schoolboy."

David stared at the hills ahead, filled with bitterness and self-loathing, he shouldn't have pushed it so hard, he thought. It had been madness really. Because whatever she said, there was little doubt in his mind that he loved her. For Christ's sake, knowing about Stone only made his longing worse. If only she would give him a chance. He had plenty to offer. Youth. Sincerity. Surely they had to count for something?

It was time to soft-pedal, time to control his emotions, start using his brain for a change. It wasn't over yet, not by a long run. He wanted her too much. He would take her away from Stone if it was the last thing he did.

"Look," he said, "I'm sorry I shot my mouth off."

"Forget it."

"No, I'm serious. I'll try not to bring up the subject again. But there's one thing I want you to promise me."

"What's that?" she asked.

"Don't rule me out."

"Rule you out?"

"I mean, don't slam the door in my face. Stone's a good man, but he's too damned old for you. One day you're going to realise that. When it happens, I plan to be around."

"You're being quite silly, David."

"Not at all. I'm being reasonable. Will you let me stay?"

She smiled. "I want us to be friends, you know that."

"Okay, then let's be friends."

"No more inquisitions?"

"I promise."

"And you won't get mad?"

"I promise that too."

"All right, a truce."

She took his arm, still smiling, and he ducked his head as a blast of icy wind battered his cheekbones. Straightening, he peered across the waters of the inlet. On the opposite side, he could see a tall hangar-like structure with a collection of wooden huts in front of it. A sense of unreality shook him. The buildings looked strangely familiar.

"What is that place?" he muttered.

Anne followed his gaze. "Moody Brook barracks, the Royal Marine encampment. The British keep nearly sixty men stationed there."

David didn't say anything for a moment. He knew beyond any shadow of doubt he had seen the huts before. And then, in a moment of blinding revelation, he suddenly realised where.

"You're quite sure?" grunted Magnus Stone.

"Absolutely," David told him.

"You could have been mistaken."

"No way. I tell you those huts were identical in every detail, right down to the flagpole. The buildings I watched the Argentine commandos raiding at the naval academy in Buenos Aires were an exact replica of Moody Brook barracks."

Stone rose to his feet and moved across the saloon, pursing his lips and looking, for the first time since David had met him, decidedly disconcerted. He was dressed in a mohair jacket and chenille slacks, and his white hair seemed to shimmer in the pale glow of evening.

Someone moved along the upper deck, their footsteps making a hollow clanging sound which echoed through the empty cabins.

"If what you say is true," Stone muttered, "it means the Argentine invasion plans are a good deal more advanced than I'd realised. I'd expected no direct action before next summer at the earliest. However, this throws a completely new light on things."

"What are we going to do, Magnus?" Anne asked from the saloon doorway.

Stone shook his head. "What we need is something positive, something concrete to shake under the noses of the Foreign Office people."

"What about David here? He's a neutral, isn't he? Supposing he described what he'd seen?"

"Not enough. They'd just say I'd put him up to it."

"I could tell them about my conversation with Galtieri," David suggested. "He specifically mentioned the possibility of a Falklands invasion."

"He was speaking hypothetically."

"Sure, but viewed in the light of the other thing, his words take on a new significance."

"What about your friends, the Farrels? They witnessed the conversation, didn't they? Would they back you up at the British Embassy?"

David thought for a moment, then shook his head. "Not a chance. Señor Farrel may look and sound like an Englishman, but he's Argentine to the core. Like Galtieri, he believes the Falklands belong to Argentina."

Stone sighed. "In which case, David's not enough. What we need is Colonel Pinilla."

David pulled out a chair and sat down at the saloon table. He stretched out his legs, resting his elbows on the polished teak surface. A daring thought was forming in his mind. It was outrageous, he knew, reckless in the extreme. It wasn't his affair, for Christ's sake, he thought he had learned his lesson on the bus. But he wanted Anne, wanted her badly. He was conscious of an excitement rising within him, an emotion generated by the awareness of love and all its myriad needs. Sure, she'd misled him, deceived him, betrayed him even, but he was ready to do anything to take her away from Stone, even risk his neck if he had to. He couldn't help himself.

"How long would it take this cruiser of yours to sail to the Antarctic Peninsula?" he inquired softly.

Stone hesitated, peering at him in puzzlement. "Providing the weather's good, three days. That's assuming the pack-ice isn't running too far north."

"Three days there, three days back?"

"Roughly speaking."

David ran his fingertip along the saloon table. "We've got the transportation," he said. "Why don't we just sneak down and grab Pinilla for ourselves?"

Stone was silent for a moment. He stood staring at David like someone in the presence of a madman. "You can't be serious?"

"Why not?"

"It's a job for experts."

"What about your crew, won't they help?"

"Not a chance. They're Italian, most of them. If their sympathies lie with anyone at all, it's the Argentines."

"Still, we do have one thing on our side. The bastards aren't expecting us. Look at it sensibly. They're running a prison camp in the middle of Antarctica. What would be safer? They know damn well that if a convict breaks loose, the cold and starvation will simply wipe him out. The guards wouldn't be human if they didn't allow security to grow a little lax."

"But what you're suggesting would mean penetrating the prison right under the sentries' noses. We're not trained for that kind of operation. We're civilians, amateurs."

Stone stopped suddenly, and his eyes began to glow. "On the other hand, I think I know how it might be done," he whispered.

David grinned. "Now you're talking."

Stone moved to the window, his face caught in the fading daylight, his hair, thick and strong, rising from his forehead in a belligerent curl, its whiteness accentuated, contrasting sharply with the flush tinging his cheekbones. David could see his eyes lighting up, could feel like a tangible force the wave of emotion flooding through him. Then Stone turned. "By God," he breathed, "I believe you're right. We've got to do it ourselves."

"It's the only way."

"You'll come with us?"

"Try and stop me."

"I thought you said you were neutral."

David shrugged. He glanced back at Anne standing in the doorway, her soft curls caught in the glow of refracted light. "Let's say I have my reasons," he grunted.

Stone laughed delightedly, his teeth flashing, his face as jaunty as a schoolboy's. "Why didn't I think of it before? There's only one answer, it's been staring us in the face from the very beginning. If the mountain won't come to Mohammed, then Mohammed must go to the mountain."

* * *

The roar of the engines throbbed in Ciro's ears. Sitting beside the pilot, he peered down at the vast curtain of ice, the sun catching the crevasses and fissures, creating pools of emptiness in places where the ferocity of the reflected rays shut out all sense of distance or perspective, taking on form and solidity in others where the ice had broken, revealing the pale blue of the sea beneath, the floes studded with great black slugs which Ciro knew to be basking seals. Antarctica, he thought. In the morning sunlight, with its features glistening, it looked enchanted, a fairyland, but only an idiot would be fooled by such deceptive beauty. It was a wilderness, chilling, awe-inspiring. If they crashed, if the engines misfired, if anything at all went wrong, their chances of survival would be next to zero. In Antarctica, there were no rescue teams, no back-up services. Only the ice, endless and implacable.

The sunlight shifted, spreading across the water's surface, picking out a glistening rampart of intricately-carved ice, the features locked into a fascinating complexity of towering pinnacles, gleaming archways and fractured buttresses. The pilot tapped Ciro on the shoulder and jerked his thumb downwards, tilting the plane to starboard. Peering through the window, Ciro glimpsed, moored in a narrow inlet between two towering mountain peaks, a small ship with a crimson hull and a white buff funnel. She looked miniscule surrounded by the shimmering sprawl of snow, and even at that distance he could see her flight deck and the massive hangar which housed her two helicopters. In accordance with the Antarctic Treaty, her solitary Oerlikon gun had been masked with a canvas covering.

Ciro waved to the pilot to take them down. The plane dipped, skimming low over the vessel's radio mast, and Ciro spotted figures on the bridge, watching them curiously. There was no longer any doubt in his mind that the vessel he was looking at was the British ice patrol ship, HMS *Endurance*. He felt a sensation of gloom assail him as he marked the location reluctantly on his map. He had been hoping they would fail in their aerial search of the Antarctic coastline, but the *Endurance*, with its red hull specially designed for easy recognition against the ice, was difficult to

miss. Now he had no excuse but to proceed to phase two of
the operation. Alert Trujillo and authorise the vessel's
destruction.

He was about to order the pilot to return to base when
suddenly he spotted, on the other side of the bay, a second
ship cruising cautiously between the drifting ice-floes. He
frowned, leaning forward to study its design. A Russian
trawler, he realised, and close—much too close for comfort.
His orders had been clear. No witnesses. When the
Endurance went down, she had to sink beneath the icepack without trace. They would have to wait. Another
twelve hours at least. Trujillo wouldn't like it, but there
was no alternative. There must be nothing left to link
the vessel's disappearance with the military command in
Buenos Aires. Trujillo would have to curb his impatience
and stand by one more day.

David lay on his bunk listening to the steady throb of the
engines as the cruiser sped swiftly through the South
Atlantic night, dipping and swaying in the heavy swell. It
was a curious sensation being at sea. He could hear Anne
and Stone laughing in the master stateroom next door, and
the sound depressed him. His thoughts lay heavily in his
head, filling him with a sense of impending loss, conscious
that through the polished veneer of the bulwark, the
woman he wanted more than anything else in the world was
locked with another man in the rhythms of love. His
imagination ran riot. He saw Stone's hands kneading her
flesh, Stone's lips pressed against her throat, her breasts,
her ears.

In the end, unable to stand it any longer, he got up,
dressed and made his way to the top deck. Standing at the
rail with spray lashing his face, he stared in silence into the
blustery darkness. It would be a long trip, he realised,
fraught with tension and danger. He had put himself in the
firing line for one reason only. To win Anne back. But first
he had to control his emotions. He hadn't won yet, so there
was no damn sense getting into a cold sweat just because
she belonged to Stone—he'd known that from the beginning. What he was planning required coolness and restaint.

When the time came, he would change everything, but for the moment, Stone's hold on Anne was something he had to live with.

For the moment, he thought. Only for the moment.

And with his face beaded with moisture, he strolled back below and crawled dejectedly into bed.

SEVEN

Next morning, they crossed Drake Passage off the tip of Cape Horn, encountering their first bout of violent weather, strong winds and giant waves which crashed over the foredeck and sent the vessel lunging and wheeling in the swell. Stone placed the upper decks out of bounds, and David spent most of his time in his cabin feeling sick and miserable. Everything that moved had to be strapped down. Even the glass on his bunkside table had to be taped securely to the cabin wall. The waves battered at the porthole window as he lay on his bunk and thought about nothing.

For two days, he scarcely touched a morsel of food. Then, on the third morning, the sea steadied. Stone explained they were nearing the pack-ice, which soothed the ocean, smoothed out the ripples and swells, brought a sensation of peace and tranquillity. In the galley, David ate breakfast for the first time.

He was feeling washed-out but decidedly better as he strolled the deck in the morning sunshine. An albatross wheeled above the foscle, squawking shrilly as David studied the gunmetal grey of the distant horizon. Just before noon, he spotted a pale blob drifting to the east. An iceberg. He hurried into the wheelhouse where Stone was working on the charts. "Seen the floe?" David said breathlessly.

Stone chuckled. His attitude toward David had warmed noticeably since they had decided to team up together. David had no idea if Stone suspected, or even cared about, his intentions regarding Anne. He continued to be friendly—a trifle aloof, but then aloofness was an integral part of the man's character, a throwback probably to the inherent haughtiness of the British upper classes and behind it all David sensed a new responsiveness, as if the Englishman, conscious of David's value as an ally, had decided to defer any doubts about his motives until their enterprise was over.

"I know how you feel," Stone smiled. "There's nothing quite like one's first glimpse of an iceberg."

David stood on the topdeck watching the glistening monument steadily approaching. Within an hour, they were almost alongside. Stone joined David at the rail, peering at the massive tower rising out of the water, its serrated flanks swelling into a multi-pointed summit. Time and the sea had carved it into a sculpture of the most exquisite beauty.

"Do you realise that nine-tenths of all the fresh water in the world is locked up down here?" Stone told him. "When we get further south, you'll see ice twelve miles thick. Imagine the effect that would have if it all began to melt."

"Why are some bits green?" David asked.

"They're the oldest sections. Some of that ice is thousands of years old, remember."

"You're kidding."

"Not at all. In our hemisphere, we think of ice as a transitory thing. Down here, it's practically eternal. I always try to grab a piece of the green stuff for the refrigerator. Tastes marvelous in a glass of gin."

By evening, they had reached the beginning of the pack-ice. It lay across the sea like a living skin, broken in places by the jagged outlines of floating bergs. In the distance, David could see a range of snow-capped mountain tips. Their flanks were coal black, and across their bases great glaciers tumbled towards the ocean, shimmering in the sunlight. In places, the ice was as smooth as frosting on a Christmas cake, in others its surface was criss-crossed with fissures, moulded into a bewildering array of funnels, towers and archways. Antarctica, he thought, his heart racing.

Stone explained that the pack looked relatively thin and with his reinforced hull he hoped to ram a way through to

clearer water. They drove at the floating ice curtain, their
prow carving a narrow passage through its brittle surface,
the stuff breaking before them with a satisfying crunching
sound as David stood in the focsle, watching the giant slabs
snap and tilt in their path. At last however, the vessel
slithered to a halt. The ice had thickened and even with the
full thrust of their engines, they could move no further.

Stone backed up and tried again. The vessel crunched to
a standstill, the ice closing around it. This time, even at full
throttle, Stone was unable to reverse. "We're stuck," he
announced.

David could hear the pressure of the ice building up on
the metal hull.

"What happens now?"

"We'll have to wait until morning. When the tide
changes, we'll give it another go. Don't worry, the ice will
shift around dawn."

With his face burned by the sun and his great shock of
white hair fluttering furiously in the wind, Stone looked
transported, as if nothing, not even the forces of nature,
could stand against him or interfere with the task he had set
himself. David studied him warily, noting the irrepressible
confidence of the man, hoping to God he knew what he was
doing.

That night, the ice's pressure tilted the cruiser gradually
sideways. On all sides, the white curtain closed in, locking
them tight until David felt like a man marooned on a distant
planet. Throughout dinner, he listened to the noise of the
ice grinding against the defenceless hull, then, towards
midnight, he wandered up on deck, staring across the
monotonous glazed vista. Their vessel had become an
island trapped in a frozen ocean. Giant bergs glistened
pinkly in the fading daylight, their awesome shapes drained
by the gentle beams of sunlight, their textures infused with
a strange, almost incandescent glow. Beauty was a strange
thing, David thought, for never in his life had he witnessed
anything so exquisite, and its allure was enhanced by its
very deadness, as if the unalterable cycles of life had
somehow halted and grown still. They seemed to have
reached a point in time and space where the entire world
was suspended. The sun and moon hung side by side in an

endless sky, and there was a feeling of peace, space, eternity.

He was aware of a change within him, a calmness, a sense of his own place in the order of things, as if the scene he was witnessing was imposing upon his consciousness visible proof of his own humanity. It was impossible to gaze across that lost, dead world and not grasp the inescapable rhythm of life. It was all around him, permeating, difficult to ignore.

When David woke next morning, the engines were already throbbing. The wind had shifted, and with the changing tide pushing the pack from below, the vessel's diesels began to haul them clear. Soon they were back in open water, chugging gracefully through the minefield of ice-floes toward the approaching mountains.

David stood in the bow, watching clusters of penguins, their bellies gleaming brightly as they streaked like darts through the crystal water swirling across their path. He spotted a whale on the far horizon, but one glimpse was all he got. The giant mammal, sensing the yacht's approach, turned with a flip of its tail and plunged for cover.

"They've learned their lesson well," Stone observed dryly. "They know now who their natural enemies are."

In spite of the snow, David felt little discomfort. Wrapped in thick woollens and heavy anorak, he scarcely noticed the cold. The Antarctic sunshine seemed almost pleasant against his cheek and he watched the mountains growing steadily nearer, mesmerised by their beauty. Jagged peaks reared against the sky. Craggy cliffs plunged to the sea. It was like creeping toward an endless range of Alps, he thought.

Soon they were in a slender channel surrounded on all sides by snow-capped tips. Stone called it Kodak Alley because of the channel's majestic beauty. It looked breath-taking in the morning sunlight. Rippling glaciers dipped awesomely and shark-toothed ridges towered above the water, but despite its attraction David knew the channel presented constant danger for it was too narrow, too restricting, there was little room to manoeuvre; the thin sliver of ocean lapping between its walls was choked with ice, and their progress was pitifully slow. Several times,

Stone had to stop the engines and pull back, seeking a new
way through. Then, as they approached the final narrows,
David felt the tension beginning to ease. The mountains
fell away, opening out as the cruiser sailed sedately into a
stretch of clear water.

By late afternoon however, they had encountered a new
hazard. Fog. It came at them in swirling strands which
seemed to hang soggily above the mainmast and funnel.
With visibility cut to a minimum, David knew pressing on
would be little short of madness. The only answer was to
drop anchor.

"We're pretty close to Bromley Base," Stone grunted.
"We'll try to reach it in the outboard."

"Supposing we get lost?"

"No problem. We'll follow the shoreline, and if my
assessment proves incorrect, we'll simply retrace our
steps."

In the small power boat, David and Anne crouched in
the stern and Stone squatted in the bow as they chugged
through the swirling wisps of fog. A single sailor guided the
craft around the maze of inlets and channels, the icebergs
distorted by the mist and looming eerily as they floated
through a world of mystic beauty.

David was trying hard not to look at Anne. He had
already made up his mind he would attempt no more
approaches, no more overtures until he was surer of his
ground. When a man made a fool of himself, he got doubly
cautious. He had controlleld his emotions nicely after that
first day out, but it wasn't an easy game he played, and he
knew contact would destroy all his good intentions. He had
to take it slowly, a step at a time. He had to be cautious and
prudent.

Suddenly, directly ahead, David saw a bizarre sight.
Perched on a rock in the middle of the ocean stood a British
telephone booth. Its scarlet walls seemed to glisten against
the towering background of ice.

Stone chuckled. "Found it," he said. "The base is just
across the inlet. The boys built that dummy phone booth so
they could watch it from their dormitory windows and think
of home."

David saw the shoreline looming through the fog.

Buildings gradually took shape, a series of wooden huts, painted green, spread across a flat-topped rock which rose above the ocean. The craggy slab of a mountain face reared behind them, and their outlines seemed dwarfed by a series of spindly radio masts etched against the snow. David studied them in silence. In such a desolate wasteland, the base seemed pitifully small.

The inhabitants showed no surprise at the visitors' arrival. Stone, it transpired, called in frequently on his wildlife expeditions and was warmly welcomed, though with a certain reserve, David noticed. He wondered if the scientists, bearded young men in woolly jumpers, resented their presence, but Stone told him not to worry. It was a natural human reaction, he said, for men who spent two-year stretches shut away in a tiny sanctuary thousands of miles from human contact. They were always a little nervous at any intrusion from the outside world.

The hut interiors proved to be primitive and functional, but at least they were warm. David felt thankful for that. The bare corridors opened into a selection of tiny offices which bristled with computers, scanners, and various intricate pieces of equipment. The walls were covered with photographs—not pin-ups, as David might have expected, but pictures of the English Lake District, the Scottish Highlands, Cotswold Villages, thatched cottages, rolling meadows. He smiled gently to himself. Men marooned so far from home knew where their priorities lay.

"What do you do here?" he asked the lead scientist, a shaggy-haired young man with a Glaswegian accent.

"Weather readings mostly," the scientist said. "We send regular reports to Buenos Aires to complete the international weather picture. We check the equipment every couple of hours day and night, all the year around. We also carry out long-term research on the upper atmosphere."

"What for?"

"Oh, we look for ways of improving radio signals, study the effects of carbon dioxide on the ozone layer, that sort of thing. In addition, we do mineral studies and survey work, including wildlife conservation. At the moment, for example, we're investigating the possibility of using krill, which thrives in Antarctic waters, for animal feed. We're also testing the feasibility of towing icebergs to countries like Saudi Arabia and Australia, though I have to admit that's pretty much of a long-shot."

"How about supplies?"

"Well, the mail ship arrives every six months. It brings our provisions and picks up our garbage."

"Your garbage?" David echoed.

The scientist smiled. "That's the trouble with Antarctica. Nothing rots. We've tried everything—septic tanks, incinerators, God knows what else. Now we seal it into special canisters and let the ship carry it out."

David spent nearly an hour wandering around the base. Somehow the stark nature of the dwellings seemed to accentuate the precariousness of man's toehold on the Antarctic continent. Space was at a premium. The men lived four to a room, sleeping in bunks in heavily-overcrowded conditions. And all the time, the complex network of equipment went on monitoring activity both above and below the endless eiderdown of snow and ice.

When evening came, they retreated to the recreation area which had been converted into a perfect replica of a British country pub, with low beams, drinking booths, a copper-lined counter, horse-brasses, even a dartboard by the window.

"The boys did it all themsevles," the lead scientist explained. "When you're a long way from home, it's amazing how important even the smallest reminders can be."

He went behind the bar and drew them each a glass of beer. Then he filled a glass for himself, swallowed it down in almost one draught, and wiped the froth from his whiskers with the back of one hand. "Now," he said, "what's this all about?"

Stone was silent for a moment as he nudged his own glass along the counter, leaving little circles of moisture on its copper suface. His face looked reflective and composed. "It's what you might call a business proposition," he said.

"What kind of business?"

"The personal kind. I'm looking for men to form a small expedition."

"We can't leave the base unattended, you know that."

"We wouldn't dream of asking you to. It's mainly yourself we need, plus perhaps about half a dozen others just to make the numbers right. You're still the official magistrate of the area, aren't you?"

"That's correct."

"And the British government representative?"

The scientist nodded.

"That means you would be quite within your rights, as emissary of the Crown, to visit all foreign bases in the vicinity, including Camp Digepol?"

The sceintist looked puzzled. "Strictly speaking, yes. We've never actually done it, of course."

"Supposing I asked you to do it now?"

"Why should I?"

"Money, for one thing. You'll be well-paid. But it's more than just a question of finance."

The scientist's frown deepened as Stone outlined the events of the past few weeks. He told the scientist about Colonel Pinilla, about David's encounter with Señor Uceda at the Buenos Aries naval academy, and about his own deeply-held conviction that a Falklands invasion was imminent.

"So you see," he concluded, rolling his glass between his fingertips, "our plan is to spring Pinilla out of the prison camp and present him to the Foreign Office as a *fait accompli*. We've worked out a plan largely involving David here which we're pretty sure will work, but first we have to get inside that compound."

The scientist's eyes were shining. "By God, you've got a hell of a nerve," he whispered. "If the Argies catch you, they'll blow your bloody brains out."

"Have you seen this prison camp?" David asked him softly.

"Only from a distance. It's further down the peninsula, about twelve miles inland. They're using convicts to carry out exploratory drilling operations."

"Drilling for what?"

"Oil. The Argies have been after the stuff for years. Of course, they're breaking the Antarctic Treaty by maintaining armed troops at Camp Digepol, but most of the other bases turn a blind eye to that."

"Well, what about it?" Stone demanded impatiently. "Will you help us or not?"

The scientist grinned, his eyes flashing beneath his heavy brows. "Don't worry, Mr. Stone, there's not a man on this camp who wouldn't jump at the chance to take a crack at those Argies. Speaking for myself, I'm so bloody bored around here, I might just decide to spring that informer of yours single-handed."

It was too late to press on any further that day so they spent the night moored among the ice and next morning, after taking on board six scientists and various pieces of equipment which Stone paid for at highly inflated prices, they sailed down the coast and dropped anchor in a narrow inlet flanked on all sides by snow-covered mountains.

That evening, as David sat in his cabin sorting out his gear, he began to regret his decision to help in Pinilla's rescue. At the start, it had seemed a marvellous idea, the perfect way to attract Anne's interest and sympathy, but as the hours went by, a pall of discomfort settled firmly in his stomach. He knew the symptoms, had experienced them often enough before. He was frightened. The first part of the operation would be simple enough, he knew, but once inside the prison camp, everything—success or failure—would depend on him. The risks would be his, the decisions his, the danger. If anything went wrong, he would be the one who would face the consequences. It seemed a high price to pay in the pursuit of love.

Soberly, he climbed into the padded overtrousers and heavy jacket provided by the research station scientists. They were the nearest they had, they said, to the clothing worn by the convicts at the prison camp. The colours were a little brighter, but with luck nobody would notice the difference.

As he zipped up the front of his jacket, David caught a glimpse of himself in the cabin mirror. He looked like something out of a horror movie, he thought wryly, for early that afternoon Magnus Stone had shaved the top of his head clean and now his skull gleamed smoothly in the pale glow of the electric light. The hairless dome seemed to imbue his face with an air of coarseness, even villainy, completely transforming his features and making him look, even to himself, strangely remote and unreal.

He pulled on the woolen cap Stone had given him, and was about to pick up his haversack when there was a light tap on the cabin door and Anne entered. She was dressed in a pair of heavy corded trousers and a thick woollen jumper and her face looked pale and serious. "We're almost ready," she said softly.

"I'll only be a minute."

She sat down on the narrow bunk. "You're still determined to go through with this?"

"Why not?"

"You're an American. It's not your fight."

"I thought we were friends. That's what you said, wasn't it? I mean, what are friends for, if not to help each other?"

"Do you take me for a bloody fool? You're not doing it out of friendship's sake. You've hardly spoken a word to me throughout this entire voyage. Now suddenly, and without any kind of explanation, you volunteer to risk your life to save a man you scarcely even know on a madcap escapade that involves a totally foreign country. It's irrational."

"Life's irrational," David stated. "Do I have to dream up logical reasons for every move I make?"

"You don't give a damn about Hugo Pinilla. You're doing it to impress me. You think I'll be so overwhelmed, I'll fall into your arms out of sheer gratitude."

"No. If you want to know the truth, I can't resist the temptation to play the hero, that's all."

Her eyes held his steadily and he sensed the determination in her, the cold, resolute certainty that, from the beginning, from the very first night they had met, had made him feel awkward and inept.

"Let's get one thing clear before we set out," she snapped.

"Anything you say."

"Whatever happens tomorrow, whether we rescue Pinilla or not, I want you to know it can have no possible bearing on my feelings toward you, nor will it alter my relationship with Magnus. It's important you appreciate that, so you will be under no illusions."

He stared at her in silence for a moment, a tightness

moving through him as he tried hard to hide his dismay. Christ, she didn't make things easy, he thought. But he still had time on his side. All he had to do was hold on to his nerve.

"Message received loud and clear," he answered evenly. "I appreciate the warning, but I'm doing this for personal reasons. You don't figure in my plans at all."

He stooped and picked up his haversack from the cabin floor. "Now let's get up on deck before the others freeze to death."

In the chill stillness of the Antarctic night, they found Stone and the scientists busily lowering four skiddoos over the side of the ship to the icepack below. The skiddoos were compact vehicles, rather like motorcycles, which ran on runners instead of wheels. Each carried two to three persons, with haversacks and equipment strapped in panniers to the flanks.

When Stone saw David, he grinned at him wolfishly, his breath leaving a hazy cloud on the ice-bound air. His hood was down and against the darkness his white hair seemed to frame his skull in a pale halo. "How do you feel?" he asked.

"Like a brass monkey," David told him. "How long before the sun gets up?"

Stone chuckled. "Give it an hour. We'll soon have you warm again. Cyril contacted the camp by radio an hour ago. They're expecting us around midday tomorrow."

"For Christ's sake, the damn place is only twelve miles away."

Stone's smile broadened. "Easy to see you're unused to Antarctic travel my friend. The skiddoos here can cover ground quickly, I agree, but we don't know the terrain. We'll have to move at a snail's pace, watch out for hidden crevasses, that sort of thing. You'll find midday is a reasonable estimate, I assure you."

David grunted and glanced back at Anne who was standing in the shadow of the wheelhouse. She was stamping her feet, her breath steaming on the chill night air. David felt a tremor ripple through his diaphragm. He was no hero, never pretended to be. A beautiful girl, a breathless memory of one never-to-be-forgotten night, and some kind of madness had overtaken him. He hoped to God he wouldn't live to regret it.

Breathing deeply, he rubbed his cheeks with his fingertips. "What the hell are we waiting for?" he snapped.

And slinging a leg over the ship's rail, he clambered down the rope to the ice below.

Colonel Moncada, commandant of Camp Digepol prison, finished his breakfast and gently dabbed at his lips with his napkin. He stared at his aide, Major Diogenes, sitting across the table opposite him. "You're sure the call was genuine?" he inquired.

"Quite sure," the major assured him. "They used the recognised call-sign."

"It seems so strange," the colonel muttered, shaking his head. "In six years, the British have totally ignored our presence here. Now, when we have on our premises an officer engaged in a secret operation to destroy a British ship, they decide to pay us a social call."

"Pure chance, I suspect," the major said with a shrug. "I feel sure there's a perfectly innocent explanation. A new leader at Bromley Base perhaps. New leaders are notorious for wanting to establish new routines."

"Can we refuse them entry, d'you think?" the colonel wondered.

The major pulled a face. "Most unwise. The British regard the Antarctic Peninsula as their own sovereign territory. They think they have a God-given right to go anywhere they please. In view of the circumstances, I consider we would be ill-advised to rock the boat at this delicate stage."

The commandant thought for a moment. "How close is Colonel Cuellar to completing his task?"

"Very close, I understand. He's spotted a Russian trawler in the vicinity and is waiting for the vessel to depart before he radios his pilot in Rio Gallegos. Naturally, there must be no question of suspicion falling on the Argentine government, which is why, *coronel*, I suggest that we make our visitors as welcome as possible and take care to observe all the proprieties."

The colonel considered the idea. He was a dull-witted

man who had been given the command of Camp Digepol because of his family connections. He picked up his cup and drained the last of his coffee, then glanced at his wristwatch.

"It's nearly eight-thirty. The work-gangs will be setting out shortly to the drilling rigs."

"In my opinion, the less the British know about what we're actually doing here, the better," the major said.

"I agree. We'll close down the rigs at least for today. All prisoners will be confined to their compounds. We'll double up the schedules tomorrow morning to make up for lost time."

"What about the flag, *coronel*?" the major asked.

The colonel looked blank. "Flag?"

"Well, it's customary in a case like this . . . that is, when one is operating on the sovereign territory of another nation, to fly that nation's flag when visitors arrive."

The colonel frowned. "Do we have one?"

"The Union Jack? I'm sure we must."

"Then get it aloft as quickly as possible. We must give our guests no cause for concern."

The major hesitated. "It's not quite as simple as that, *coronel*. The Union Jack must be flown above the blue-and-the-white. It's a question of protocol."

The colonel stared at him, affronted. "Never," he snapped. "Whatever the British claim, the Antarctic Peninsula belongs to Argentina."

The major sighed. Leaning forward, he said insistently: "What we are discussing here, *coronel*, is a question of political necessity. We must avoid a confrontation at all costs. We have too much to lose to risk upsetting our callers over a pointless gesture. I say, let us observe protocol to the letter."

The colonel pushed away his plate and sat back in his chair. His face looked flushed and angry, but there was a gleam or resignation in his eyes as, sighing, he rose to his feet, lifting his tunic from the coat-peg. Through the windows, he could see the barbed-wire compounds and the rows of prisoners' huts beyond.

"As usual you are right, my friend. My responses in such

matters are altogether too emotional. Where would I be without your level head, I wonder?"

The major smiled. "You are a soldier, *coronel*. It is part of a soldier's nature to uphold his country's honour. This is a political issue and no one expects you to be a politician."

The colonel paused in the act of pulling on his tunic. "You do realise we have the traitor Pinilla in our care?"

"I have thought of that, *coronel*."

"Is it possible . . . just remotely possible . . . that this so-called goodwill visit has something to do with that?"

"I don't see how," the major answered.

"Supposing they ask to see Pinilla?"

The major shrugged. "Even if they know of his existence, which seems extremely unlikely, we will simply deny all knowledge of the man."

The colonel scratched his cheekbone. "Is he still in solitary confinement?"

"Of course. The orders were quite explicit. He is to be held in maximum security and allowed no contact with the other prisoners."

"Just the same, in view of the circumstances I think we should take special care when our guests arrive today. It's not that I don't trust our security arrangements, Ramon, but I want the guard doubled on Hugo Pinilla, at least until this evening."

The major nodded slowly. "Very well," he promised. "I'll see to it right away."

Magnus Stone lowered his field glasses. From their position on the hilltop they could see the camp quite clearly, sprawled in the snow-filled saucer beneath them. The sun glinted on the metal roofs and David could discern the barbed-wire perimeter fences, the stark watchtowers, the guards patrolling the prison compounds. He glanced at his watch. It was ten minutes to noon. Stone's estimate had been right all along.

"We'll leave the skiddoos here," Stone said. "Don't want the Argies to know what equipment we're carrying."

"How many remain behind?" David asked.

"Only Anne. She can wait until our return."

"Shouldn't someone stay with her?"

"She'll be all right. We need as many faces as we can
muster so the Argies won't notice the difference when you
disappear."

"If everyone goes, that'll make seven of us altogether."

"That's right. Try and slip off the minute you get a chance.
If they invite us for lunch, they might start counting."

David nodded. Stone's face looked tanned and fit. Not
once throughout the long journey inland had he faltered,
even for an instant, and despite the maturity of his years,
David realised Stone was probably the most robust speci-
men among them. Ageing he might be, but there was no
denying the life and energy that flowed in him yet. He
made a powerful rival.

"You're clear about what happens when you get Pinilla
out?" Stone asked.

"I think so. We make our way to the derelict whaling
station down the coast."

"Correct. No point heading back to the cruiser. It's the
first place the Argentines will look. We'll pick you up early
tomorrow morning."

David turned to say goodbye to Anne but she studiously
avoided his eyes. A flash of anger moved through him. He
wasn't going to cry on her shoulder, for Christ's sake. If she
wanted to play dumb and hard to get, to hell with her. He
had enough on his mind without worrying about her.

They set off when they were ready, the scientists at the
front, Magnus Stone bringing up the rear. David positioned
himself roughly in the middle where his bony frame would
be less conspicuous. He still wore the stocking cap to hide
his shaven skull.

In the brilliant sunlight, he watched the prison compound drawing steadily closer. The barbed-wire fences and
the functional starkness of the prisoners' huts looked grim
and austere.

David glimpsed soldiers gathering in the area around the
main gate. He spotted a man in colonel's uniform waiting
patiently in the entrance. He was grey-haired, and the gold
braid around his cap-band seemed to shimmer in the
sunlight. His high boots were brightly polished, and
beneath his tunic he wore a rolltop sweater instead of a
shirt. He saluted smartly as they marched up.

"Welcome to Camp Digepol," he announced, shaking each of their hands in turn. "Our amenities here are somewhat primitive but entirely at your disposal. We trust your visit will prove a friendly and constructive one. Please accompany me to the reception centre where the necessary documentation can be completed."

He shepherded them through the gates into the prison camp proper, and David felt his pulses beginning to race. They were in. Now there could be no turning back.

A small knot of worry gathered in his diaphragm, swelling outwards. Somehow—and he had no idea precisely how to manage it—he had to lose himself in the camp's interior before the Argentines established precisely how many scientists were in their party. There were guards everywhere, though none of them were armed, David noticed. The commandant had clearly decided to observe the rules of the Antarctic Treaty, at least until his visitors had departed.

He steered them toward a large timbered building which David took to be the camp's administrative section; it looked more spacious and elegant than the sombre rows of huts behind it, and its approach paths had been carefully cleared of snow.

The colonel ushered them through the front door and along a passageway into a pleasant well-ordered office where a tray of drinks, ready-poured, stood on a polished cocktail table. The colonel invited his guests to help themselves while he opened a drawer and pulled out a large official-looking visitors' book. David glanced quickly around. He knew there was no sense in waiting any longer. It was time to move. Time to show what he was made of. He felt very small. A small man in a huge world.

His body tingling with tension, he ducked back into the passageway, pretending to look for the washroom. He pulled off his stocking cap, pushing it into his jacket pocket, then with his heart beating wildly and his shaved skull clearly exposed, he stepped from the administrative building and began to cross the crowded square. The buildings opposite see-sawed in his vision. Heat-waves seemed to ripple off the crusted snow and his whole body trembled with fear and apprehension.

He had almost reached the other side when a harsh voice jerked him to a halt. "You there," it bellowed. "Stand where you are."

David felt his heart sink as he froze to attention. Panic rose inside his chest, funnelling upwards, deadening his senses until he could scarcely think or breathe. He saw a soldier strolling toward him, his bulky figure enclosed in a padded khaki jacket. He was a thick-set man with a heavy brutish face and a thin moustache which barely concealed the traces of a hair-lip. His eyes were small and close together and his brows met at the bridge of his nose. He peered at David suspiciously. "Who gave you permission to walk here? You know all prisoners are confined to their quarters."

David's heart leapt and his mind raced desperately. "I . . . I'm on a special detail, señor," he whispered.

"What detail?"

"Snow clearance."

"Snow clearance?" The soldier's tone was incredulous. "Are you mad? Prison duties have been suspended for twenty-four hours. What is your name?"

"Campos, sir," David muttered miserably.

"And your hut number?"

"Twenty-four."

The soldier pursed his lips, his small eyes fixing intently on David's face. He had the air of a man to whom life's small precise details offered a constant source of fascination. "Who is your compound leader?"

Oh Christ, David thought. He was not prepared for close scrutiny, had gambled everything on a clean uncomplicated break-in and an even cleaner getaway. In desperation, he chose the first name that came into his head, the name of his father's friend. "Alberto Farrel."

"Farrel?" The soldier's eyes narrowed. "I know of no compound leader called Farrel."

"He is . . . a replacement. Our usual man has fallen ill."

The soldier seemed slightly reassured, but his expression was still wary and suspicious. "Who issued the order for snow clearance?" he snapped.

"The commandant himself, señor. The colonel wanted

the area in front of the messhall cleared before his guests arrived for lunch."

The mention of the colonel seemed to have a calming effect upon the soldier who peered at David closely, sniffing through his nose. When he spoke again, his voice was softer and had a slight lisp to it. "Well," he said, "what do you expect to clear it with, your bare hands?"

"I . . . I was on my way to pick up a shovel, sir."

"In this direction?"

David felt panic rising in his chest. He stared at the soldier, dumbfounded, unable to speak.

"You know where the toolshed is. Over by the cookhouse. Where the hell do you think you are going, man?"

"To relieve myself," David said breathlessly.

"Relieve yourself?" The soldier's eyes widened. "The colonel orders you to clear the snow from the front of the messhall and you wander off to relieve yourself?"

"It's an emergency," David protested.

"Do it in your pants, *cabrone*."

"My pants? Yes, sir."

"Now turn around and get back to that toolshed on the double."

His body trembling, David trotted back the way he had come. The soldier stood watching him in silence, his hands on his hips. He waited until David had covered nearly thirty yards, then he bellowed: "Stop, you idiot. Where the hell do you think you're going now?"

Miserably, David turned, straightening to attention. The soldier was shaking his head in exasperation. "Are you blind as well as mad? There's the toolshed man, right in front of you." He pointed to a small wooden shack, his cheeks mottled with fury. "If I see you clowning around again, I'll make you curse your mother for giving you birth."

Gulping hard, David scrambled to the tiny shack and let himself inside. Pickaxes, shovels and assorted digging tools lined the walls, but to David's relief, the hut was empty. He sat on the floor holding his breath, his whole body shaking violently. It had been a close call, dangerously close. He had been a hair's breadth from disaster. Barely thirty seconds in the compound and already he had been challenged. But at least the man hadn't noticed the difference in his clothing. That was one thing in his favour. He inhaled slowly, filling his lungs, expelling the air through his nose as he struggled to regain control.

He waited almost an hour until he was sure the compound was relatively clear, then easing through the door, he began to move in the opposite direction. From this point, he could see the prisoners' quarters clearly. Their huts stood in orderly rows, the austere fronts comfortless and chilling. He spotted the convicts themselves strolling around their narrow enclosures or gathering in groups inside the barbed wire. Each hut was fenced off individually from the others, but the wire strands were set wide apart and served more as a demarcation line than an actual physical barrier.

David hesitated as he glanced swiftly around, his eyes seeking out the soldiers in the square behind him. No one appeared to be looking in his direction. In a single movement, he ducked beneath the strands of barbed wire and straightened cautiously, mingling with the convicts on the other side. His nerves were at screaming point as he waited for someone to challenge his presence, but no one did. Moving to the corner, he squatted on the ground, resting his spine against the fencepost. For a while, he scanned the inmates' faces. They looked a rough and seedy lot, their shaved head burned by the Antarctic sun. There was no sign of Hugo Pinilla.

At last, feeling his confidence returning, he rose to his feet and ambled casually toward a solitary convict standing with his arms hooked over the wire strand, peering across the compound beyond. He was a small man, very thickset, with a villainous face and a heavily-jowled chin. For a moment, David stood at his side staring in the same direction. Then he said casually: "What's going on out there?"

The man glanced at him, his face expressionless. "Don't you know?"

David's eyes picked out Magnus Stone and his friends coming out of the admin. building. "Looks like some kind of delegation."

"For Christ's sake, you must walk around with your eyes shut. Why do you think we're not working today? Because the colonel thinks we need a little shut-eye? He's pulled us off the drilling rigs because the British scientists from Bromley have decided to pay him a call, and it wouldn't do, would it, to let our dear neighbours know that we're drilling for oil?"

"Yes, well I'm sort of new around here," David explained.

"New?" The man peered at him suspiciously. "When did you arrive?"

"Yesterday morning. They . . . they flew me from Rio Gallegos."

"I didn't see any plane arrive. Normally we get our intakes every fortnight. We're not expecting the next bunch for another ten days at least."

"This was a special flight," David said hurriedly, "authorised by the central office in B.A. Straight in, straight out. The pilot didn't even wait for supper. I guess you must have missed it."

"Yeah," the man's eyes were still fixed shrewdly on David's face. "I must have."

David hooked his arm over the wire rim, trying hard to look nonchalant.

"I've got a friend down here," he said. "They brought him in about a month ago. Name of Hugo Pinilla."

The convict shook his head. "Never heard of him," he stated.

"Tall man, sort of loose and gangly. Around the forty mark."

"I told you, there's nobody called Pinilla in this camp."

"He probably walks with a limp," David insisted. "He got shot in the thigh when he was arrested."

"Oh." The convict frowned. "That sounds like number 652. Don't you know we go by numbers here? They like to dehumanise us as much as possible."

David hesitated, picking at the wire points with his fingernail. "Any idea where I'll find him, this 652?"

The man laughed shortly. "You can forget that," he said. "Nobody's seen the bastard since he arrived. They're keeping him strictly under wraps. Over there." He nodded at a hut standing near the opposite end of the compound, almost directly in line with the toolshed. As he watched, David saw the door open and a soldier peer outside.

"That's his personal guard," the convict explained. "There's always at least two of them on duty, night and day. This morning, they doubled the sentry roster. Now they've got four in there, and they're all armed. Try and get near the place, they'll blow the top of your head off."

"He must come out sometime," David murmured.

"Don't you believe it. Everything the man does takes place inside that hut, eating, sleeping, pissing. They don't even let the poor bastard into the daylight. I don't know what crime your friend committed, but the way they're treating him he might as well have been buried alive."

David was silent as he stared across the compound, his optimism fading. A sense of profound depression took hold of him. He had counted on contacting Pinilla by evening. Now everything—the plan, the escape, the proposed rescue—seemed on the point of disintegrating. With his segregated quarters and armed guards to protect him, their Argentine informer looked more remote and unreachable than ever.

EIGHT

Stone and his companions left in the late afternoon. David watched them setting off across the snow-covered plain, their outlines blurred against the glare of the sun, the colonel smiling, shaking each of their hands in turn, waving from the gate as they moved diagonally towards the rim of the distant ridge. Somehow the sight of the scientists' departure filled David with a sense of desolation. He felt like a marooned sailor watching his last hope of rescue fading across the horizon. Nothing was working out the way it was meant to. The first part had gone all right. Oh yes, the first part had been fine. He'd gotten in without any trouble, but now he was trapped, shut off and friendless, with the man he had come to spring sealed up and guarded like Fort Knox, for Christ's sake.

He moved back to the perch against the fencepost, sick with worry, sick with the hopelessness of his situation. He wished to God he was free again. But there was no way out. Not yet. He had nothing to do but wait.

Just before six a buzzer sounded above the camp's administrative block, the noise echoing shrilly across the crowded compound. Without a word, the prisoners shuffled into orderly lines and stood waiting patiently. David joined them, positioning himself in the centre of the row, reflecting on the fortunate caprice of nature which had made him lean and cadaverous-looking, allowing him to mingle unobtrusively with his haggard companions. After a moment, soldiers arrived to marshal them to the messhall. Now that the British visitors had left, the soldiers openly sported their carbines.

In the chow-hut, David queued with the others at the hotplate where convicts in white aprons passed out dishes of steaming food. A large sign hung beneath the raftered ceiling. "Eat All You Want," it said, "But No Waste."

David took his plate, gathered a handful of cutlery, and made his way to the nearest of the long trestle tables. The noise inside the messhall was deafening. Men were talking and eating at the same time, scraping their forks against the metal tableware as they scooped up mouthfuls of food.

David chose a chair set slightly apart from the others and settled himself down, trying to look inconspicuous. He was hoping no one would notice the subtle difference in his clothing. He had scarcely begun to eat when he suddenly became aware that the conversation at the table had halted and everyone was staring at him, their eyes curious and intent. David felt his stomach lurch. Putting down his fork, he swallowed wildly, peering back at the faces gazing into his.

"What are you doing?" a man asked. He was lean and bony with a huge Adam's apple which bobbed against the muscles of his throat.

"Eating," David answered uncertainly.

"Expect to eat again?"

Confusion flooded David and he felt the colour mounting in his cheeks.

"I . . . I don't understand," he muttered.

"Don't you know whose chair you're sitting on?"

David peered wildly down at his seat.

"That chair belongs to Papá Grande," the thin man said. "Let him catch you in it and he'll snap you into little pieces."

David rose hurriedly to his feet. "I'm sorry," he stammered. "I'm kind of new here. Part of the recent intake. I guess I don't know the rules yet."

He picked up his tray and moved to another table, selecting a place that was suitably integrated with the main body of diners. His hand was trembling as he started to eat. Close, he thought. The masquerade was proving more difficult than he'd expected. In fact, he must have been crazy to think he would get away with it, the hours alone, desperate, isolated, struggling to survive in an unfamiliar environment. How simple the idea had seemed in the comfort of Stone's stateroom. Nothing to worry about. In at noon, out at midnight. But what about the hours in between? And what about the man he had come to get? Trussed up and guarded to the eyeballs. It was madness. A fiasco. And for what? A girl who didn't give a damn if he lived or died. Who regarded him at best as an amusing diversion, at worst as an insufferable intruder.

The meal over, the convicts again formed orderly lines and were marched back to their barrack huts. At the prison enclosures the men dispersed to their individual quarters and David, with his heart beating wildly, mingled with the nearest group, entering their billet. It was long and angular, with wooden bunks arranged around the walls. Two stoves stood in the centre of the floor, their metal bellies glowing with the heat. David moved toward them and sat down, pretending to warm himself. The others gathered around their beds.

When the prisoners were all inside, the troops moved along the line of huts locking each of the doors in turn. David saw the man on the adjacent bed peering at him intently and felt his spirits plummet.

"Who the hell are you?" the man hissed.

David pretended to look around in a show of sudden confusion. "Christ, I must have entered the wrong hut," he exclaimed.

A murmur ran through the cluster of skeletal faces and the prisoners gathered around him, their eyes tense and hostile. He could smell the odour emanating from their unwashed clothing and their shaved heads gleamed in the glow of the electric light.

"I've never seen this man before," someone stated. "He's no prisoner. Look at his clothing."

David felt his heart sink as they tore open the front of his padded jacket.

"Look at his shirt. That's not prison issue."

Their hands seized him from every side. He made no attempt to struggle. He knew resistance would be useless.

"Who are you?" the first man hissed, thrusting his face close to David's. His cheeks were narrow, and there was a thin scar tracing the corner of his forehead.

"I told you," David gasped. "I came into the wrong hut. I'm part of the new intake."

"Like hell you are," the man snapped. "You must take us for a bunch of bloody fools. You're another spy."

"No," David protested weakly. "You've got it all wrong."

The man turned to look at his companions. "When will those buggers learn? It doesn't matter how many of their snoopers we smash up, they still keep sending them in."

"I'm telling the truth," David insisted. "You've got to believe me."

The man punched David hard in the stomach. The blow was unexpected and he felt the pain radiating through his diaphragm. He doubled over, coughing hoarsely.

"What are we going to do with him?" a voice asked.

"What do we always do with spies? Break his legs, of course, and toss him out into the snow. Fetch the rope, hurry."

David heard the sound of a bunk being lifted. He straightened and tried to bolt for the door, but someone stuck their foot between his ankles, sprawling him full-length on the floor. The convicts dragged him to his feet and he felt the lean man fixing a piece of rope around his throat, the coarse hemp scraping the lobe of his left ear. It was like being caught in a nightmare dredged from the inner recesses of his mind—the constriction on his windpipe, the rough faces scorched by the Antarctic sun, the bald heads gleaming in his vision—nothing seemed real, only the fear. He felt that all right. It was flooding his senses, shutting off responses, blotting out thought, reason, awareness.

"Please listen to me," he hissed wildly. "I lied to you, I admit it. I'm not a prisoner, but I'm not an informer either. I came here for a reason. I'm trying to rescue a man called Hugo Pinilla. I have nothing to do with the camp authorities. I'm not even Argentine, if it comes to that. I'm from the United States."

"You're all the same, you government snoopers," the lean man murmured. "When you realise you've been tumbled, you chatter like monkeys. Well, we have our own methods for dealing with spies."

David was dragged, still choking, to the corner of the stove and his left leg was jerked roughly over the surrounding brickwork. Hard fists fastened on his ankle, holding the limb determinedly in position, and David's eyes widened in panic, as he glimpsed the lean man looming above him, wielding a massive block of wood, standing with both legs braced wide apart as he took careful aim on David's lower shin.

"Hold on a minute, Manuelo," a prisoner said, "we can't break his legs without Papá Grande's approval."

"Papá won't mind. He knows what we do to infiltrators. He was the one who started it."

"Just the same, we ought to let him know. I mean, when they find this bastard smashed up in the morning, it'll mean punishment for the entire camp. Papá Grande's not going to like that. He could turn nasty."

The lean man thought for a moment in silence, his eyes studying David warily.

"He's right," another prisoner insisted. "All punishments have to be authorised by Papá Grande himself. It's the rule."

"Very well," the lean man conceded. "Fetch Papá Grande immediately. Tell him we've caught another intruder."

David lay helplessly, the rope stretched taut around his neck, and watched two men carefully prise up the floorboards on the other side of the stove. They slipped into the open sliver of space and he heard them scrambling beneath the hut foundations. A curious lassitude seemed to take hold of him. What kind of a set-up had he gotten into? he wondered, where the prisoners operated with a complete disregard for the camp authorities, running their own mini-society on vigilante lines, carrying out brutal punishments, ignoring consequences, discipline, retaliation? He stared dumbly upwards as silence gathered among the assemblage of shaven skulls. The minutes stretched. He had no idea how long he had been lying there, his throat straining against the pull of the rope, when he heard once again a scrambling noise and two figures appeared through the opening in the floor. A third followed swiftly. He was dressed like the others in convict's clothing, but his body and limbs were immense. His bullet head seemed to sit like a concrete bunker in the centre of his shoulders and his hands looked heavy and corded, the wrists thick, the fingers strong and powerful. Papá Grande, David guessed.

The giant walked slowly toward David and stood above him, studying his features intently. His eyes held a curious flatness which David found disconcerting. "Who are you?" the giant demanded gutturally.

David tried to speak. The rope was hurting his throat so much his voice sounded strained and distorted, but with a desperate effort, he managed to blurt out his story.

Papá Grande was silent for a moment, as he scrutinised David's face. There was something almost hypnotic about the intensity of that stare, and as though he could not help himself, David found himself gazing back, feeling the last vestiges of concealment being ripped from him. He was under no illusion about what would happen if Papá Grande decided his story was false, and the prospect of imminent pain, of crawling crippled through the snow, looking for warmth, comfort, help, filled him with a paralysing torpor.

"How did you get here?" the giant demanded.

"I smuggled myself in on the supply plane."

"That's impossible."

"I had help. A mechanic at the airport. He pushed me into the cargo hatch when no one was watching."

"In these temperatures, you would freeze to death."

"I damn near did. Another half-hour and I wouldn't have made it."

"And you risked all that because of this man Pinilla? Why is he so important?"

"Because they are planning to kill him. If I don't get him out, he'll go the way of all the *desaparecidos*. Escape is his only chance."

Papá Grande was silent for a moment. He turned his back on David and walked slowly to the other side of the room. For several seconds he stood staring at the wall while David's nerves stretched to breaking point and sweat gathered on his neck. He knew his fate was being decided.

The giant swung on his heel. "I think he is telling the truth," he declared.

Relief flooded David's senses, and a murmur of disappointment rose from the watching men.

"How can you be so sure?" the lean convict protested.

"Because his story is too outrageous to be a lie. Because he speaks with an accent. Because I feel sure he is an American."

He walked back to David, studying him closely. "This man Pinilla, you realise he is under heavy guard?"

David nodded.

"After you get out, where do you plan to go? There is nothing beyond the perimeter fence but wilderness. Snow, ice, temperatures below zero. You'll be dead in a couple of days."

"Pinilla is doomed anyhow if I leave him here," David stated, "I plan to strike northwards for the British base at Bromley."

"For God's sake man, that's sixty miles away. Without food, without shelter, you haven't a hope of making it."

"I'd still like to give it a try."

The giant's neck seemed to sink even deeper into the collar of his jacket. His eyes, no longer wary, looked curiously out-of-focus as he said: "A man who would risk his life for a friend does not deserve to be trussed up like a chicken. Let him go."

David felt the rough hemp scraping his cheeks as the rope was dragged over his face and ears. The hands clutching his clothing released him and sighing gratefully, he struggled to his feet, massaging his throat with his fingertips.

"You are a fool," Papá Grande told him bluntly. "You've got more courage than brains."

"I have to do it," David grunted. "I have no choice."

"You could stay and work with the rest of us. When the supply plane returns, maybe you can get out the same way you got in."

"Too late. By then, Pinilla will be dead."

"So you're set on breaking out of here?"

"I told you. A man's life depends on it."

"Very well. We'll do what we can to help."

For the first time since entering the camp David, staring at the heavy shoulders, the thick neck, the awesome musculature of the figure standing in front of him, felt a sudden flash of optimism. He'd thought his chances finished, kaput. But now, overwhelmed by the sheer animal presence of this man, he told himself excitedly that with such a formidable ally, who knew what might be possible?

First though, he had to establish exactly what he was up against. "How often is the camp patrolled?" he asked.

"Spasmodically. The soldiers don't like to strain themselves. They spend most of their time keeping warm around the cookhouse stove."

"What about the machine-gun towers? Are they fully manned?"

"Not since two of the guards froze to death one night. The sentries take it in turns to occupy them an hour at a time. There are never more than two in operation at any given moment."

"Searchlights?"

"None. No need in the Antarctic summer, it's not dark long enough to make it worthwhile."

David thought for a moment. "I'll need help. They're holding Pinilla in solitary confinement and under heavy guard. He's got at least four men with him day and night."

"Wrong," Papá Grande corrected, "the guards were doubled for the British scientists' visit. Now they have resumed their customary rota. There will be only two sentries, and we will deal with them in our own special way."

His face relaxed into a smile and David saw his cracked teeth gleaming between his beefy lips. "At midnight, after the sun sets," Papá Grande said, "then we will go and rescue your friend."

"It's time," Papá Grande said.

Moving to the stove, he carefully removed the floorboards. He had chosen a second convict to accompany them, a man almost as big as the giant himself. His name was Guiterrez.

Papá Grande signalled to David to lower himself through the opening and, with the other prisoners watching, David, swallowing hard, squeezed through the narrow space and crouched beneath the hut's foundations, peering at the dim outline of the adjacent enclosures and the buildings beyond. There was a scraping sound above his head as Papá Grande and Guiterrez followed swiftly, then together the three men ducked into the moonlight and flattened themselves carefully against the building's flank. THe camp seemed deserted. Beyond the distant wire, David could see the mountains etched against the sky.

Moving as delicately as they could, the three men trotted across the open space, darting from hut to hut, taking advantage of each available patch of cover. They clambered through the wire separating the prisoners' section from the central compound and skirted the roll-call area, their breath steaming on the frostbound air. David scarcely noticed the cold. His heart was pounding furiously.

Suddenly Papá Grande caught his sleeve, pulling him back into the shadows. Footsteps approached and David sucked in his breath as a detachment of troops marched by, carbines dangling loosely from their shoulders. The midnight patrol. He watched them tracing the line of silent huts, their outlines curiously bulky beneath their padded Arctic jackets, their heads muffled inside fur-lined Cossak-style hats.

Papá Grande gave David a dig, and they moved off again, leaving the roll-call area behind and cutting obliquely across the open ground. When they reached the toolshed they stopped and tested the door. The metal catch was locked, but Papá Grande jemmied it in an instant and they squeezed inside. In the darkness, David could just discern the shovels lining the walls. His nostrils caught the odour of kerosene and spirit fumes. For a moment he stood breathing hard, trying to quell the tension gathering inside him, then, before he could grasp what was happening, he felt something crash into his spine, thrusting him violently against the wall, and as his eyes widened in surprise he glimpsed Papá Grande closing in on him, his massive bulk blotting out even the dim periphery of his vision, his fingers fastening savagely on David's throat.

Stunned and bewildered, David gasped at the air, his tongue flapping between his flaccid lips. Papá Grande's face was barely inches from his own, and he could see the small

eyes smouldering fiercely. "You lied," Papá Grande hissed.
"Back there in the hut, you lied. The supply plane arrived
three days ago. You could not have survived three days
without knowing about the guards, the nightly patrols, the
absence of searchlights."

Panic gathered in David's chest as he realised Papá
Grande had simply been biding his time, waiting for the
moment he would have David at his mercy. He could feel
the strength of the man in the relentless pressure of his
fingers. If he doesn't loosen his grip, David thought wildly,
he'll bloody well kill me.

"You came this afternoon," Papá Grande insisted, "with
the scientists from the British base."

David nodded his head, realising it was pointless denying the truth any longer, and Papá Grande's fingers
slackened minutely. "Why did you lie?"

"I had to," David choked. "I couldn't tell you everything
without implicating other people. But the rest of my story
is true. I *am* an American, and I *have* come to rescue Hugo
Pinilla."

"You have help? Outside help?"

"Yes."

"The British?"

"Correct."

"What happens after you get Pinilla out?"

"There's a disused whaling station eighteen miles down
the coast. They're picking us up by ship tomorrow at
midday."

Papá Grande let David go and he collapsed against the
wall, rubbing his neck with his fingers.

"I knew it," the giant whispered, studying him intently.
"You were too determined, too bullheaded. There had to be
someone on the other side."

Excitement glittered in his eyes and his massive chest
began to rise and fall rapidly, the breath escaping in little
wisps of steam which trailed into the rafters above his head.
"We're going with you," he declared.

David blinked. "You're crazy."

"I've waited years for a chance like this. You think I'd let
you escape alone?"

"Impossible, I tell you. You'd never make it to the whaling station on foot."

"We'll travel with you."

"You can't. We've got a skiddoo picking us up, a vehicle. It looks like a motorcycle except that it moves on runners like a toboggan. It'll never carry us all."

"I could snap your neck like a chicken's," Papá Grande told him coldly. "Guiterrez and I could take your place. In this light, the skiddoo driver would never know the difference."

David swallowed wildly. "You'd never get anywhere near that skiddoo. You're too big, for one thing. And even if you did, even if you managed to reach the whaling station, how would you persuade the ship to take you on board?"

Papá Grande considered this for a moment, his great head bowed in thought and David waited, conscious of the giant's uncertainty, aware now that he held the advantage but unsure of how to exploit it, wondering what he would do if the Argentine decided to abandon him or, worse still, kill him out of pique.

"You've got to take us," Papá Grande stated. "You owe us that."

David sighed, shrugging his shoulders. "Listen, I'm grateful to you, I really am. But I tell you apart from the driver, that skiddoo can carry only two people."

"You refuse?"

"It's not a question of refusing. It's simply what's feasible and what isn't. Two men can go, only two. And let's face it, Pinilla's need is greater than yours."

Papá Grande sighed. David saw the light fade from his eyes and felt himself gently relax as the giant spat on the ground. Silently, he moved across the hut and picked up a heavy shovel, hefting its weight in his hand, testing it for balance. He nodded at Guiterrez who did the same thing.

"I don't know what your game is," he said to David, "and I don't really care. But anyone who breaks out of this rattrap scores a victory for the rest of us. I gave you my word and I won't let you down. If we can't go with you, the least we can do is take care of the guards."

David felt relief flooding through him as, clutching their

shovels, they ducked into the moonlight. For a moment, one panic-stricken moment, he'd actually believed the giant would kill him back there. There was an air of indomitability in Papá Grande that was difficult to ignore, and the memory of those muscular fingers made David's skin crawl.

The rasp of boots reached them over the crusted snow. Another patrol. Startled, they ducked around the toolshed corner and flattened themselves behind a line of refuse containers.

The guards marched by, five men in padded fur caps with the flaps turned back to resemble wings, their breath hissing on the chill night air.

Papá Grande waited until the sound of their footsteps had faded into the darkness, then he rose from his hiding place and led the way across the compound toward the dark outline of Pinilla's hut. David could see a light blazing in one of the windows.

Papá Grande slowed his pace, easing to the left where the entrance lay. Immediately opposite stood a tiny cupboard shelter with a red cross painted on its flank. It was the dispensary where the medical supplies were stored. Papá Grande paused, leaning his shovel against the shelter's wall as, bending down, he moulded a snowball and hurled it hard against the prison hut door.

A moment passed, then the door opened and a head popped out. David could see the soldier quite clearly peering into the semi-darkness. The man's eyes lit on the tiny patch left by the snowball on the wooden panel and, frowning in puzzlement, he eased into the open, raising his rifle in front of him. They watched him move across the trampled snow, peering warily from left to right. Papá Grande waited until he was almost level with the dispensary corner, then he stepped into the open, swinging the shovel in a savage arc. The soldier's eyes widened for a fraction of a second before the shovel's head connected with the side of his skull in a heavy metallic clang and he thudded into the snow like a fallen treetrunk.

Papá Grande darted across the opening and flattened himself at the side of the doorway. Seconds passed and

David waited in a paroxysm of uncertainty until, attracted by the noise, a second sentry appeared. He blinked as he glimpsed his companion lying face-down in the snow and an exclamation of surprise issued from his lips. He stepped forward to investigate and Papá Grande drove the shovel between his ankles, tripping him expertly. The man sprawled to the ground, his rifle falling from his fingers, and before he had time to shout an alarm, Guiterrez sprang forward and brought his own shovel down with a terrifying crack.

David stared at the two motionless figures stretched out at his feet. Blood trickled from the first man's skull, tracing livid patterns in the trampled snow around the doorway.

Papá Grande burst through the hut door, Guiterrez following in almost the same instant, and after a moment, Guiterrez's head appeared in the opening, motioning David inside.

The hut was smaller than the oblong barrack rooms and there was a solitary stove gleaming at its centre. There were a couple of chairs, a small table with an assortment of unwashed dishes scattered across it, and a cigarette tray cluttered with cheroot ends. Mugs containing stale coffee dregs stood in various parts of the room.

Against the opposite wall, stretched out on a narrow bed, lay Hugo Pinilla. His head had been shaved, and his elongated features carried the sickly air of a man in the grip of some terrible illness. His left wrist had been handcuffed to a metal ring on the wall above. The noise of Papá Grande's violent entry had woken him up, and now he was staring at the intruders with a startled expression on his face.

"You remember me?" David hissed.

A flash of recognition appeared in Pinilla's eyes. Silently, he nodded. He looked wary and apprehensive, but mingled with the caution David detected a faint glimmer of hope.

"I'm David Ryker, the American. We met on the bus."

Pinilla moistened his lips with his tongue. "What are you doing here?" he whispered.

"I've come to get you out."

"Out? How can that be possible?"

"We're going through the wire. Can you move?"

Without answering, Pinilla peered pointedly at the handcuff on his wrist. His arm was hooked across the head of the bed to the ring on the wall. David swore under his breath. "Who's got the key? The sentries?"

Pinilla shook his head. "It's kept in the guardroom," he said. "They only release me twice a day to go to the head."

"Christ," David said, "we haven't got time to mess about."

Gently, Papá Grande nudged him aside. Leaning forward, he examined the chain intently, then he motioned Pinilla to stretch it tight against the wooden planks and stepping back, took careful aim with the sharp edge of the shovel. David held his breath as he drove the shovel forward, smashing the heavy blade against the slender link of chain. Once, twice, three times he swung, and on the last blow, the handcuffs parted with a metallic ping. David expelled the breath from his lungs, helping Pinilla to his feet. "Come on, let's get the hell out of here," he said.

"How do we break though the wire?"

"With these." David fished in his jacket pocket and drew out a small pair of metal cutters.

"You're mad," Pinilla told him. "That perimeter fence stands right in the open. There's no cover for thirty yards at least."

David glanced at Papá Grande. "What time is it?"

Papá Grande looked at his watch. "A quarter after midnight."

"At half-past, there'll be a diversion on the eastern corner of the camp. Something spectacular to distract the sentries' attention. When that happenes, we slip out the western side."

"And then?" Pinilla murmured.

"Don't worry about then. Just trust me. I followed you here, didn't I?"

They left the hut, Papá Grande and Guiterrez leading the way through the semi-darkness, David helping Pinilla along on his damaged leg. Though the Argentine's thigh wound had healed, he was very stiff from the lengthy period of inactivity.

When they were almost in line with the perimeter fence, they huddled against the wall of the adjacent heating plant and waited. David could see the stretch of open ground and the grim outline of a machine-gun tower rearing against the sky.

Papá Grande swore under his breath. "You're out of luck," he hissed. "The tower's occupied."

"You're sure?"

"Look closely. You can see the shape of the sentry's head. He'll probably vacate the place after an hour, but by then it'll be too late."

"Well, let's hope the diversion keeps his attention elsewhere," David said.

He had scarcely finished speaking when suddenly, far to the east, a rapid volley of shots rang out. They sounded harsh and discordant on the still night air, their rattle reverberating strangely over the empty compound. Almost simultaneously, signal flares streaked into the sky, turning the semi-darkness into brilliant day. David blinked as the green fluorescent balls hung motionless above the silent huts. For a moment, nothing happened. Then, with an ear-splitting roar, the camp siren burst into life. Its wail was deafening as from the direction of the cookhouse sentries tumbled into the open in a welter of confusion.

"Run," Papá Grande urged, "run for the wire."

David turned to look at him, feeling an unaccountable thickening in his throat. "I don't know how to thank you," he said quietly.

"Forget it. You're not out yet."

David seized his hand and squeezed it hard. "Sorry we couldn't take you along. I hope to God they release you soon."

The giant grinned, his teeth gleaming faintly in the semi-darkness. "What the hell, it's not such a bad life," he said. "The bastards like to think they've got everything under control, but we run things pretty much the way we want to. I can't wait to see their faces in the morning. They're going to look pretty damned sick when they find that hut empty. Now move. You want them to grab you before you make it to the wire?"

With David clutching Pinilla's arm, the two men stumbled the few yards to the first perimeter fence, David warily watching the tower poised against the sky. The sentry's attention appeared absorbed by the commotion at the opposite side of the camp, but for how long? David wondered. Panting hard, he reached the wire fence and flopped into the snow, his breath rasping in his throat as he struggled with the cutter, clipping the taut strands and bending back the ends until he had fashioned a large enough hole to crawl through. He slithered underneath on his belly, hearing a faint scraping noise as Pinilla followed in his wake. David crossed the open ground and went to work on the second fence, his movements fevered and erratic. He was painfully conscious of the machine-gun post at his rear. One downward glance was all it would take, a single shift in the sentry's eyeline. Against the snow, caught between the fences, he and Pinilla would be trapped like squirrels in a cage.

Pinilla knelt at David's side, helping him pry back the metal strands, then David flattened out and wriggled through the narrow opening, waiting while Pinilla followed, his pale face wincing as his injured thigh scraped along the ground. They rose to their feet and began to run, Pinilla hobbling desperately with David's arm supporting him at the shoulder. David saw the mountains, their craggy tips looming against the sky. He saw the empty expanse of snow. Where the hell was the skiddoo?

The rattle of an engine rang in his ears and dimly through the shadows, he spotted a vehicle careering toward them, kicking out great fountains of spray as it hurtled across the slippery surface. Thank God, he thought.

A shout echoed on the chill night air as the sentry in the watchtower, his attention drawn by the skiddoo's approach, glimpsed David and Pinilla scurrying through the semi-darkness, and David's stomach bunched in alarm as he heard the metallic rasp of the man's gun barrel swinging into alignment, then—rat-tat-tat-tat-tat-tat-tat—David's eardrums shuddered as a hail of bullets trailed them across the empty expanse, kicking up tiny spurts of snow.

David saw the skiddoo skidding to a halt, and Anne's

padded figure waving to them through the gloom. "Come on," he snapped, grabbing Pinilla's shoulder.

The two men stumbled into the open, machine-gun bullets scything the air above their heads, and David felt his spine cringing as he listened to the staccato blasts. He forced Pinilla into the leather saddle, then clambered over the vehicle's rear. "Move," he bellowed, his voice hoarse with fright.

And in a blinding curtain of spray, they thundered furiously into the night.

NINE

Lieutenant Trujillo was fast asleep when the orderly came to wake him. He blinked up at the man framed against the narrow window. Outside the sun was shining. "What time is it?" Trujillo asked.

"Five a.m.," the orderly told him, "we've just had Colonel Cuellar on the line."

Trujillo propped himself up on his elbow, all trace of sleep vanishing from his eyes. "Yes?" he whispered. "Tell me man, for God's sake."

"Operation immediate," the orderly said softly.

Trujillo felt his pulses starting to pound. He threw back the bedclothes and dressed quickly, conscious of a strange hollowness in the pit of his stomach. It was not fear, he knew that. Anticipation rather. Excitement. The knowledge that the long wait was over. At last he could do what he had been sent to do. The prospect made his senses tingle for he was a simple-minded man, the youngest son of an affluent landowner, and from the time he had been old enough to appreciate such things, he had been imbued with all the arrogance and conceit wealth and privilege can engender.

He had always known his life was earmarked for some great and noble purpose. Some men were born to be forgotten, others were bound in destiny. It was right that he, of all people, should strike the first blow in the liberation of the Malvinas. It was no more than his due.

He pulled on his flying suit, fastening the straps. "Is the aircraft ready for take off?"

172

The orderly nodded, surprised at Trujillo's eagerness. "I thought you might care for some breakfast first," he said.

Trujillo stared at him. "Are you mad? We are on the point of changing world history and you expect me to eat breakfast?"

He opened his locker and rummaged among the things inside. Turning, he handed the orderly a bottle of champagne. "Put it on ice for me," he ordered. "I want it chilled and waiting by the apron when I return."

The orderly nodded, watching Trujillo stride towards the doorway. He was like a Samurai from centuries back, secure in the knowledge of his own inviolatability, his young face flushed and eager. He paused for a moment on the threshold, breathing deeply in the chill morning air. Then he stepped into the sunlight and was gone.

In the radio room, the operator turned to Ciro and said: "He's taken off, *coronel*."

Ciro nodded. The events had been put into motion. Now they would follow their inevitable course. In an hour—two at the outside—his friend Captain Barker and the entire crew of HMS *Endurance* would vanish beneath the Antarctic ice-pack.

Ciro felt weary, bitter and disgusted. Killing in the field he could readily accept. Destroying an enemy out to destroy you, there was a certain purity in that, a certain dignity, for a man facing an efficient foe played by a different set of rules. But this was not war. This was not the profession he had trained for. It was hard and vicious. Unscrupulous, degrading.

Rubbing his fingertips against his temples, he peered through the window across the prison compound outside. The roll-call area was packed with men. The convicts had been lined up in squadron formation and armed guards were patrolling the perimeter fence, their bodies muffled beneath their padded overjackets. Ciro could see more guards systematically searching the rows of huts, one by one. During the night, a prisoner had escaped, the sergeant said. Top security. Somebody's head would have to roll. Ciro didn't doubt the sergeant for a moment. He had a nose for calamity, for the imminence of wrath from above.

His judgement was unshakable. Ciro scarcely cared one way or the other. Until a few days ago, he hadn't even heard of Camp Digepol.

He strolled into the outer office, trying to shift his mind from the thought of Trujillo's aircraft skimming across the South Atlantic waters. A corporal sat typing at a desk in the corner and Ciro glanced idly through the folders in his OUT tray. "What is this?" he murmured, picking up the file.

"Photocopies," the corporal said.

Ciro thumbed through the sheets inside, frowning as his eyes caught the name "Chris Salvesen." "These papers are written in English."

"That's right, *coronel*. They represent permission from a British shipping company to dismantle their disused whaling stations on the island of South Georgia. The contract has gone to an Argentine scrap-metal firm."

"But what on earth is the file doing down here?"

"We automatically get copies of all documents relating to activity in the South Atlantic area. It's routine."

Perching on the edge of the desk, Ciro read through the papers carefully. His English was a little rusty and he had to mould the words syllable by syllable with his lips. "Is this all?" he muttered when he had finished.

"Yes, *coronel*."

"But this permit comes from the shipping company only. South Georgia is a Falkland Islands' dependency. Shouldn't there be a separate clearance from the governor in Port Stanley?"

"Correct, *coronel*. That is the next step. Now that the contract has been awarded, it is up to the company itself to seek British authorisation."

A daring thought entered Ciro's mind. Maybe it wasn't necessary to destroy the *Endurance*, after all. Maybe with a little judicious manipulation, she could be lured safely out of harm's way without the loss of a single life.

He felt the blood mounting in his cheeks as, clutching the folder in his hand, he hurried back into the radio room. "Get me General Ramirez in Buenos Aires," he commanded. "I don't care where he is or what he's doing, I have to speak to him immediately."

It took almost thirty minutes to locate the general and get

him to the transmitter. When his voice, cracked and distorted, came over the air, he sounded terse and irritable. "Is that you, Ciro? Do you know what time it is?"

"I'm sorry general, but this is important."

Quickly, Ciro outlined his idea and waited for the general's reaction. There was a long pause as Ramirez considered the suggestion and Ciro, standing behind the operator's seat felt his heart thumping against his ribcage, then Ramirez muttered: "I don't know, Ciro. We'd be taking one hell of a chance."

"We're already taking a chance, general. If the news ever gets out who sank the *Endurance*, the repercussions could reverberate around the world."

"But your plan depends entirely on luck."

"Not luck, general. It's a studied assessment of the situation as it stands."

"Supposing the British don't react in the way you anticipate?"

"They'll have to react. They'll have no other choice."

"Understand me, Ciro, I'd give my right arm to avoid sending that ship to the bottom."

"Then try it my way, general. We won't have to kill a single man."

"Damn you, Ciro, it's my neck on the chopping block if anything goes wrong."

"Mine too," Ciro reminded him.

Ramirez sighed and for a long moment, Ciro heard nothing but the crackling of the receiver. Then Ramirez said: "Very well, in the name of humanity, I'll accept the risk. Recall Lieutenant Trujillo."

"You won't regret it," Ciro said jubilantly.

To the operator he snapped: "You heard the order. Contact Lieutenant Trujillo and instruct him to return to base immediately."

Sitting in the cockpit, Lieutenant Trujillo saw the light flashing on his radio console. He pressed the selector switch to the ground fequency and spoke into his headset microphone. "Camp Digepol, this is Etendard zero-one. I am climbing to five thousand metres and holding. The weather is good, and I expect to be inside the target area within twenty minutes. Over."

A voice crackled in his ear. "Etendard zero-one, you are commanded to return to base. Over."

Trujillo blinked. The message didn't make sense. He pressed the switch again. "Etendard zero-one to Camp Digepol, will you repeat please? I did not understand the order. Over."

"The mission has been aborted. Understand? The mission has been aborted. You are to return to base at once. Over."

Trujillo felt stunned. It was some kind of mistake, it had to be. They couldn't call him back now, not now when he was on the verge of making history. He took a deep breath, his features hardening. To hell with them, he thought. He knew where his duty lay. It was clear and inescapable. Reaching down, he flicked the console button to "off."

For several minutes the operator fingered the controls, his pale young face tense with concentration, then he took off his headset and peered up at Ciro earnestly, his dark hair tumbling over his brow. "I'm sorry, *coronel*, I cannot raise him."

"What do you mean you can't raise him? You spoke to Trujillo only a second ago."

The operator sighed and shook his head. "We've lost contact, *Coronel* Cuellar. I do not understand the reason, but Lieutenant Trujillo appears to have switched off his radio."

It was after nine when the skiddoo floundered to a halt. The engine had been hiccupping for hours and several times had almost spluttered to a standstill, but on each occasion Anne had managed to kick it back into life. Now however, David knew with a chilling certainty that the vehicle was finished.

Cursing, he clambered from the saddle and knelt to peer at the engine.

"Could be something simple," he said hopefully, "like a fuel leak."

"Not a chance," Anne replied. "I checked the whole thing thoroughly before we started out."

"Well, it's screwed up now, that's for sure. How far do you think we've come?"

"We've been driving half the night," she said. "We must be almost there."

Glumly, David peered around the surrounding mountains. They looked grey and hostile, their snowy flanks riven with dark streaks where the fractured rock nudged through. Wisps of cloud nestled in the gullies or trailed lazily from the mountain crests, smudging their outlines into a bleary haze that blended into the sky with no dividing line. Closer, the sun glistened on verglas coating the rippling plain at their feet and the starkness of the surrounding countryside was emphasized by its sheer sweep and magnitude. There was nothing to see in any direction but desolate inhospitable wilderness.

"Let's take a look at our position," David said, holding out his hand.

Anne gave him the sketch map Stone had scribbled out the night before. Raising the paper to the light, David studied it carefully, trying to relate the markings with the features of the surrounding landscape. In the end, he gave it up as a bad job. Stone's drawing was too vague. The country through which they were travelling was immense. It was impossible to ally one with the other.

He thrust the map back into his pocket, shivering in the chill morning air. Somehow they had to find the coast, he thought, it was their only chance of escape. But the land mass seemed endless. There was no sign of a break in the continuous curtain of ice.

He sighed. He had never wanted to run for the whaling station in the first place, had argued against it from the beginning. To his mind, it would have made more sense to have doubled back and headed for the cruiser. But Stone had been adamant. The first spot the Argies would look, he'd said. Damned idiot. Anything would have been better than this, lost at the end of the world in the middle of nowhere.

"Well, we'll freeze to death if we stay here," David

announced. "We'll just have to start hoofing it." He glanced at Pinilla. "Think you can walk?"

The Argentine nodded grimly, his cheeks pale, his eyes heavy with weariness.

"I can try," he promised.

"We'll move as slowly as we can. If we head north-north-west, sooner or later we're bound to hit the ocean. Anne has the compass, she can plot our route as we go along. Watch out for crevasses. They tend to get hidden under the snow."

They retrieved the emergency supply pack from the skiddoo's baggage-pannier and moved off with Pinilla clutched supportively between them. Walking was easier than he'd anticipated, for the snow, despite its depth, had crusted in the sunlight, and they were able to move relatively quickly except when the brittle surface broke beneath their feet, sending them floundering helplessly up to their knees.

The land altered subtly as they pushed steadily on, the endless plain streaked with black volcanic outcrops and even—in places where the ice had not touched—patches of occasional moss. In sections, the snow's skin was lined and serrated with an almost mathematical precision, as if the terrain had been carefully divided by some giant hand, whilst in others there was nothing to see but an endless expanse of shimmering white.

David's spirits sank as they continued northward. Though the sun rose steadily, the cold seemed to intensify until by noon his body had begun to tremble despite the thickness of his padded overclothing. He could see both Pinilla's and Anne's faces were lined with weariness. The long night's drive, the strain of tumbling and slithering across the endless snowscape had drained their last resources of energy. No one had made allowances for the unexpected. If they got out alive, it would be a miracle.

By late afternoon, they were utterly exhausted. Behind them, their tracks marked a ragged trail through the thick blanket of snow. Ahead, the hills merged into a sharp ridge rising against the sky. There was no sign of a break in the wilderness. It was like wandering across the surface of some long-dead planet.

He left the others sprawled on the ground and floundered desperately toward the ridge top, the last frantic pull-up taking every ounce of strength he possessed until, by the time he reached the summit, he was reeling drunkenly from side to side and his breath was rasping audibly in his throat. Ahead, the ground dipped gently downwards and there, nestling in the lap of the surrounding mountains, lay a narrow bay. Its shores formed a perfect half-circle, and at the deepest point of the curve he glimpsed a cluster of tumbledown wooden shacks and a line of metal storage tanks rusting in the sun. The whaling station, he thought. For a moment he almost wept with joy, then the sobs caught in his throat and a wave of desolation swept through him. In the pale light of the afternoon the buildings looked grim and austere. Along the beach of volcanic ash, ancient whale-oil casks lay open to the sunlight, their buckled flanks peeling outwards like the skeletal remains of some long-forgotten species. The tiny bay lay empty and deserted. There was no sign of Magnus Stone or his cruiser.

They strolled wonderingly down the hillside until they had reached the first of the battered buildings. The roofs were sagging, and in places had crumbled away altogether. Gaping holes reared between the window frames, and the great metal vats where the whale blubber had been melted into oil stood cracked and derelict, their flanks daubed with cryptic messages left by visiting sailors. Ahead, steam rose from the waters of the little bay, drifting eerily across the foreshore. Stone had said the bay was the mouth of a submerged volcano. In 1957 it had erupted unexpectedly, and the ocean had boiled, stripping the paintwork from the hulls of three whaling vessels moored in the harbour. The men in the huts had fled in panic, leaving everything intact. Now, like the *Marie Celeste*, the whaling station was a crumbling relic frozen in time.

David tried the first of the huts. The door had gone, and the wall at one end had splintered under the wind, but the others were in no better shape and at least it offered a sanctuary of sorts, a flimsy refuge against the bitter cold. They helped Pinilla in and settled him comfortbly in the nearest corner. His eyes were slack with exhaustion as he peered around the ruined room. "What is this place?" he muttered.

"Looks like the radio centre," David grunted, eyeing the line of equipment against the opposite wall. He visualised the operator sending out his frantic message of destruction as the earth shuddered under the volcano's impact. Wires dangled from the instrument panels and plugs hung loosely from their sockets. An empty bottle, discarded and long-forgotten, stood on the corner of the console.

Pinilla's eyes seemed to click into focus inside his skull. "This *is* the radio room," he croaked excitedly. "Help me up."

"What for?"

"Some of that equipment might be worth salvaging."

"You know something about radios?"

"I ought to. I spent the first two years of my career as a radio operator. If I can get this thing working, we should be able to send out an SOS, contact the ship."

They helped Pinilla to the instrument panel and he sat for a while tinkering with the wires and leads, his hands flicking buttons, twisting dials, tapping transmitters, his dark head bowed in concentration.

"What do you think?" David asked.

"Well, it's knocked about a bit, but some of this equipment has been replaced already. Maybe the scientists from Bromley keep it up to scratch just in case of emergency. Who knows, I might get it operating."

"Okay, do what you can. Anne and I will take a look around. They must have stored food someplace. If we intend to go on living, we're going to have to eat."

They left Hugo working furiously and moved into the sharpness of the open air, walking side by side through the derelict encampment. David was conscious of a bond between them, forged by their helplessness, their mutual dependence upon each other, their instinct to survive. The huts looked strangely ghostlike with the clouds of steam rising over them from the narrow harbour, and behind their roofs the hills rose in an unbroken line.

"I wonder what's happened to Magnus," Anne muttered.

"Midday at the latest," he said."

"Well, for God's sake, we're six hours late in getting here. Maybe he's been and gone already."

"No, that's not possible. He'd have waited a day at least. Something's happened. Something I don't understand."

"You trust him?"

"Magnus? Don't be silly. He'd never let us down. The Argentines must have detained him. There's simply no other explanation."

"In British Antarctic Territory? They wouldn't dare."

"The Argentines don't recognise British claims, remember."

"Well, if he doesn't turn up pretty damned soon, we're in one hell of a jam."

"Don't worry, he'll come. I know it."

They found the food store still intact, its walls piled high with tinned goods of every description. David borrowed Anne's knife and tentatively opened a can of tomatoes. He sniffed cautiously. The contents were still good. "At least we won't starve to death," he said. "This place is a natural icebox. There's enough grub to keep us alive for the next twenty years."

"Heaven forbid," she grunted. "I couldn't stand another day in this dreadful place."

He stared at her standing just inside the doorway, her spine pressed hard against the boxes of canned food. She was trembling visibly, and her cheeks looked pale and stained.

"You okay?" he asked.

She nodded. "Just . . . cold," she hissed. "I'm sure I'll never feel warm again."

He stood studying her in silence for a moment, then without a word began to drag debris from the lower end of the hut, searching for a stove. He found one at last, half-buried under an avalanche of food cartons, its belly still packed with ancient grey ashes. David scooped them out and, tearing strips of cardboard from the boxes, pushed them into the grate to serve as kindling. He found a couple of chairs and smashed them into servicable pieces, stacking the timber carefully inside the stove's interior. Then he took out his cigarette lighter and kneeling, set fire to the cardboard strips. Flames crackled through the makeshift fuel and smoke billowed into the narrow chimney. David closed the stove door and rose to his feet. "Come here," he ordered.

Without a word, Anne moved toward him and he took her in his arms. Her fists clung to the heavy material of his padded overjacket, her body shaking violently as he enfolded her tightly as he could, willing the heat from his chest and limbs to seep into her chilled flesh. He could smell the gentle fragrance from her hair. After a while, as the stove's warmth began to infiltrate the room, her shivering slackened. Her arms slid slowly to her sides, but David did not let go. His own body had started to tremble now, the aching inside him too strong to ignore. For days, he had turned his mind from that, looking inward, seeing only himself, but now he was suddenly conscious of a fierce physical awareness, a tightening sensation deep in his stomach. He pulled back her head so he could look at her face. She peered up at him impassively, her eyes neither friendly nor hostile, and unable to help himself he stooped and kissed her gently on the mouth. There was no response. He increased the pressure, feeling her lips parting beneath his, feeling the warm moistness of her tongue. Something started up inside him then, a kind of madness that was impossible to control, an emotion charged with long-deferred need, and groaning deep in his throat he tore at the front of her Duvet jacket, pulling up her jumper, cupping her breasts in his palms.

"You mustn't," she whispered, gripping his wrists, trying to pull his hands away.

But he was already beyond the reach of reason, and suddenly they were on the ground together and David was tearing at her clothing as they rolled furiously over the windswept floor. He felt the yielding softness of her flesh burning his skin, the fevered scouring of her nails against his spine and suddenly she wasn't struggling any more but writhing against him, desperately, hungrily, her mouth opening, warm and breathless against his ear, emitting a low quavering moaning sound as he entered her, and outside steam rose from the gently lapping water and drifted in wispy, lingering strands across the barren cluster of derelict huts.

* * *

Lieutenant Trujillo glanced down at his instrument panel. The air-speed gauge showed three hundred knots. He banked the aircraft thirty degrees, setting it on a southeast heading. The altimeter indicated five thousand feet. Off the starboard wing he could see the circular outline of Deception Island, the mountains tipped with snow, the shoreline frothy where the waves crashed against the forebidding rock. Bang on course. Soon he would reach the tip of the Antarctic Peninsula, then another fifteen minutes and the *Endurance* would be a blip on his radar tube. The gun-metal sprawl of the ocean whipped beneath Trujillo's nose, the pale blobs of the drifting bergs blurring into each other in a blinding streak of white.

Trujillo felt no compunction for what he was about to do. Only a kind of dizzy excitement. It was like being drunk, he thought, but without the sour feeling in the pit of the stomach.

He had taken a chance, switching off the radio like that. Had been asking for trouble. He would be reprimanded on his return to Rio Gallegos. Court-martialled even, if anything went wrong. But he'd had to do it. Had to. The idiots were calling him back, pulling the plugs out. They had no right, after all he had gone through. This was his destiny. It was what he had been born for. No one could interfere with that. No one.

Trujillo lowered the nose of his plane, levelling out at six thousand feet, making a mental note to watch out for mountain peaks as he approached the Antarctic coastline. Impulsively, his hand reached out and gently patted the weapon-control console on the instrument panel. Soon he would lock the missile on to target, set the relay switches and send the Exocet winging on its way. Long after he was dead and buried, his name would be revered and remembered. Ramon Trujillo. Liberator. A court-martial was a trivial price for a little place in history. His pulses pounded at the thought. Not long now, he told himself. Not long now.

On the bridge of HMS *Endurance*, Captain Nick Barker studied the ice-bergs ahead with speculative eyes. The

massive chunks of green and white were lying motionless in
their path, not drifting with the wind and tide. Barker knew
the signs, he had seen them many times before. The bergs
were not really ice-bergs at all, but the tips of submerged
mountain peaks directly beneath their hull.

The *Endurance* was plotting out uncharted waters off the
Graham Land coastline. Though outwardly everyone appeared casual enough, a sense of tension had settled over
the officers standing on the bridge for they knew that just
below the surface jagged peaks were brushing the *Endurance's* keel and one mistake could rip open the vessel's belly
like a gutted fish. The next few miles would take a degree of
skill and precision that went far beyond the limits of normal
seamanship. Everything depended on the practised eye of
their captain.

Barker watched the curtain of ice building up gradually
in the *Endurance's* path. The *Endurance* had been specially
constructed for this kind of operation and installed with
scientific and surveying equipment. She also had a reinforced bow, and where the pack was thin he knew he could
ram the ice head-on, but the manoeuvre would be a
delicate one, requiring judgement and careful navigation.
He was contemplating the route ahead when a rating
entered the bridge and saluted smartly.

"Message from the radio room, sir. We've picked up an
sos from the old whaling station on Arturo Bay."

Barker frowned. "That place has been derelict for years.
Are you sure?"

"No doubt about it, sir."

"It doesn't make sense. There's nobody in these waters
that we know of."

"Could be a castaway from one of the Russian trawlers,"
the rating suggested.

"We've no word of anyone missing, have we?"

"Not on the record sheet, no sir."

Barker looked at his navigational officer. "What do you
think, Bill?"

The officer shrugged. "Sounds pretty odd to me, sir."

"Some kind of hoax, do you think?"

"Possibly. On the other hand, supposing it's for real?"

"That's just the point. We can't take that chance."

"Investigate?"

"We'll have to. We'll leave the charting for another day. Let's turn this thing around. And Bill?"

"Yes sir?"

"Get a chopper in the air, will you? I'll need an extra pair of eyes. I don't want to run aground in this icepack. If we hang about too long, somebody might die out there."

Lieutenant Trujillo was puzzled. Though he had followed his instructions to the letter, he had failed to pick up any sign of the *Endurance*. The screen on his radar tube remained inscrutably blank. Trujillo felt his nerves beginning to tighten. He knew he was right on target. If Colonel Cuellar's calculations had been correct, he should be within a mile or two of the vessel's original location. Even allowing for a change in course, his radar should have picked her up. Dammit, she couldn't have vanished into thin air.

Lieutenant Trujillo cursed under his breath. He knew his aircraft was stretched to the limit of its fuel capacity. There was time for one sortie, nothing more. If he failed to locate the vessel within the next five minutes, he would be forced to turn back and head for land. The thought appalled him. In his mind, Trujillo had already elevated himself to the role of national hero. It was cruel, cruel that he should be thwarted so close to his goal.

Angrily, he pounded the radar screen with the side of his fist. The plexiglass covering remained distressingly blank.

And then, as he watched, a solitary blip appeared at the left-hand side of the combined television and cathode ray tube. Trujillo felt his heart leap. The *Endurance*, it had to be the *Endurance*. There was no other vessel within a hundred miles. No wonder he had failed to find her. She had altered course dramatically and was steaming north at a breakneck pace. But now at last, she was lying directly in his sights.

He forced himself to remain cool. He had to check, make sure. He couldn't take a chance on this, there was too much to lose. Radar contact wasn't enough. He needed visual confirmation. If he sank the wrong ship, there'd be the devil to pay.

He switched the knob beneath the navigational instruments from positon one to position two and the aircraft turned slightly to the right, the blip moving into the centre of the target zone. Swiftly, Trujillo checked the reading on the radar screen and set the dials on the data processor to the same designates. The read-out screen flashed the words: "You have acquired target."

Below, the Antarctic coastline streaked dizzily by. Trujillo could see the vessel now. It was lying directly ahead, almost lost in the dour sprawl of the surrounding ocean. As he closed rapidly, he was able to pick out the details of its scarlet superstructure, the triangular outline of its foremast, the markings on its flight deck, where its helicopters were launched. The gates of the massive hangar were open and Trujillo felt his senses racing. The ship lying in his target zone was indisputably HMS *Endurance*.

Moving as quickly as he could, he pressed the relay switches at the top of the weapon-control console. The circuit was almost complete. Another second and the Exocet would be winging on its way.

Suddenly, a second blip appeared on the radar screen. Puzzled, Trujillo peered blankly at the tiny blob flickering beneath his nose. An unidentified craft directly in his flight path. Impossible. The sky was clear for a thousand miles. It was simply beyond credibility that another plane could be buzzing around down here. What the hell? he thought.

He squinted through the windshield, ignoring the ship below, focusing his gaze on the empty space in front. On his radar screen, the blip was converging rapidly. Then he saw the machine looming out of the shimmering sky. It was a tiny Wasp helicopter, its massive blades thrashing at the air, its plexiglass dome sparkling in the sunlight. Terror engulfed him.

"Mother of Christ," he yelled.

He hauled on the controls, gritting his teeth as the aircraft banked swiftly, turning to starboard in a crazy curve. The earth seemed to tilt and his senses reeled, his brain swimming wildly inside his skull. He saw the jagged peaks of the snowcapped mountains streaking up to meet him, then he was skimming between them, battling to bring the aircraft under control. The cliffs were hemming him in on every side. He was in an alley with no way out. Altitude, he thought. He had to gain altitude.

He dragged on the controls, his stomach tightening into a solid bunch of muscle and sinew. Ahead, the sky seemed to darken. He sensed the danger even before he glimpsed it through the windshield, and his mouth opened in a soundless scream as the mountain rose before him, blotting out the sun. He saw the jagged fissures, the hanging icefields, the sharktooth ridges, then the plane struck the cliffside in a tumultuous eruption of flame and smoke, and Lieutenant Trujillo never saw anything ever again.

David sat on a hilltop watching the water in front of him. The sea lay in a flat grey sheen broken here and there by feathery slivers of pack-ice. In places, David could see tiny penguins scuttling over the slippery surfaces, staining the ice with their droppings. There was no sign of Magnus Stone's cruiser, no sign of any vessel at all, and David knew instinctively that Stone wasn't coming. Something had happened. Maybe the Argies had caught him, blasted his boat to bits before he'd had a chance to slip his moorings. Whatever the answer, it could be years before another vessel pulled in at the whaling station. Years. David's senses froze at the prospect. How would he stand it, trapped in such desolate surroundings? Even the thought of Anne failed to cheer him, for he saw their predicament as a further twist in a pattern so entrenched he had almost come to expect it as his natural way of life. Whenever he found something he really wanted, one way or another it always got spoiled. That moment in the store hut had been no temporary assuagement, he knew that, no impulsive satisfying of some transitory need. She'd meant it body and soul, his instincts told him so. But life, with its customary irony, had turned the tables neatly, abandoning him to a future without comfort or hope.

Groaning softly, he rose to his feet and began to walk down the hillside, moving hard to keep the blood circulating through his limbs. Westward, the land lay in an intricate network of dark fractured rock, the late afternoon sun picking out the glaciers and ridges, giving an almost ethereal tranquility to the moment. They made a beautiful sight, those mountains, David thought, a perfect blueprint for a century of Christmas cards. But to a man lost and abandoned, their austerity was spine-chilling.

Ahead, the slope began to level out as he approached the outskirts of the whaling station, and something on the ground caught his eye, causing him to pause. Directly in front he glimpsed a pair of parallel lines running through the snow. Ski trails.

Impossible, he told himself, catching his breath, the station had been derelict for years. If there'd been any trails at all, they would have been obliterated ages ago by the snow and ice. But the twin runnels were unmistakable. They led in a meandering line between the cluster of battered huts.

David broke into a run, sprinting toward the radio shed. The trails could mean only one things. Pinilla's desperate sos had been picked up after all.

The buildings fell back and David saw the radio hut set slightly apart from the main encampment, then a coldness spread through his stomach as he glimpsed, seeping in a steady drip over the wooden step, the unmistakable trickle of blood. He slackened his pace, moving forward warily, his heart beating more slowly now. He could hear its thump, heavy and precise, like the murmur of a distant ocean.

He reached the hut door and spotted Pinilla still slumped at the radio console, his head thrown back, his body tilted to the side, his left arm dangling. His throat had been cut, and blood was dripping from his fingertips on to the bare floor.

David felt sick. In the far corner, he could see Anne crouching against the ruined wall, her eyes blank with terror, and standing beside her, dressed in a heavy white anorak and waterproof overtrousers, was Segunda. His dark hair fell in a tangle across his handsome forehead, and in one hand he clutched his *facón*, the blade still covered with blood. In the other, he held a tiny pistol, its barrel pointing directly at David's chest. For the first time since David had met him there was no sign of laughter in Segunda's eyes. His face was dark and serious as he watched David enter. "Hello, *compánero*," he said softly.

David was struggling hard to recover his composure, but

he knew he was not being entirely successful for across the front of his skull his muscles had begun to tremble. "How did you get here?" he demanded.

"I followed your tracks."

"You picked up our SOS?"

"Did you imagine we wouldn't?"

David turned his head slowly, nodding at the corpse beside him. "Was that necessary?"

"He was a traitor. I had no choice."

"You could have taken him back to Camp Digepol."

"Too late."

"Too late?"

"He knew too much. He had become too dangerous to live."

David was silent for a moment as the awful implication sank slowly into his consciousness. Then he said: "We too carry that knowledge."

Segunda nodded. "I know," he agreed sadly.

My God, he's going to kill me, David thought.

Despite the seriousness of the situation, he felt remarkably calm. His brain seemed to be operating on two distinct levels. In one, he contemplated the moment of destruction, wondering how it would feel when the bullet entered his body. In the other, he struggled to think of a way to avert the inevitable.

"I like you, *camarada*," Segunda said. "Twice, you saved me from much embarrassment. But there are things which must be done in duty. A man in my profession can have no room for personal sentiment."

David felt as if his senses had deserted him. He seemed unable to respond in any way whatsoever.

He saw the flash as the gun went off and without understanding why, found himself lying flat on his back with the ice-coated rafters floating above him. There was no pain, that was the strangest thing, only a cold numbing sensation which crept through his limbs and lower trunk. He saw the ceiling shimmering and undulating eerily. Then his eyelids drooped and his brain sank into a pit of blessed oblivion.

* * *

Ciro stood in the commandant's office and carefully opened the bottle of champagne. It had been given to him by the commandant himself who seemed to feel a celebration was called for. Ciro tended to agree. His passionate last-minute appeal had saved the *Endurance*, for which he felt thankful and relieved. He knew the vessel was still intact, for they had picked up a series of radio messages on her frequency, and Lieutenant Trujillo, after switching off his set in a fit of pique was, Ciro assumed, now hightailing it back to Rio Gallegos with his tail between his legs.

It was not Lieutenant Trujillo however who occupied Ciro's thoughts at that precise moment, for an extraordinary thing had happened. The prisoner who had escaped the evening before had aroused considerable consternation on the Argentine mainland. A government agent had been flown in by special plane that same afternoon with orders to locate the fugitive at any cost, and almost immediately after his arrival, the Camp Digepol radio operator had picked up a transmission from an old whaling station on Arturo Bay. Equipped with skiddoo and skis, the agent had set off at once to investigate, and for the first time Ciro had discovered the agent's identity. Martin Segunda. The man he suspected of infatuating his wife. Ciro's brain was in a turmoil. It was like an omen, as if fate were presenting him with an opportunity to put his world in order. Segunda, the Gaucho, here in this trackless wilderness, unprotected, unsuspecting—unencumbered by the restrictions of law and order. It was a chance Ciro knew he couldn't afford to miss, and his hand was trembling as he passed the commandant the bottle of champagne.

Smiling, the colonel took it and turned to the third man in the room, carefully filling his glass. The man was slim and elegant with a deeply tanned face and prominent nose. His cheeks were hollow, the bones high and accentuated, imbuing his features with a certain elusive dignity. His eyes were bright, and in the thin glow of the electric light they seemed to glitter beneath his heavy grey brows. He wore a V-necked sweater with a ribbed collar and a pair of heavy tweed slacks.

"What happened to your scientist friends?" the colonel asked.

The man shrugged expansively. "My captain is taking them back to their research station. They suspect nothing. The cruiser will return first thing in the morning."

"We must congratulate ourselves then. Everything is going to plan."

Magnus Stone nodded, raising his champagne glass high. Beneath his shock of thick white hair, his face looked strangely flushed. "We are in the process of making history, gentlemen," he said. "The liberation of the Malvinas can now begin."

TWX US STATE DEPARTMENT BUENOS AIRES TO WASHINGTON OFFICE;

HEAVY MOBILISATION STILL CONTINUING AROUND ARGEN-TINE PORTS. AIRCRAFT CARRIER AND FOUR DESTROYERS NOW ASSEMBLED IN B.A. HARBOUR. REASON GIVEN QUOTE ROUTINE EXERCISES CARRIED OUT JOINTLY WITH URUGUAY-AN NAVY UNQUOTE DOES NOT STAND UP. ADMIRAL CARLOS BUSSER HAS BEEN CALLED TO THE CASA ROSADA FOR CONSULTATIONS. MEANWHILE ARMOURED PERSONNEL CAR-RIERS BEING FERRIED OUT TO WAITING FLEET. ALL EVI-DENCE SUGGESTS ARGENTINA PREPARING FOR WAR.

TEN

It was broad daylight when David woke up. The sun beamed through the porthole window and he lay for a moment blinking at the ceiling, the low throb of engines echoing in his ears. He was on a ship, but which ship? Tentatively, he peered around the tiny cabin. It was barely the size of a railroad compartment, its deck bare, its bulwark varnished a deep sombre brown. There was a locker, a padded seat, a small serviceable table which doubled as a writing desk and a tiny washbasin. David's clothes hung on the front of the door.

He carefully pulled back the blankets, wincing as a sharp stab of pain lanced under his ribcage. The lower half of his torso was covered with a heavy gauze dressing. When he touched it, his pain increased.

He heard a sudden piping sound just above his head and a distorted tannoyed voice announced: "All hands, all hands, all hands. The keep-fit class is now meeting in the forward hold. There will be bingo in the Senior Ratings' Mess at 1500 hours this afternoon. Tonight's film is *American Gigolo* with Richard Gere."

David frowned. An English voice. He was not then a prisoner of the Argentines. Suddenly he remembered Anne crouching against the radio hut wall, her features frozen with terror, and the memory sent a spasm of shock through his frame. Had Segunda shot her too? He must have, he realised despairingly. Everything David knew, Anne knew also. Segunda would have no alternative. Oh Christ. David felt his neck turn icy. If Segunda had killed Anne, there was no point to anything. His life was shattered. Everything he hoped for had become a nonsense.

Throwing back the bedclothes, he eased himself to the floor, his side throbbing. He moved to the washbasin and stared at his face in the mirror. There were dark rings under his eyes and a heavy coating of beard stubble covered his chin and throat. Several days' growth at least, he estimated. He had been unconscious for some considerable time.

Moving as delicately as he could, he pulled on his clothes, wincing as the exertion hurt his damaged side. He had almost finished and was in the process of buttoning up his shirt when there was a light tap on the door and a young man with tousled red hair peeked in. His eyes widened when he saw David standing there. "You're awake, sir," he said.

"That's a matter of opinion," David said dryly.

"You do look a bit green around the gills."

"Quite frankly, I can't imagine how anyone can feel as bad as I do and not be dead."

He glanced around the tiny cabin. "Where am I?"

"HMS *Endurance*, the Royal Navy ice patrol ship. We picked up your SOS at the whaling station. Our marines found you lying in the radio hut."

"Was I alone?"

The young man hesitated. "I'm afraid your companion was dead, sir. They found him with his throat cut."

"What about the girl?"

The seaman looked blank. "Girl?"

"Didn't they find another body? A young woman? Slim, blonde?"

"There was no one else, sir. Only the male corpse and yourself."

David took a deep breath. A sudden wave of hope flooded through him. He shook his head in an effort to clear it. If both Pinilla and himself had been worth killing because of what they knew, surely Segunda would not stop at Anne? Unless he had a reason. But what reason? David wondered. Segunda was ruthless and dedicated. Nothing would divert him from his murderous goal. Except perhaps the one weakness in his make-up. David remembered Señor Farrel's description of the man. "He has an exorbitant

sexual appetite," Farrel had said. Was it possible Segunda
had kept Anne alive for personal reasons? David tried not
to think about that. The idea made him shudder. Instead,
he concentrated on the happy possibility that Anne, for
whatever reason, had by some miracle managed to survive.

"I was planning to bring you a little lunch if I found you
awake," the seaman said. "On the other hand, since you're
already up, perhaps you'd prefer to dine with the officers in
the wardroom? You'll have to move carefully though, sir, so
as not to open up that side."

"Who stitched me up?" David asked.

"Oh, the MO did that. He's a dab hand with bullet
wounds. You were lucky actually. The shot was fired from a
very small calibre pistol and your padded overjacket slowed
down its velocity. We'd have stuck you in the sick bay but
we're running a little short of space down there. We've got
Lord and Lady Buxton plus a film crew on board, so we
moved you into the only spare cabin we had left. I've been
feeding you nothing but soup for the past five days, which
probably explains why you're feeling a bit shaky on your
pins."

"Well, I'm grateful," David said as he followed the young
man along the narrow companionway.

"All meals are taken in the wardroom mess," the seaman
explained. "You've been allocated mess number 30. You
must use that number for signing bar chits and laundry
bills. The laundry is collected daily. Visitors are requested
to bundle up their dirty linen and enclose a list of contents
showing their mess number. Clean laundry is returned by
the laundryman, usually the same day."

The sailor paused at a glass door and motioned David to
enter. "The others will be along in a moment, sir. Lunch is
served at 1200 hours."

The wardroom was bright and spacious. A long polished
table stood just inside the door, and there were padded
seats lining the outer walls. A small cocktail bar, complete
with a pressure pump for daught beer, occupied one corner.
Beyond it, David could see photographs lining the oak
panelling. One was a picture of an old-fashioned sailing
ship, starkly projected in vivid black-and-white, and
framed at its side hung a portrait of a handsome man in his

early thirties with dark wavy hair and a strong masculine chin. David was studying it curiously when a voice from the doorway made him jump.

"Ernest Shackleton . . . He was a British Antarctic explorer. They simply don't make them like him any more."

David turned to find a tall, well-built, good-looking man in British naval uniform standing beside the table. He strolled over, smiling, and stopped at David's side, peering up at the picture of the sailing vessel.

"That's his ship," he explained. "The first *Endurance*. She got stuck in the ice in the Weddell Sea back in 1916. Shackleton brought out every one of his men alive after living on the ice for a year and a half. An incredible story. Beyond credulity really. If you read it in a novel, you'd never believe it."

He grinned at David, holding out his hand. "I'm Tony, one of the helicopter pilots."

"David Ryker," David said. "Glad to know you."

"Good to see you up on your feet at last."

"Well, I'm still kind of shaky around the knees."

"That's understandable. You've scarcely eaten for the past five days. Liquid diet only. You were coughing up everything we poured into you."

"I guess I'm a pretty lucky man."

"Lucky's the word all right. That coat of yours made an admirable flak-jacket. When the MO got you on the operating table, he found the bullet lodged just below the surface. Don't make any sudden movements though. Don't want those stitches tearing loose. Fancy a beer to steady you up?"

"I'd like that. Thanks."

The officer moved behind the bar, and taking a glass from a hook on the wall, filled it expertly at the pump. The cool liquid frothed over the glass rim. David took the proffered drink and sipped at it cautiously—British beer was a taste he wasn't too sure of yet.

"I guess I ought to thank you," he said.

"For what?"

"Not asking too many questions."

The officer grinned. "Not my job, old son. That comes later, when you meet the captain. I gather he wants to see you in his quarters directly after lunch. You'll have some explaining to do then all right."

David hesitated, sliding his glass across the bar top. "What happened to the corpse you found, the one whose throat was cut?"

"Our marines buried him at the whaling station. We've little enough room as it is, without hauling a dead body on board."

"There was no sign of anyone else around? A lady, for instance?"

The officer peered at him shrewdly. "Lady?"

"I thought . . . well, I just thought something might have been left behind. A glove, a handkerchief, something like that."

"Listen, chum, you were alone when our boys discovered you. Just you and the corpse. I know nothing about any lady, and until the captain questions you, I suggest you leave off discussing the matter any further. Security and all that."

David stared at him, nodding slowly. "Okay," he agreed.

The other officers arrived in dribs and drabs, young men for the most part who greeted David with friendly good humour. They dined on steak and kidney pie and a kind of thick raisin pudding covered with custard sauce. Afterwards, David was taken immediately to the captain's quarters on the deck above. The captain's cabin was almost as large as the wardroom itself, the walls covered with pictures depicting street scenes, bridges, dockyards, riverfronts. David was peering at them curiously when a man walked into the room through the side door. He was medium-sized with short dark hair, merry eyes and a pleasantly sculptured face. He was dressed in blue trousers and a dark blue jumper with a captain's epaulettes on the shoulders. He smiled as he followed David's gaze.

"They're photographs of Tyneside," he explained. "It's one of England's big ship-building centres. I was stationed there for a while. Found the people marvellous. It was one of the happiest periods of my life and I like to remind myself of the place."

He held out his hand. "Nick Barker," he said. "I'm the captain of this ship."

David smiled, warming to the man instantly. "I'm David Ryker."

The captain chuckled. "At last we have a name. You've been our man of mystery for the past five days. Sit down, let me get you a drink."

"Thank you, but I think I'd better take it easy for a while. I'm still feeling kind of rocky."

"Not surprising. That bullet wound in your side wasn't serious, but by the time we reached you, you'd lost a lot of blood. We were too late to help your companion, I'm afraid. His wound was a little more . . . permanent."

"I know," David whispered. "I saw his body."

The captain sat down and studied David shrewdly. The smile had left his face and his manner was suddenly hard and businesslike. "You're American," he said.

"That's right."

"Would you mind telling me what on earth you were doing wandering around at Arturo Bay?"

"Well, it's kind of a complex story."

"Then let's start at the beginning, shall we?"

As briefly as he could, David went through the events of the past few weeks. He described his meeting on the bus in Argentina with Hugo Pinilla, his subsequent arrest and his dinner with Galtieri. He described his relationship with Anne, his involvement with Magnus Stone, his attempt to break Pinilla out of prison, Segunda's arrival at the whaling station and the moment he realised he had just been shot.

When he had finished, Captain Barker stared at him in silence, his face dark and serious. "That's quite a story," he said at last.

David nodded. "I wouldn't blame you for not believing me."

"Oh, I believe you all right. It's too outrageous not to believe. The question is, what happened to Miss Danby?"

"I don't know," David admitted. "It doesn't make sense at all. Why would Segunda go to the extent of killing both Pinilla and me, unless . . ." He hesitated.

"Unless what?"

David sighed. "This man Segunda has quite a reputation as a lady killer. It's not beyond the bounds of possibility that he decided to ignore instructions and keep her for himself."

The captain leaned back in his chair, twisting his face sympathetically.

"If that's true, I'm afraid the future doesn't look too rosy for your girlfriend. He'll have to carry out his orders sooner or later."

David nodded miserably. He was thinking the same thing. His first flush of hope began to fade. "Where are we heading?" he asked.

"The Falkland Islands. After that, the *Endurance* sets out on her last voyage. We're sailing home, England. The poor old lady's being scrapped. Part of the government's new defence cuts."

David stared at him in surprise. The captain shrugged, smiling grimly.

"Big mistake, if you want my opinion."

"How's that?"

"Well, the *Endurance* represents the British presence in the South Atlantic. Take her away, and we've nothing left."

"But captain, with all due respect, she's not much of a presence, is she? One ship."

"You're wrong. As long as she flies the white ensign, she's a symbol, a declaration of intent. Something to make our enemies think twice."

"Enough to stop a Falklands invasion?"

"Enough to start one, if we pull her out. In Buenos Aires, the military junta sees the British decision to withdraw as lack of interest. You can't blame them for setting their sights on the Falklands."

He paused, eyeing David keenly. "That's what surprises me about your story. Your friend Magnus Stone wields a great deal of influence in Britain. He includes among his friends a number of cabinet ministers. I happen to know through certain . . . private sources that he was a major influence in Westminster's decision to withdraw this ship."

David looked at him. "Stone? You can't be serious."

"I am deeply serious. Several months ago, Stone was approached by the Ministry of Defence to carry out a detailed study of Britain's role in the South Atlantic. He's no military expert, you understand, but he does have a certain reputation as an Antarctic expert. It was his report which persuaded the Defence people that *Endurance*'s role had become obsolete."

"I can't believe it."

Captain Barker smiled humourlessly. "Hard to accept, isn't it, when you hear him ranting on about patriotism and his hopes for Britain's future? However, I haven't told you it all yet. I don't know how much you understand about the way the British government is run, but there are, in Westminster, a group of people the press have labelled the 'Persuaders.'"

"Politicians?"

"Not in a direct sense. They're a collection of professional lobbyists hired by big-business concerns to influence decisions taken in the House of Commons. They have no direct power themselves, but they do know how to apply the right kind of pressure, and they also know which MPs are most likely to respond."

Captain Barker paused.

"Your friend Magnus Stone has spent a small fortune hiring these 'Persuaders.' He's been trying for months to get the government to withdraw from South Atlantic waters completely."

"But that doesn't make sense. Stone's utterly obsessed with the idea of an Argentine takeover. Why would he want to weaken Britain's position?"

Captain Barker crossed his legs, gently dusting the top of his thigh with his palm.

"I suppose you do realise Stone is Argentine himself?"

David felt his stomach contract, and he swallowed hard, staring at the captain wildly. "What?" he whispered.

"Oh yes, he's one of the Anglo community. His father sent him to England when he was four years old and he's been there ever since. In almost every respect, he's the quintessential Englishman. He carries a British passport, for instance, and there's no denying his patriotic fervour. But old roots dig deep, and in a situation like this, one can't help wondering where his true allegiances lie."

David sank back in his chair, stunned. A whole new dimension had opened up in front of him. Was it possible, just remotely possible, that Stone had been lying all along? If that was the case, where did it place Anne? She was a

Falklander born and bred, fiercely independent, dedicated
to the welfare of her islands. But she was also under Stone's
influence. Mentally and emotionally. Had Stone fooled her,
just as he had fooled David?

David's brain was in a turmoil. Weakly, he rubbed his
temples with his fingertips as Captain Barker rose to his
feet and moved into the inner office. When he returned, he
was carrying David's wire cutters and a small sheet of paper.
"These constitute your entire possessions, apart from the
clothes you're wearing," he said. "I've been keeping them
until you'd recovered enough to give an account of yourself.
I'm now satisfied in my own mind that what you've told me
has been the truth, so when we reach Port Stanley we'll
deliver you to the hospital there. It will be up to the
governor to decide whether or not to carry the investigation
further. I shall certainly pass on your story to my superiors
in London, but in view of Magnus Stone's reputation, I
hardly imagine they'll take much notice."

Dumbly, David unfolded the paper and looked at it. It
was the sketchmap he had taken from Anne, the one Stone
had drawn for her. Still in a state of confusion, he sat talking
to the captain for a little while longer, then excusing
himself, made his way toward his cabin. He was halfway
along the companionway when a sudden thought struck
him. He stopped in his tracks, and reaching into his pocket,
drew out the battered sketchmap and turned it over,
studying the other side intently in the corridor light. He
hadn't been mistaken. Something was written on the
opposite side of the page. A few scrawling sentences had
been hastily jotted down by someone using a ballpoint pen.
Probably a radio message, David decided. But the words
were meaningless, as indecipherable as hieroglyphics.

On an impulse, he stopped a sailor who directed him to
the radio room. He found the operator sitting in front of his
console, a headset over his ears. David placed the message
in front of him. "What do you make of this?" he asked.

The operator removed his earphones and glanced briefly
at the words on the sheet. "Looks like some kind of word
code," he answered, "A museum piece. The sort of stuff we
were using fifteen, twenty years ago."

"Can it be unscrambled?"

"Sure. But it'll take time. You have authorisation?"

David sighed. "I guess not. To tell the truth, I don't even know if the damned message is important. It might be nothing more than the monthly grocery list."

The man thought for a moment, then shrugged. "Leave it with me," he said. "I'll do what I can. I can't start until I go off-duty though, and even then it's largely a matter of luck."

"I appreciate your trying, anyhow."

Suddenly David felt very tired. He'd had to absorb too much too fast. He was still weak from blood-loss and the effects of his ordeal. But one thing he felt sure of. Anne Danby was still alive. Why or how, he could not figure, but Magnus Stone might hold the answer. If Stone was, as he now suspected, a British traitor, David intended to prove the fact, confront him with the evidence, show Anne the true nature of the man she was working for.

But that would come later. Right now, he was dead on his feet. All in all, it had been one hell of a day. He went to his cabin and took off his clothes. Then, drawing the curtain across the porthole window, he crawled into bed in the dark.

Ciro stood at his dormitory window and watched Segunda crossing the prison compound. He had recognised him instantly from the photograph in his wife's bedroom, but when the commandant had introduced them, he had taken care to exhibit no sign of hostility or resentment. Segunda, he knew, suspected nothing. They had dined together, drunk together, played chess together, and all the time Ciro had been at pains to show nothing but courteousness and conviviality. He was surprised to discover Segunda was an easy man to like. He had an infectious sense of humour and an irreverence for all things military which Ciro both admired and approved of. Even now, he experienced no sense of hatred as he studied Segunda's movements through the window, only a grudging feeling of respect. It was easy to guess what Tamara saw in the man. Segunda carried an air of recklessness that was almost a positive force.

Nevertheless, Ciro had no intention of allowing the opportunity to pass. He was caught in the grip of *machismo*, that sense of masculine pride which dominates the

Argentine character, making it impossible to ignore an insult, no matter how trite. In his heart he wished Segunda no harm, but in his mind the inescapable patterns of the past, the noble heroic virtues of masculine myth and legend demanded his honour be satisfied. *Machismo* had to find expression. It was his duty and his birthright. A miracle had placed them together in this isolated setting. He would not get the chance again.

First, though, he had to establish Segunda's guilt. For all he knew, the photograph in his wife's drawer might be nothing more than coincidence. He needed positive proof. Something clear and indicting. Then he could move.

He watched Segunda disappear into the messhall and, putting out his cigarette, reached for his coat. Shivering in the cold, he crossed the compound to Segunda's quarters. He found the room in a state of some disarray. Segunda had apparently just got up. His blankets lay twisted into an untidy tangle, and the clothes he had been wearing the previous evening still hung over the solitary chair.

Swiftly, Ciro went through his things. It did not take him long to find what he was looking for. The charm was small and dainty, fashioned in the shape of a miniature wolf. It was made of fourteen-carat gold and studded with tiny diamonds. There was a delicate chain attached so that it could be fastened to a bracelet or key-ring. Ciro had bought the ornament for his wife several years earlier on the anniversary of their wedding. He had told her it would bring her luck.

Now he felt tears dimming his eyes. There was no longer any doubt, he realised. The evidence was conclusive. For a long moment he stood in silence, the charm clasped in his hand, then carefully he replaced it where he had found it.

When he left fifteen minutes later, there was nothing to show the quarters had been entered. His anguish had diminished, and in its place was a new sensation, startling in its intensity. He had a goal now. Something to accomplish. He felt almost jaunty as he crossed the compound toward the commandant's office.

On March 24th, a group of intelligence officers and military attachés met at the British Embassy in Buenos Aires to discuss the situation in the South Atlantic. The reason for their meeting was a series of bizarre happenings on the island of South Georgia, eight hundred miles away. British scientists on a reconnaissance trip from their research base at Grytviken had spotted a party of Argentine scrap-metal men unloading supplies from an Argentine naval vessel moored in the harbour. The Argentines had claimed they were in the process of dismantling a disused whaling station there. They had refused to lower their national flag or to sail to Grytviken to have their passports stamped.

When the news of this strange incursion had been radioed to the Falkland Islands, the governor, Rex Hunt, had ordered HMS *Endurance*, which had just arrived at Port Stanley, to set sail immediately and either eject the intruders or force them to comply with British regulations. The *Endurance* was now steaming on its way, happily unaware that in Argentina heavy military mobilisation was taking place throughout the eastern provinces. The intelligence officers concluded their meeting with the agreement that the South Georgia incident had been a deliberate diversion designed to draw the *Endurance* away from Port Stanley prior to a full-scale Argentine invasion of the Falkland Islands. This news was passed immediately to their head office in London.

No acknowledgement was received. No action was taken.

From Director, South American Division, CIA, to Washington Office:

Dear Bill,

Yesterday at dawn, the Argentine carrier *Veintecento de Mayo* left Buenos Aires together with four destroyers for an unnamed destination. The officer in command of the fleet is Admiral Carlos Busser. There is now little doubt at this Embassy that the Argentines intend an armed take-over of the Falklands. Do you want us to contact London, or can we leave that to you?

David sat in the conservatory at Port Stanley hospital staring over the narrow inlet. The hospital doubled as an old people's home and for the past two weeks he had been the youngest patient in the building, a fact which had considerably enhanced his popularity among the nurses but done little to alleviate his boredom. Though his wound was healing nicely, and though the governor had declined to carry the investigation further, accepting his story verbatim and giving him the freedom of the islands, there seemed little prospect of getting a flight home again. Minus passport, money and papers, he was still trying to sort out the legal complications by telephone, a process not helped by the tension aroused through the landing of the Argentine scrap-metal men on the island of South Georgia.

There was, however, another reason for David's depression. He had satisfied himself in his own mind that for one reason or another, Anne Danby was still alive, but knowing the fact, or rather "believing" it, was one thing, understanding was something else again. He missed her all right, more than he'd ever imagined, and he clung desperately to the belief that sooner or later, in whatever circumstances, they would somehow meet again. But in the meantime, he had to live with the awful torment of ignorance. That was the worst part, he decided, not knowing. Had Segunda spared her for some devious purpose of his own? Or was it Stone's work? Was she still helping with his grand design, still playing her role, still unaware of the man's true nature, of her own complicity?

David was contemplating this when he heard the conservatory door open and turned to see a fair-haired young man in a pair of dusty jeans picking his way between the rows of elderly patients. David had met the young man twice before. His name was Johnson and he worked as a sound engineer at the local radio station.

Johnson's eyes were smiling as he reached David's wheelchair. "How are you feeling?" he asked.

"Lousy."

"You look pretty good."

"Looks are deceiving. I'm bored to death. If I don't get out of here soon, I'll probably blow my mind."

Johnson laughed as he peered around for a spare chair and sat down opposite David, the smile still playing on the corners of his lips. "Any luck with your passport?"

"Not so far. Getting through on the telephone's the

toughest part. The Argentines seem to shut the lines down at a moment' notice."

"Yes, they're getting to be something of a menace. We've just had word that one of their submarines has been spotted heading toward Port Stanley."

David frowned. "Think it's the start of an invasion?"

"No, they're probably just playing at silly buggers again. They've been piling on the pressure ever since those scrap-metal men landed on South Georgia."

"What's the news from London?"

"It looks as if they're beginning to get worried at last."

"About time."

"Well, you can't really blame them for being skeptical. I mean, we're not actually at war with Argentina, are we? They like to rattle their sabres a bit just to keep us on our toes, but that's as far as they've ever gone."

David grunted. "We'd be in a hell of a mess if they decided to go further, with the *Endurance* nearly a thousand miles away."

"As a matter of fact, that's what I've come to see you about."

Johnson fumbled in his jacket, taking out a slip of neatly-folded paper and spreading it out on his lap. "This message arrived for you this morning from one of the radio operators on the *Endurance's* crew. Frankly, it doesn't make a damn bit of sense to me."

David took the paper from Johnson's hand and held it to the light. It was a decoding of the writing he had found on the back of Magnus Stone's map.

It said:

February 21st. Subject: Fat Gladys.

To: Morning Star.

From: Cousin Teapot.

Gladys visiting Aunt Eva, but expected home for tea. Could prove obstinate if Arthur comes a-courting. Could you send her to the picture show?

David read the message twice, then handed it to Johnson. "What do you make of it?" he asked.

Johnson shook his head. "It's double-dutch to me. Where did it come from?"

"I found it scribbled on the back of a piece of paper given
to Anne Danby by Magnus Stone."

"Stone?"

"You know him?"

"Of course I know him. Everyone in the Falklands knows
Magnus Stone. He spends practically half his life here."

"How does he strike you? As a man, I mean."

Johnson shrugged. "Seems pleasant enough."

"But do you trust him?"

"Trust him? Why not?"

David hesitated. Why not indeed? he thought. What was
he trying to prove? That Magnus Stone was a traitor? Well,
he knew that all right, could feel it all the way to his shoes.
But try telling it to people who'd regarded the man as a
hero for the past twenty years. No question about it, Stone
would be a tough nut to crack.

The answer had to lie in the message at his fingertips. It
was coded, wasn't it? People used codes because they had
something to hide. He had to concentrate, had to make
sense of this meaningless gobbledygook. It was his only
piece of real evidence.

"Let's consider for a moment," he said, "Assuming Stone
wrote this message, whom do you imagine Fat Gladys
might be?"

"I've no idea."

"What about Aunt Eva? Know anybody by that name?"

"Not a soul."

"There's always the possibility of course that Aunt Eva
refers to the Antarctic."

Johnson blinked. He seemed surprised by David's suggestion. "That's rather fanciful, isn't it?"

"Let's think about it. Just for the sake of argument, let's
suppose that Fat Gladys is the *Endurance*. She's gone to
Aunt Eva's—in other words, to the Antarctic—but she's
expected home for tea. Home being the Falkland Islands.
She could prove obstinate if Arthur comes a-courting, so
could she be sent to the picture show?"

Johnson stared at David dumbly. The laughter had faded
from his eyes.

"What if Arthur is really the Argentine invasion force?"
David added, pressing on quickly. "Is it possible, just

possible, that those scrap-metal men have been placed on South Georgia to lure the *Endurance* away from Port Stanley?"

Johnson did not answer for a moment. His tongue came out, gently moistening his thin pale lips, and the jaunty air in his features was replaced by something David couldn't quite decipher—uneasiness, he imagined. His own pulses were pounding furiously. It had been so easy, so elementary, so childishly simple, yet he felt sure he was right. It all fitted. There was no other explanation.

Excitement flooded David's senses, but Johnson still looked unconvinced.

"It's illogical," he said. "Magnus Stone is a great champion of these islands."

"You know that he's an Argentine by birth?"

"He was born in Buenos Aires, yes, but his parents were British, and he was raised and educated in England. For God's sake, he's been trying for years to persuade the British Foreign Office to take a stronger stand in the South Atlantic."

"If that's true, why did he propose the scrapping of the *Endurance*?"

Johnson looked startled. "Magnus Stone would never do such a thing."

"He did it all right. In a special study conducted for the British government, he claimed the role of the British ice patrol ship had now become obsolete."

"I find that hard to believe."

"It's easily checked."

"Look here, you're assuming an awful lot on the basis of a highly dubious message."

"You're right, I *am* assuming. But let's assume a little more, shall we? Let's assume, just for a moment, that what I'm suggesting is true, that Magnus Stone, incredible though it may sound to your disbelieving ears, really is a British traitor. Where would he be now?"

"God knows."

"Well, put yourself in his shoes."

Johnson thought for a moment. "Here probably," he said. "Port Stanley?"

"The Falklands anyway."

"Right. He knows these islands better than anyone alive. Who else would the Argentines use for relaying information to their invasion fleet?"

"You're crazy."

"Where does Stone stay when he comes to the Falklands?"

"On his boat, of course."

"Does he have a more permanent base?"

"Well, he's got a hut on Falkland Sound. Sometimes he moors his cruiser in Tyrrel Bay and uses the building as a shore headquarters."

"How far's Tyrrel Bay?" David asked.

"A good day's drive overland."

"Can you lend me a Land Rover?"

Johnson blinked at him. "You're not fit enough for a journey like that."

"I'm as fit as I'll ever be. I'll need a map and compass too."

"You idiot, what the hell do you think you're going to do?"

David stared at him grimly. "If what I believe is true," he said, "if Magnus Stone is setting these islands up for invasion, if he's sitting at this moment radioing information to the Argentines, I'm going to find the evidence and rub the bastard's nose in it."

The cruiser rocked gently in the swell. Ciro stood on the topdeck and stared across the narrow harbour. Moonlight flickered over the dancing waves. On two sides, green hills rose into the gathering darkness. A cold wind blew and Ciro shivered. The weather was damnable, he thought. Even in summer, the savagery of the gales seared a man's skin.

Almost five days had passed since he had been ordered north on Magnus Stone's boat to establish a base on Falkland Sound and relay strategic information to the Argentine invasion force poised along the mainland coast. They were now moored in a narrow inlet shown on the map as Tyrrel Bay. Nestling against the hillslope above was the wooden hut Stone used as his shore headquarters. Ciro could see its radio mast poised against the sky.

Segunda too had sailed with them. He was standing now on the bridge, talking to the young blonde woman who served as Stone's companion. She was a beautiful girl, Ciro thought, an obvious target for Segunda's attention. Yet though Segunda chatted charmingly, waving his hands in expressive gestures, the girl's features remained stony and aloof. Clearly she disliked the man. In fact, judging by the cold glitter in her eyes, was even repulsed by him. Ciro felt his curiosity stirring. An unusual woman indeed.

He lit a cigarette, shielding his match from the buffeting wind. His resolution had not weakened. He knew what had to be done. When the moment came, the right moment, he would not hesitate. But he wanted it right. Not hurried, not flustered. Segunda must know what he was dying for. He had to follow the custom. Tradition, emotion, they were all inter-related.

In a strange way, Ciro felt a certain sadness for the act he was about to perform, a sense of regret. He did not want to kill Segunda, liked the man if the truth were known. But there could be no turning back. His duty lay clear. He would bide his time until the invasion started, when there would be chaos and confusion. Then he would strike.

Shivering in the wind, Ciro drew hard on the cigarette, watching the smoke curl from his lips and vanish into the night. A shout reached them from the radio hut on the hill above. The operator was standing just outside the doorway, waving a slip of paper in his hand. Attracted by the noise, Magnus Stone came up on deck, followed by three Argentine soldiers. The operator ran down the hill, scurried up the gangplank and handed Stone the sheet of paper. He read it quickly, then smiled at Ciro, his cheeks flushed and elated.

"Our waiting is over," he said with excitement in his eyes. "The fleet is on its way at last."

David drove as fast as he dared, guiding his vehicle across the undulating landscape, trying hard to follow the track as it bobbed and dipped around the inclines of the surrounding hills. He had been travelling for hours, picking his way through clumps of tufted moorgrass, peat bogs, boulder-strewn riverbeds, ragged gulleys and jagged outcrops.

Several times he had floundered in the mud, but always, by pushing the vehicle into overdrive, he had managed to drag himself through.

It felt good to be moving again, good to be free of the suffocating confines of that tiny hospital. It stopped him thinking for one thing. Made him concentrate on doing something for a change. He was trying hard to put Anne out of his mind. He'd thought about her endlessly over the past few weeks. Torturing himself. Going over the possibilities again and again. But it did no good. Nothing did any good except action. Hard and direct. Hit the bastard where it hurt. That was what he was working on now.

He drove with the map spread across his knee, following the track as it wound over the open moorland. The hills looked grey beneath the empty sky. The Land Rover lurched as its front tyre caught a piece of rock, and David's fingers tightened instinctively on the steering wheel. Then shuddering and jerking the vehicle righted itself, and with David working the gearbox with his left hand, it trundled on across the rolling carpet of peat.

ELEVEN

By the evening of April 1st, there was little doubt left in the minds of the Port Stanley residents that something serious was going on which would have a direct effect upon their futures and their livelihood. The news from London was grim. British Defence Secretary John Nott had received word that Argentine warships were loose in the South Atlantic and an Argentine submarine was said to be picking out landing sites around the Falklands capital.

In Washington, the British and Argentine ambassadors had been summoned to the State Department and prevailed upon to settle the dispute peacefully. President Ronald Reagan had telephoned General Galtieri at the Casa Rosada in a last minute attempt to avert tragedy and bloodshed, but though the gesture had been a noble one, Galtieri's response was a garbled monologue on Argentina's right to Falklands sovereignty and President Reagan had known in his heart as he hung up the receiver that the phone call had been made too late.

At 10 Downing Street, Mrs. Thatcher and members of her military advisory committee met to discuss plans for retaliatory action. That same afternoon, the British Foreign Office informed Governor Rex Hunt that a massive Argentine invasion force would be within striking distance of Port Stanley before dawn. To avoid panic and alarm, the news was kept from the people themselves, but few of Port Stanley's residents failed to detect the subtle changes in the behaviour of the security forces.

The Royal Marines, though they expected to be outnumbered twenty to one, deployed themselves around the town outskirts, with the main detachment guarding Government House. Beaches were booby-trapped and gun emplacements situated at strategic points surrounding the airport, ready to pour fire into any troops which attempted to land.

At seven-thirty that evening, Falkland Islands Radio began its transmission with the news that Governor Rex Hunt was about to make an important broadcast. For the people of the Falklands, this information in itself was enough to confirm their deepest fears. They knew then beyond any shadow of doubt that the battle for their islands was about to begin.

Excerpt from transcript of radio broadcast by Governor Rex Hunt to the people of the Falklands, April 1st 1982, 8:15 p.m.:

> Good evening. I have an important announcement to make concerning the state of affairs between the British and Argentine governments over the Falkland Islands dispute. We have now sought an immediate emergency meeting of the United Nations Security Council on the grounds that there could be a situation which threatens international peace. I have alerted the Royal Marines and I now ask for all serving members of the Falkland Islands defence force to report to the drill hall as quickly as possible. I expect to declare a state of emergency before dawn tomorrow. I shall come on the air again as soon as I have anything to report. In the meantime, I would urge you all to remain calm, and stay off the streets.

Night lay heavily across Mullet Creek. In the shadows, the soldiers looked grim and intense. Their faces had been blackened to merge with the darkness, and clusters of grenades dangled from their combat tunics. They were members of the *Buzo Tactico*, Argentina's elite commando force who had been dropped on the beach by helicopters from the aircraft carrier *Veintecento de Mayo*. They worked without speaking, checking weapons and equipment, their movements crisp and precise. Each step had been carefully rehearsed a thousand times over, and every man knew the part he must play in the overall design.

When they were satisfied everything was in order, they split into two groups, the first moving to the east, following the coast to attack Port Stanley from the rear, the second heading north, climbing the steeply-ragged incline of the nearby hillslope until they had reached the summit. They stood on the line of rocks which ran like a plume along the narrow ridge and stared at the cluster of buildings below. Moody Brook Barracks. In the darkness, the wooden huts looked pitifully small. Only the exercise hangar conveyed any sense of size or dimension.

The commandos' equipment clattered softly as they moved through the night, picking their way down the steep grassy incline, their breath steaming on the frosty air, their faces, almost obscured beneath their sooty coatings, blank and featureless, only the eyes discernible in the starlight, glinting fiercely with a mixture of excitement and fear. Approaching the huts, they fanned out, spreading in a pincer-like formation to surround the camp from all sides. The wind plucked at their tunics, battering their cheeks as they lay among the grass tufts.

Their leader checked that his men were in position, then gave a short sharp blast on his whistle. The commandos knew their instructions blindfolded. Rising, they covered the last few yards to the walls of the barracks, scrambling over the flimsy perimeter fence, their boots crunching on the gravel, their black combat suits mingling with the shadows as they zig-zagged toward the silent row of huts. Windows were smashed, grenades hurled in. Explosions split the night.

The commandos kicked open doors, riddling the rooms with bullets. The din was deafening as woodwork splintered under the hail from their machine-guns.

For nearly twenty minutes the clamour went on, the men bursting from room to room, tossing in grenades, waiting with heaving chests for the thunder of detonation, then hurling themselves into the billowing pall of smoke and firing their weapons in a compulsive frenzy. When the commander finally called a halt, the buidings had been completely devastated. Stumps of fractured timber creaked

ominously in the shadows and fire blazed through the open
window frames.

Grim-faced and silent, the commander moved through
the decimated dormitories, anger blazing inside him. Their
intelligence reports had been faulty, the attack had been a
futile waste of time. The barracks were empty. There was
no one at home.

Two miles away, blockaded in Government House, Governor Rex Hunt heard the racket as the Argentines attacked.
Grimly, he took out the pistol he was carrying and checked
to see that it was loaded. His chauffeur and personal friend
Don Bonner had commandeered his only shotgun and was
sitting at the window now, the weapon across his knees, his
head slightly tilted as he listened to the din on the other
side of the inlet.

Governor Hunt moved to the door and peered into the
passage outside. Two marines were standing in front of the
Shackleton Room, their faces dark and intense. They too
had heard the explosions and knew what they meant.
"Christ," one of them commented, "thank our lucky bloody
stars we wasn't in there, sir. They'd have chopped us to bits
by now."

"There'll be plenty of time for that," Governor Hunt said
gently.

"They've finally gone an' done it then? Invaded, I mean."

Hunt nodded, peering dubiously up at the ceiling. The
building, he knew, would never withstand a prolonged
siege. Though its exterior looked impressively like an
English country mansion, its walls were built of clapboard
on wood. Against a high-velocity bullet, they would be next
to useless.

Governor Hunt felt anger rising inside him. He had no
intention of surrendering, he thought. If the Argies wanted
a fight, he would give them what they'd come for.

A party of marines clattered down the stairs and shuffled
into the governor's study. Hunt joined them, looking grim
and thoughtful, and at that moment, the rattle of gunfire
abruptly halted. It was startling in its suddenness. One
moment the air had been filled with the chatter of machine-
guns, the next a heavy silence had settled over the harbour.

For a long moment, nobody spoke. Outside, the night seemed quiet as the grave. They looked at each other sombrely, their faces pale and intense. Governor Hunt knew what they were thinking.

"We're next," he said.

David brought the Land Rover to a halt, peering cautiously through the heavy curtain of darkness. The land rose in a series of small craggy hills, their crests forming a perfect ridge which bobbed and undulated southward, vanishing into the swirling gloom. At their feet, like a pale jewel gleaming through the shadows, he could see the waters of Falkland Sound. If his calculations had been correct, Tyrrel Bay would lie directly beneath.

He switched off the ignition and clambered into the mud, wincing as the wind bit through his padded jacket. His side was aching from the long drive, and he was already regretting the decision to tackle Stone alone. The constant lurching and shuddering could easily have opened up his wound, he realised, and without help in this miserable wilderness, he'd have been in a sorry pickle indeed. What a country. Nothing but peatbogs and wind. He couldn't understand why the bloody Argentines wanted it in the first place.

Moving carefully through the gloom, he followed the tilt of the hill, the ocean lying dimly on his left. Heavy clouds hung over the neighbouring peaks. He spotted the bay below and felt his heart jump. There was a vessel moored to the shorelines and he forgot the ache in his side, forgot his fleeting moment of regret as he recognised Magnus Stone's cruiser. So his theory had been right all along. The boat's presence was an indictment in itself. Proof positive of perfect guilt. The traitorous bastard.

At the moment of realisation, a new emotion rose through David, recognisable now for what it truly was. Jealousy. The timeless hatred of a man for his bitterest rival, and, feeling it, David knew there was no point fooling himself any longer. Everything he had planned, everything he had worked towards had been for one purpose only. To win Anne for himself. Now, glimpsing the evidence of his opponent's infamy, David's resentment became a burning desire for revenge.

His eyes picked out the line of a tiny hut. Stone's shore base. He would have to move more cautiously. The building might be occupied.

David edged closer, using what cover he could find. When he had reached a point some thirty yards from the hut's entrance, he lay flat on the ground and studied it warily. The building appeared to be deserted. Down in the bay, he could hear the murmur of voices, but here on the shoreline there was no sound, no movement, only a heavy pall of silence.

Satisfied the area was clear, David rose from where he was lying and darted across the patch of open ground, flattening himself against the building's flank. He peered fearfully into the shadows. No one challenged him. The only signs of life were the noises drifting up from the vessel below. The sailors appeared to be making preparations to depart.

He tried the hut door. It was unlocked and warily he stepped inside. The room was small and divided into separate compartments. Several contained bunks and primitive pieces of furniture, and at the far end stood the customary peat stove, its narrow funnel disappearing into the raftered ceiling. A radio transmitter stood on a nearby desk, the headset still plugged to the transmitting console. It looked as if it had been recently used. In front lay a profusion of papers. David took out his cigarette lighter and flicked it, holding the flame low as he checked each of the papers in turn. They were covered with hastily-scribbled messages, some of them in code. Others were written in Spanish, and running his finger along the lines David was able to discern details of weather conditions, Falkland currents, suitable landing spots, British defence positions. His face settled into a cold mask. There was no longer any doubt which side Stone was fighting on, and the realisation that he had been treated like a fool, had been utilised, manipulated, exploited, filled David with a slow burning anger.

He went through the desk, trying all the drawers. In the bottom, he found a heavy cardboard file, and placing it in front of the radio set, he examined it carefully in his lighter's glow. A sense of indignation rose inside him as he turned the pages. It appeared to be a report carried out by Stone for the Argentine junta. Skimming from sheet to sheet, David's fury grew. The report was a travesty. It assured the Argentines that in the face of a full-scale military invasion, Britain would have no recourse but to negotiate the best deal she could for the islanders and accept the situation with grateful relief.

"The British," it concluded, "though by nature ready to unite strongly against a common enemy, are always quick to discern where their best interests lie, and it is the opinion of this writer that they would consider an armed counter-attack along conventional lines to be self-defeating in purpose."

For a moment, David stood staring down at the papers in mute disbelief. Even now, with the evidence lying in front of him, he seemed unable to grasp the enormity of what he had discovered. If what he suspected was correct, if the file was indeed a detailed assessment of the Falklands situation carried out by Stone for the Argentine military, then these papers could prove dynamite in the hands of the press.

David tore the report out of its cardboard folder and pushed it down the front of his shirt. He had his proof now, all he needed. He could destroy Magnus Stone in the headlines of the world, show Anne once and for all—if God willing, she was still alive—the true character of the man she had given herself to.

He moved to the door, his heart thumping wildly. Suddenly, the muscles contracted in his stomach as he spotted coming up the footpath from the cruiser a party of Argentine soldiers and, striding along in front of them, a tall man with a thick shock of unruly hair. The man's features were almost obscured in the darkness, but David recognised the tilt of his head, the fluid elegance of his movements. Segunda.

His heart sank. His Land Rover was parked on the hillside above. He had no hope of reaching it. The only escape route lay in the opposite direction.

He could see Segunda clearly now, his face unusually sombre in the starlight and, taking a deep breath, David plunged through the open doorway and ducked around the side of the building, his body shuddering as he remembered how easily the Argentine killed. There was a momentary pause as the soldiers stared after him in stunned surprise. David heard shouts of anger and alarm, then a shot rang out, the bullet hissing past his ear, and he slipped in the mud, sprawling flat on the ground, the dampness seeping through the padding of his heavy overjacket. Gasping frenziedly, he dragged himself to his feet and scrambling as hard as he could, tore into the night, the Argentines furiously following.

Corporal Monaghan moved along the line of housefronts, scrambling deftly from garden to garden. Behind him, his five-man squad followed at his heels, their faces charcoaled to merge with the dark. Agaisnt the blackness of their skin, he could see their eyes bright with fear.

Immediately ahead, the battle for Government House was raging fiercely. Corporal Monaghan had heard the gunfire from the opposite side of town, and had moved back as swiftly as he'd dared, using the buildings as cover, conscious of his orders that no fighting was to take place in the vicinity of the streets themselves, watching fearfully for any sign of movement, any thickening in the shadows which might indicate the presence of enemy soldiers.

Corporal Monaghan and his squad had been detailed to watch the inlet for signs of Argentine assault craft. They had glimpsed the dim shape of a vessel drifting through the narrow channel and had opened up immediately, scouring the metal decks with a murderous fusillade of machine-gun fire before withdrawing to the relative cover of the town.

Now Monaghan's intention was to rejoin the main detachment of marines ensconced around Government House. But the sounds of battle told him that the Argentines had already out-manoeuvred their gun emplacements, landing at the lower end of the island and crossing overland to launch their attack on Government House from the rear. Most of the assault force appeared to be grouped on the hill at the building's back, hiding amongst heavy clumps of rhododendron bushes.

Monaghan spotted the little post office rising to his right.

The wooden walls were still intact, and displayed in the window he could cearly see the sign: "The Falklands are Beautiful—and British."

He raised his hand, bringing his squad to a halt. They gathered around him, their faces tense and watchful, blending with the darkness.

"We're stuck," Monaghan told them simply. "This is as close as we can get without having our cobblers shot off."

The marines looked at each other. "If we stay where we are, the bastards'll be up our arses in half an hour," one of them said.

"Right," Monaghan agreed. "Which leaves us with only one alternative that I can see. We've got to make a run for it."

The marines looked doubtful. "Through that lot?" a man muttered.

"Dicey, I realise. But from what I can tell, most of the Argies seem to be grouped on that hillside on the rear. If we can pin them down for a few seconds, give them something else to think about, maybe it'll grab us the breathing space we need. Are you willing to give it a try?"

The marines stared at him, their dark faces tense and drawn. Silently, they nodded. "Okay, a fresh magazine per man, and when I give the word, make the bastards' eyes water, understand?"

They fanned out, positioning themselves in the grass, peering through the darkness at the slope behind Government House. Corporal Monaghan cradled his weapon, switching the safety catch to "fire". Pressing the stock against his chin, he took careful aim at the ragged sweep of hillside. "Now," he ordered, and gently squeezed the trigger. The weapon purred against his shoulder. He saw the green tracer bullets arcing into the night and his eardrums shuddered as his squad opened up with their own machine-guns, pouring fire into the shadows above.

The sound of fighting halted. The Argentines, realising they were under attack from a completely new direction, were desperately scrambling for cover.

"Come on," Monaghan yelled, rising to his feet, and without waiting for the squad to follow, he hurtled across the tiny garden, his machine-gun clutched at his hip. He

saw the fence looming up and took it at the gallop, crashing
on to the road beyond. His heart was hammering fiercely
agianst his ribcage, and bile spurted into his mouth,
tainting his tastebuds with a harsh bitter flavour. Sprinting
as hard as he could, his legs moving by pure instinct, he
watched the front garden of Government House drawing
nearer, the glass windows of the conservatory catching the
starlight, the dark clumps of rhododendrons rising menac-
ingly through the gloom.

Suddenly Monaghan's senses jumped, for directly in his
path he glimpsed a British marine crouching in the shrubs
at the garden periphery, struggling to draw a bead on the
front of Monaghan's chest.

"What the bloody hell do you think you're doing? We're
on the same bloody side, you stupid sod," Monaghan
yelled, taking the fence in a single bound.

Without hesitating, he swung his machine-gun, feeling
the butt shudder as it contacted bone and gristle. The
marine fell backwards into the bushes and Monaghan drove
his knee into the man's face, hearing a grunt of pain as the
soldier collapsed in a heap on the ground.

Then, as Monaghan's squad scrambled wildly over the
fence to join him, the night was suddenly alive as, with a
fearful earsplitting din, the Argentine guns opened up
again.

David scarcely knew how long he had been running. His
brain seemed to have congealed inside his skull and he was
conscious only of the frantic need to escape. The Argentines were still behind him, somewhere at his rear, but he
had managed in that first determined burst of speed to gain
a fractional lead, and now they seemed to have fallen back
out of sight. From time to time, they fired their carbines
into the darkness, but happily, since they had no idea of
what they were aiming at, most of the shots went wide.

David paused for a moment, clutching his hip. The pain
beneath his ribcage was excruciating. His hand came away
wet, and when he peered at it in the darkness, he could see
dark blood staining his fingers. His wound had opened up
again.

He mounted a tiny ridge and peered down at the sea

below, its metallic greyness gleaming through the gloom. There were men down there. He could see them moving across the beach, carrying boxes from an assault craft moored to the shoreline. Argentines.

David stood gasping, the pain rippling through his body in waves which seemed to jar agonisingly with the rapid movement of his lungs. So it had happened at last. This was no isolated landing, he felt sure. The Argentines were here. Tomorrow, the whole world would know.

Behind, he could hear his pursuers gaining. They'd catch him eventually, the bastards, he couldn't keep this up, the pace they were setting. Then Segunda would kill him. One more casualty in a ludicrous war in the middle of nowhere. He couldn't allow that to happen. He had too much to lose, too much to gain. The proof. Hidden inside his shirtfront. Now he had what he needed, the power to hit back. He could destroy Magnus Stone in a single stroke, if only he could shake off Segunda. He stared down at the soldiers below, their shadowy outlines blurred and indistinct as they moved to and fro, depositing their equipment above the rocky foreshore. A daring plan entered his mind. It was dangerous in the extreme, but he had to grab himself a breathing space. Wounded as he was, his strength would sooner or later disintegrate. He had to escape while there was still time.

Moving as delicately as he could, he descended the precipitous hillslope toward the troops below. To his rear, he heard a murmur of voices as his pursuers reached the top of the ridge. He picked his way through the fluttering grass-clumps, moaning softly as the pain lanced up through his ribcage and his hand, gripping his side, became slippery with blood. The wind scoured his face, tugging at his hair, and his nostrils picked up the salty odour of the sea mingled with diesel fumes from the Argentine assault craft. He could see the landing party taking shape now, their shadowy outlines gathering form and substance, their faces, blackened for concealment, obscured beneath their bulbous combat helmets.

His neck tingling with tension, he slowed his pace, picking his way more carefully as he crept to within twenty feet of the beach's rim and stopped, breathing deeply. He felt terribly exposed as he squinted into the darkness looking for an escape route. On one side lay a shallow defile where heavy seas had whittled away the surface of the sand. Pebbles and seaweed had gathered thickly along the defile's rim, providing a natural trench where a man, crawling flat on his belly, might be protected and concealed from the soldiers in front.

David hesitated, summoning his nerve. Leaning forward, he rooted among the stones at his feet and choosing three or four, weighted them carefully in his hand. Above, his pursuers had started down the incline and were drawing steadily nearer.

He took a deep breath, trying to quell the fear rising inside him, then ignoring prudence completely, he leapt from the shadows, and hurled the pebbles with all the force he could muster. A soldier yelled as a rock bounced off his skull. A second cursed savagely as he was struck in the middle of the chest.

David dove into the darkness and began to scurry along the shallow defile as the confused Argentines opened up with their carbines and the night erupted in a barrage of sound. Bullets whined and whistled above him as, burrowing as low as he could, David dragged himself along by his elbows. He heard an answering burst from the hillslope behind and grinned savagely. Each of the two parties of Argentines thought it was under attack from the other. Spurts of flame split the darkness, and the rattle of gunfire became almost deafening as a furious dogfight developed.

David rose to his feet, chuckling insanely and, still clutching his side, staggered off into the night.

The heavy fire kept Ciro remorselessly pinned down. He had found a spot behind a jagged boulder and was crouching as low as he could, his right hand clutching the heavy service revolver he had drawn from his holster. Around him, the men were firing in a frenzy of panic, and bullets wailed through the air, pinging off rocks, thudding into the sand beneath their feet.

He had no idea who their assailants were. According to their intelligence reports, the British marines were assembled around Port Stanley. A terrible thought entered

Ciro's mind. Was it possible, just remotely possible, that in the darkness they had been attacked by their own side?

Sweating, he eased his head around the rim of the boulder. Through the shadows, he spotted Segunda almost directly in front. The Gaucho had found a narrow defile in the sand and was worming his way along it, bullets whistling harmlessly above him.

Something cold seemed to settle in Ciro's chest. Segunda made a perfect target. In the turmoil, the Argentine confusion was total. He, Ciro, would never get a better chance.

Ciro felt something in his throat begin to throb. He had almost forgotten why he wanted Segunda dead. In the beginning he had hated the man with a blind unreasoning passion, but Segunda was a stranger no longer—he was a human being, with the same strengths and frailties as every other human being. In different circumstances, he might even have been a friend.

Ciro was not by nature a vindictive man. Killing was something he found distasteful and abhorrent, even as a soldier. But there were things a man must do in the name of honour. It was born to into him, that inescapable code of conduct and principle. Segunda represented the embodiment of everything he had suffered over the years. The pain, the anguish, the humiliation. The disdain of his wife Tamara. They all found a focal point in that figure crawling away in front of him. He could not weaken and still call himself a man.

Ciro brought up the revolver, holding his wrist steady with his free hand. He could barely see Segunda now, the man's outline had blurred with the night. Ciro fired, once, twice, three times. He blinked, squinting into the darkness. It was impossible to tell if he hit Segunda or not. There was nothing to see but the beach and the ragged trail in the empty sand.

A bullet zipped past Ciro's skull and he jerked back, shivering violently, huddling against the boulder with the revolver clasped in his sweaty palm. He had to find a way out of here. It wasn't over, not yet. He had to know if Segunda was dead. He had to see the body, touch the coldness of the flesh. Until he did, he couldn't rest.

* * *

At the front of Government House, Marine Martin Tolan crouched behind a rhododendron bush and studied the building in front of him. It looked black and contourless in the eerie darkness. Along its front, he could see the glass conservatory, and to the right, where the governor's office lay, a cluster of cars and Land Rovers parked on the cindered forecourt. The Argentines had flash-diminishers fitted to their carbines, making it impossible to determine exactly where they were lying, but judging by the sound Tolan calculated they had occupied the ridge and copse behind. Most of the action had taken place at the rear of the house, and by comparison the front portion had remained relatively quiet.

Marine Tolan had scarcely managed to convince himself that this was actually happening. They'd talk about it a lot, the Argies invading, but nobody had really believed they would. When the news had come through that they were actually on their way, everything had been hazy and dream-like. The bloody Argies had come out of nowhere, sneaking in by the back door, ignoring their gun-emplacements entirely and hitting them from the rear. He wondered what they would say about it back home.

Marine Tolan tried not to think about home, because the commander had said they were outnumbered by about twenty to one, and any hope Tolan had that he might see his home again seemed a remote one in the circumstances. Instead, he concentrated on doing what he'd been paid to do, and rising from his hiding place, he ducked around the side of the house, carefully skirting the Mini and Cortina which had been parked there, and clambering over the wooden gate which divided the front and the rear sections of the garden. The Argentine fire seemed to intensify as he dropped to the other side, and he scuttled for cover against the side of the staff quarters. Dimly through the darkness, his eyes picked out the figures of a corporal and two marines crouching there.

"What are you playing at?" the corporal whispered, "You came over that fence like a battery of 115s. Who the hell do think you are, John bloody Wayne?"

"Sorry," Tolan muttered. "It's too quiet around the front. I thought I'd be better off where something's happening."

Suddenly, a series of explosions erupted on the lawn and instinctively the four men ducked low, hugging the ground as the night flared into brilliant day. Phosphorous stun grenades, Tolan thought. In their glare, he spotted three black-clad figures scrambling over the wall of the vegetable garden and sprinting wildly toward the back of the house, swinging their carbines across their chests. Without speaking, the four marines rose from where they were crouching and opened fire—crack, crack, crack—the bullets exploding in a steady reverberating roll as they ejected old shells and chambered new ones, feeling the recoils jarring their armpits as they loosed off their shots without really aiming. The first of the Argentines somersaulted forward, his body cartwheeling into the concrete path which bordered the edge of the lawn. The second was tossed into the air like a piece of carelessly-flung confetti. The third pitched forward as the top of his head came off, hitting the ground with a stomach-churning thump. None of the bodies moved again.

The corporal's face looked weird in the fading glow of the stun grenade.

"Where's the governor?" he snapped at Tolan.

"Inside the house, I think," Tolan answered tersely, his throat unnaturally dry.

"Better check."

Marine Tolan nodded, and without a word, ducked back the way he had come, entering the building by the rear door. Water pipes, ripped to shreds by the hail of automatic fire, were disgorging liquid down the bullet-riddled walls. He passed the Shackleton Room and swung into the governor's office.

Governor Hunt was under the table, clutching a pistol in one hand. He was speaking into the telephone, clarifying the situation in different parts of the island. Marine Tolan stared at him in amazement. Look at the bugger, he thought. We've got the whole bloody Argentine army outside, and he's chatting away on that thing like he was checking who won the three-thirty at Cheltenham.

* * *

David staggered as he limped through the now brightening darkness, blood trickling in a steady stream down the outside of his thigh. He knew he could not last much longer. His body had already begun to lose co-ordination, stumbling and weaving dizzily from side to side. Soon he would collapse completely.

The land dipped and he looked down on the sea again. A broad bay stretched beneath him and the breath caught in his throat as he spotted a beach crowded with thousands of tiny figures, their white bellies gleaming. Penguins. A bustling Emperor colony, scrambling and scurrying in earnest confusion. The entire shoreline was a vast teeming throng.

David stood gasping as the rocks see-sawed in his vision. There was still no sign of his Argentine pursuers. It had been a stroke of inspiration setting one agaist the other, but his advantage couldn't last for ever. They'd be after him soon, following his tracks through the endless maze of peatbogs—their task made easier by the dawn light. But he had to rest. He had to recuperate. If he could lose himself in that myriad sprawl, he would be just one more figure in an endless multitude. It was worth a try.

Still clutching his side, he hobbled down the bank and cautiously stepped on the beach, moving more slowly as he approached the first outer stragglers of the flock, placing his feet with almost mincing care, first one, then the other, pausing for a moment after each individual step before pressing on again. The penguins made no attempt to flee from his path. Unused to man, they felt no fear. A foul fishy smell pervaded David's nostrils, but he turned his mind from that, picking his way as delicately as he could through the curious swirling throng. Some of the penguins wriggled comically toward him and stood peering up at his face.

When he had reached the centre of the mass, he sat down gently in the sand and let his limbs and muscles relax. For a while, the penguins clustered around him, puzzled by this strange intruder, but at length, having satisfied themselves he was not about to do anything more spectacular than sit, they drifted back about their individual business.

Southward, David heard a distant rattle like rolling

thunder. Port Stanley, he realised. The capital was under attack. Things were happening more quickly than he'd realised. The battle for the Falklands was already under way.

Segunda spotted the blood leading across the muddy hillside and making his way toward it, squatted down, studying the peat intently. So the man was wounded. That threw a new complexion on things. A wounded man couldn't get far, not through this terrain. Sooner or later, he would have to stop, rest, gather his strength. It was tough going through the endless beds of mud, the see-saw sprawl of the tufted hillsides. Hurt, a man's energy would quickly dissipate. He would collapse out of sheer exhaustion.

Segunda was about to straighten when a strange shiver settled on his neck. It was nothing he could put a name to, an emotion too instinctive to follow any logical pattern, but he knew he was being watched. Slowly, he turned his head and his stomach tightened. A man stood on the slope above, his body framed by the brightening dawn. His outline was stark, vividly emotive with the lifting sunrays picking out the folds of his clothing and the ravaged hollows of his cheekbones. Segunda recognised the figure instantly. Colonel Ciro Cuellar.

The colonel's uniform was muddy and bedraggled and his hair was dancing crazily in the wind. He was standing in the classic firing position, one arm fully extended, the other gripping his wrist, his finger curled around the trigger of a heavy service revolver. Silently, afraid to say anything in case the simple act of speaking invoked an involuntary response, Segunda watched the colonel draw back the hammer. My God, he's going to shoot me, he thought. Segunda was nonplussed. He had no idea what had prompted the colonel's strange behaviour, for until this moment, their relationship had been a harmonious one. They had played chess together, discussed world events together, and in some cases (though the colonel's experience in such spheres was clearly limited) the relative attractions of women of mutual acquaintance. Segunda found Cuellar a reflective man, quiet and responsive, the kind of companion he instinctively warmed to. Why he

should provoke this bizarre confrontation in the middle of
nowhere was beyond Segunda's understanding. Perhaps
the man had gone mad?

Segunda was not afraid to die—he had lived with death
all his life, had inflicted it with such random detachment
that the act had almost lost its relevance, and he stood in
silence, calm, immensely contained, waiting for the moment the bullet would enter his chest, shatter his breastbone, rupture his insides.

Nothing happened. Colonel Cuellar was still standing in
the same position, but his teeth had begun to chatter wildly
and his body was shuddering all over. In the pale gleam of
dawn, Segunda saw sweat glistening on his features. He's
lost his nerve, Segunda thought. He can't bring himself to
squeeze the trigger.

Segunda did not pause to ponder the colonel's motives.
Crouching swiftly, he reached inside his jacket pocket,
pulling out his Starfire .38, flicking the safety catch with his
thumb. Holding the pistol at arm's length, he loosed off a
single shot, feeling the recoil jerk against his fist, glimpsing
the flash as the gun went off, catching the faint acrid odour
of cordite in his nostrils. The bullet took the colonel in the
centre of the abdomen and he jerked backwards into the
mud. Segunda heard him moaning softly, his voice distorted by the wind.

Frowning, Segunda climbed the hillside until he was
standing by Cuellar's head. The colonel lay on his back, his
arms outstretched. Muddy peat oozed around his neck. His
eyes were open and his lips fluttered helplessly as he
struggled for breath. Segunda could see the hole where the
bullet had penetrated leaving a widening patch of scarlet
under the colonel's ribcage.

"You damn fool," Segunda muttered. "What the hell
made you do that?"

Cuellar's breath wheezed in his throat and his eyes
seemed to widen until they were bulging from their
sockets. The wind plucked at his hair, scattering fragments
of powdery earth across his tortured cheeks. "I . . .
wanted to . . . kill you."

"I thought we were supposed to be friends?"

"This was . . . different. Something personal."

Segunda squatted on his haunches. He could feel the heat radiating from Cuellar's forehead. Sweat beaded the colonel's skin and trickled down the steep curve of his throat. Cuellar seemed to be concentrating very hard, as if something deep within the recesses of his brain was struggling to get out.

"Colonel," Segunda said softly, "until two weeks ago, I'd never met you before in my life. What could I have done to offend you?"

"My wife."

"Your wife?"

"Tamara. I found your picture in her drawer."

Segunda thought quickly. There was only one Tamara he could think of, a dark girl with angular cheekbones to whom once, many years ago, he had been engaged. The affair inevitably had broken up and she had married somebody else. Six months ago he had met her at a café on the Florida. He had been seeing her spasmodically ever since, casual assignations over almost as quickly as they began.

"You are Tamara's husband?" he whispered, amazed at his own stupidity.

The colonel did not answer. He looked almost beyond the reach of rational response. Segunda could see he was fading quickly. His breath rasped in his throat, and his eyes had assumed the glassy milkiness of encroaching death.

Sighing, Segunda said: "Colonel, with me women are a pleasant diversion, nothing more. There was no danger to your marriage. You should have seen that."

"I loved her," Cuellar whispered simply.

"Love?" Segunda exclaimed. "What's love? A woman is something to bring pleasure. Never to kill for."

"She was the best thing . . . in my life. I couldn't . . . I couldn't let you take her away."

Segunda nodded. He understood. The colonel had had no choice. It was all part of the ancient ritual, *machismo.* What a crazy people we are, he thought. We let our minds and hearts be ruled by attitudes and ideals which have no place in our true consciousness yet form the very essence of our character, forcing us to take up arms against our friends.

But faced with the enormity of his deed, Cuellar had found his conscience even stronger than tradition. There was a gentleness in the colonel Segunda had seldom witnessed in other men. He hated to watch him die.

The sun rose steadily, picking up warmth as it flooded the hillslopes with golden light. The peaks looked crystal clear, every creek-bed, every peat-gulley almost too sharply-etched to be real. Sparkling burns trickling merrily through slopes of heather and gorse. Moor grass filtered down the inclines, or clung like smoky spirals to jagged outcrops of rock. Great screes tumbled towards the sea like the folds of immense bridal veils. Still Segunda waited, watching the colonel's features settle into a waxen mask. His eyes still bulged, his lips sagged, but something had altered, some elusive spirit seemed to have left his body and departed. In less than an hour, Segunda, pressing his fingertips against Ciro's throat-pulse, realised the colonel was dead.

Sighing, he rose to his feet. The wind plucked at Cuellar's hair and mud oozed across his cheeks, mingling with the blood trickling from his mouth.

Segunda stuck the Starfire angrily into his pocket and stumbled off down the hillside, his features dark and wintry. He was getting too old for this game, he told himself. He recognised the symptoms, had glimpsed them often before in others.

He was beginning to experience pity.

TWELVE

Corporal Willoughby of Section Two sat in the garden of the little bungalow guarding the road to Port Stanley airport. Dawn was just beginning to break and a pale streak of light showed in the eastern sky. For the past two hours, he had heard the sounds of great activity around the area where the airstrip lay, but so far there had been no physical sign of the invaders themselves.

A steady rattle of gunfire told him Port Stanley was still under attack. Government House, he guessed. Their orders had been to avoid fighting in the streets wherever possible, so the lives of the civilians would not be endangered. He hoped the bloody Argies appreciated that. There would be hell to pay when this night was over.

Willoughby heard the sound of movement behind him and turning, glimpsed Marine MacInnes wriggling up to his side, his thin face sweaty in the pale light of dawn. In his hand, he clutched a thermos flask. "Fancy some coffee?" he whispered. "Warm the old cockles a bit."

Willoughby grunted, and eased his rifle into his other arm. He took the plastic cup MacInnes offered and sipped at it gratefully. The coffee was harsh and bitter, and Willoughby pulled a face. "Who made this muck?" he demanded.

"Cranston. He used to be a brickie in civvie life. He can't tell the difference between coffee and cement."

MacInnes was silent for a moment, peering up the road ahead. "Anything happening?" he muttered.

"Christ knows. They've been at it for hours, bashing and

clanging around. No sign of the bastards though. Not yet.
Where's the lieutenant?"

"Around the back. He's checking the inlet."

Willoughby stared at the flush in the sky. "Looks like the
start of a glorious day."

MacInnes nodded, following his gaze. "I hope to God
we're still alive to appreciate it," he remarked dryly.

"Sssshhh. Listen."

MacInnes held his breath, tilting his head in the icy
dawn. A dull metallic clanking noise came drifting across
the open moorland.

"Something's coming up the road," Willoughby hissed.
"Sounds like a convoy. Get the lieutenant, quick."

MacInnes scuffled away and Willoughby narrowed his
eyes, squinting into the lifting sun. Dimly, he spotted a line
of slow-moving vehicles, their incongrous metal shells
shuffling beetle-like along the narrow highway. "Amtracks,"
he breathed.

From a distance, the vehicles looked large and unwieldy,
their armoured flanks studded with metal handles, their
window visors raised, revealing the narrow slits at the front
of the cabins where the drivers sat, their gun turrets open,
the mountings clearly visible in the pink flush of dawn.
Willoughby counted eighteen in all. If that lot hits Port
Stanley, they'll rip the place to shreds, he thought.

The lieutenant came scurrying towards him through the
garden, his cheeks pale in the early morning.

"Amtracks, sir," Willoughby whispered. "A whole bloody
fleet of the bastards."

The lieutenant swore under his breath. Beneath his
jacket, he wore a thick army pullover with a bright silk scarf
tucked into the V-necked collar.

"Get that anti-tank launcher over here," he shouted to
his marine squad.

Willoughby lay on his belly clutching his rifle and
watched the gun-team swing their weapon into alignment.
The Amtracks were clearly in their line of vision now, the
leading vehicle barely three hundred yards away. He could
see the giant treads biting at the tarmac as the massive
monster lumbered ponderously forward.

The gun-team checked their sights, the lieutenant

crouching behind them, resting on one knee. The seconds stretched as the Amtracks rolled nearer.

"Fire," the lieutenant breathed softly.

There was a harsh belching sound as the anti-tank shell burst from the metal tube. Dry-mouthed, Willoughby watched it arc through the dawn, carrying its message of death in a feathery shower of sparks. It hit the leading Amtrack and the vehicle seemed to lunge, skidding sideways across the road. Then, as Willoughby stared in awed fascination, the armoured walls buckled outwards and a great mushroom of crimson flame erupted into the sky, scattering fragments of twisted metal, blazing rubber and scorched flesh across the barren moorland.

Dawn had broken when David woke up. His body felt chilled and he shivered miserably as he peered across the beach at the ridge above. There was no sign of movement, and grunting with pain, he eased himself gingerly to his feet. The penguins gathered around him, their white bellies gleaming in the sunlight, their little red eyes peering up with beady incomprehension.

David touched his side. The blood had crusted while he slept, but he felt weak and sickly, and his limbs were stiffening in the biting chill.

He studied the hills around him, picking out the sharp lines of gullies and cliffs, grey now in the flush of the early morning. There was no sign of life. He had lost the bastards, thank God. They had given up the pursuit, or had gone past him in the chill pre-dawn hours.

He pulled himself together and began to pick his way through the scurrying penguin flock, leaving the beach behind and following a winding, erratic course up the rim of the rocky buttress which wriggled to the elongated humps of the surrounding hills. The sun glared in his face, its rays gathering warmth as the morning lengthened, flooding his limbs with a new sense of life. A smattering of snow glistened on the distant peaks.

David reached the top of the ridge and paused, gasping heavily, his eyes sweeping the fells dipping away in front of him. There were no trees, only the valleys and slopes, their colours changing noticeably in the pale sheen of day. The summits looked vividly clear, and the air was charged with a freshness that filled David, despite his deteriorated state, with a sense of the world renewing itself.

The shimmering of the sun solidified, taking on form and density, moulding into the figure of a man moving toward him out of the glare. The man's body looked strangely familiar, and his hair was thick and tousled, dancing in the wind. The light changed, drifting across his features, and the breath seemed to choke in David's throat. Segunda.

The Argentine was moving with an almost tireless grace, homing in on him like a remorseless unbeatable force. David felt a sense of utter despair. He had been so sure he had shaken off his pursuers that now, faced with the imminent prospect of capture, he almost wanted to drop in his tracks, but something, some indeterminate instinct for survival spurred him on, and he turned and began to scuttle along the crest of the narrow ridge. His body twisted awkwardly as he tried to favour his damaged side, but despite his efforts he felt fresh blood welling between his fingers and trailing down the outside of his thigh.

The ridge's sides steadily steepened and soon he was tracing the rim of a jagged cliff, the earth plummetting to the waves far below, their white crests breaking fiercely as they crashed against the seaweed-cluttered rocks. A wild thought occurred to David. Maybe he could clamber down the precipice. It looked a terrifying drop, the rock brittle and unstable, but if he could negotiate those perpendicular slabs, Segunda might be unable to follow.

Without hesitating, without pausing to consider the wisdom of what he was doing, David eased down the steep clay bank until he had reached the edge of the cliff-face. The rocks were cracked and fractured, their surface brown, covered with dust, little trails of hanging clay winding between them. In places, David could see splashes of white where birds nested on the narrow ledges.

Gently, using his backside as an anchor, he lowered himself gingerly down, his heels reaching out in front, seeking holds, cracks, tiny nobbles on the splintered surface. Fear clutched at his throat, and his vision seemed to swim, the rocks below blurring and swaying in a strange see-saw motion that made him feel desperately sick.

The cliff tilted into a dangerous overhang and David
paused in his descent, crouching with his spine against the
hard rough rock, his legs splayed, his heels digging at the
miniscule footholds. He had gotten himself into a hell of a
position, he realised. He wasn't sure if he could retrace his
steps even if he wanted to. He knew the slightest tilt would
throw his balance out of alignment. Suddenly he felt
himself slipping and realised his feet were giving way.
Christ, I'm coming off, he thought.

He spotted a grass-tuft growing above the overhang's rim
and, twisting his body sideways made a lunge for it, his
fingers clutching the stiff coarse strands as his heels and
backside slid from their perch and his body plunged
downwards. He was dangling over the precipice, his legs
thrashing, his fists gripping the grass until the knuckles
gleamed white through the skin.

He saw Segunda easing down toward him, drawing his
facón carefully. The sunlight glinted on its vicious fourteen-
inch blade. Bitterness welled inside David. The bastard.
Even at this moment, the Argentine would not leave him to
die in peace.

David watched Segunda position himself at the precipice
top, clutching the weapon with both fists. Driving hard, he
swung the *facón* downwards, the metal hissing through the
swirling air. Thwunk, its tip drove savagely into the clay
above the overhang's lip, burying it almost to the hilt.

"Grab the handle," Segunda snapped.

David blinked. Puzzlement rippled through him, but
obediently, he switched one hand from the grass-tuft and
wrapped his fingers around the *facón's* bone grip.

"Now give me your other hand," Segunda ordered.

David felt Segunda's fist fasten on his wrist. The Argentine was leaning backwards, digging in his heels as he
struggled for balance, hauling hard on David's left arm.
David's toes scratched at the rock and he wriggled hard,
using the *facón* handle for purchase as he heaved and
floundered his way upwards.

Segunda dragged him across the overhang and helped
him to the top of the ridge. Gasping, David collapsed on
the ground. A wave of sickness spread upwards from his

stomach and he swallowed it back, struggling to maintain control.

Segunda scrambled down to retrieve his *facón* and, when he returned, he was grinning wildly. "I am delighted to find you still alive, *camarada*," he said. "I thought I had killed you at the whaling station. I've never missed like that before. It must have been the toy gun those idiots gave me at Camp Digepol."

David stared at him, his chest rising and falling. "Why did you save me?" he choked.

Segunda shrugged as he carefully cleaned the *facón* blade and slipped it into its leather sheath. His cheeks looked flushed with exertion, his eyes dancing, filled with their old familiar humour. "You looked so pitiful dangling there. I couldn't bear to watch you fall like a bundle of helpless firewood."

"But goddamit, you already tried to kill me once."

Segunda chuckled. "That was weeks ago. Then you knew too much for your own good. Today your knowledge is useless. Our invasion has already begun. By tonight, the whole world will know the truth. You can harm us no longer."

David fell back on the ground, letting his head rest among the grass clumps, peering at the sky. He was almost afraid to ask the next question. But he had to know. "What did you do with her?" he croaked.

"Segunda looked puzzled. "With who?" he muttered.

"The girl. Anne. Miss Danby."

"You mean Señor Stone's companion?"

David nodded.

"Nothing."

"Nothing?"

"Of course not, *companéro*. I had no reason to harm her."

"You mean she's still alive?" David felt his heart beating wildly.

"She was the last time I saw her, several hours ago."

David propped himself on his elbow. "What about me? Are you going to let me live too?"

Segunda shrugged. "Why not?"

"When the press arrive, I can ask some very embarrassing questions."

"Without proof? Who's going to believe you?"

"I have proof."

Segunda smiled. "But only for the moment," he said. Leaning forward, he tugged open David's jacket and rummaged inside his shirt. Still smiling, he drew out the document David had stolen from the radio hut. The sheets were soggy with blood, and Segunda shook his head remonstratively.

"It would not do for this to fall into the wrong hands," he chided.

He held the papers to the light, frowning as he studied the crimson stains. Then he leaned forward, peering at David's side. "You seem to be in quite a mess," he said.

"My wound's opened up again. It's been running all night."

"Well, we can't have you bleeding to death, *amigo*. It would be such a waste. I'd better take you back to our medics and get that side stitched up. Give me your arm."

Stumbling to his feet, David stared at him soberly. How ironic, he thought, that at this moment of need, the man he had feared so much was the one person he could turn to for help.

Leaning forward, he slid his hand across Segunda's shoulder, and with the Argentine supporting him on one side, began to limp painfully across the ragged hillside.

Governor Hunt sat on the edge of his desk and stared at the marine commander wearily. With dawn, the firing had slackened and was now limited to a few spasmodic bursts. For the moment, the grounds were relatively quiet. Governor Hunt rubbed his fingers dejectedly over his forehead. "What did you say?" he whispered.

"They're bringing up Amtracks," the commander repeated. "Armoured personnel carriers packed with troops and armed with 30mm cannon. Section Two knocked out one of the bastards on the airport approach road, but they've got a whole fleet out there. When they get them into position, they can blow this entire building sky-high."

The governor sighed. "I just can't stand the thought of surrender."

The marine commander nodded. "I quite understand.

My men will fight on as long as you deem it necessary. But I must point out that against those Amtracks, we don't have a chance."

Governor Hunt pulled a face, running his fingers through his short dark hair. He knew further resistance would be pointless. The battle for the Falklands was over. The moment for decision had finally come.

With a sigh, he straightened from his desk and reached for his jacket, pulling it on. His eyes looked weary and resigned. "I suppose I'd better go talk to the beggars," he said.

The Land Rover rattled along the approach road to Port Stanley, and David saw the houses building up, the angular streets climbing the narrow hillside, their metal rooftops reflecting the pink and gold of the fading sun. He was sitting beside Segunda, his side encased in plaster. The Argentine medics had been brusque but thorough, stitching up his wound and dressing it carefully. They had fed him bully beef and coarse black beans, then Segunda had driven him back to the capital, a journey which had taken most of the day. Now evening was falling as they entered the outskirts of Port Stanley. There was little to see of the pre-dawn battle. The gaily-coloured buildings looked barely touched, and David spotted Government House rising on their right, the walls riddled in places with shrapnel holes, but the glass conservatory which adorned its front miraculously intact. Argentine troops wandered over the carefully trimmed lawns, and the Argentine colours fluttered from the flagpole.

As the road entered the town proper, David saw Argentine soldiers everywhere. They carried an air of quiet jubilation as they moved through the network of little streets, grenades and mortar shells bobbing from their belts. Camouflaged vehicles trundled along the waterfront, and officers in combat clothing bellowed out orders in harsh, discordant voices.

Segunda drove past the cathedral and swung to a halt at the wooden jetty. David spotted a vessel moored alongside the quay. Its hull was gleaming sleekly and its superstructure was aerodynamically-shaped, the bridge and wheel-

house slanting backwards to the trim promontory of its
radar mast and funnel. As he stared at it, David felt a
tremor ripple through his body. Stone's cruiser.

Frowning in puzzlement, he turned to peer at Segunda.
The Argentine smiled.

"He sailed around the coastline during the night," he
explained. "Orders."

"What's he doing here?"

"Waiting for you. Somebody's got to get you out of here.
To tell the truth, *camarada*, you are something of an
embarrassment. We'll be happy to see you go."

David was silent for a moment, watching Segunda
fumble in his pocket and bring out a packet of thin
cheroots. He offered them to David who shook his head,
then he placed one between his own lips and lit it carefully,
cupping his hands to shield the match from the wind.

Segunda had surprised David during the long day's drive.
He was a man of many contradictions, each one difficult and
ingrained. But in spite of everything, David could not
forget his inherent ruthlessness, or the part he had played
in the events of the past few weeks.

"I guess you're feeling pretty damned pleased with
yourself," David said.

"Why not?" Segunda admitted. "We are the new *conquistadores*."

"But for how long?"

Segunda's lips twisted into a thin smile as a detachment of
troops marched by, their boyish faces absurdly youthful
beneath their heavy round helmets. Their sergeant was a
dark-skinned man with a fierce moustache who was barking
out instructions on the cool night air.

"The Malvinas are Argentine," Segunda said. "They will
always be Argentine."

"The British government might have something to say
about that," David remarked dryly.

Segunda shrugged and went on smoking casually, a glint
of humour in his pale grey eyes. David was silent for a
moment. Throughout the long day's drive, he had turned
his mind from thoughts of his immediate future, but now at
last he could avoid the subject no longer. "Am I free to
leave?" he asked.

"You sail with Stone on the evening tide."

"And you?"

"My job is finished here. I will return to Buenos Aires."

"To carry on your profession?"

Segunda shrugged. "I am an instrument, nothing more. A soldier in civilian clothing."

"You really believe that?"

"I assure you *companéro*, it is true. One day, you will understand."

David stared at him in the gathering twilight, then he eased himself from the passenger seat and clambered to the ground. The pain in his side had largely diminished but the heavy dressing made his torso feel stiff and unwieldly.

"I guess you think I ought to thank you," he said. "I would have died on that cliff if you hadn't pulled me up."

Segunda grinned. "That is not necessary. If I had not been following you, you would not have been on the cliff in the first place."

David nodded. "That's true. I'll just say goodbye then."

"Good luck *amigo*. I am glad we did not kill you."

"Take it easy with those women," David warned, shaking his hand.

"I will try," Segunda promised seriously. "I strive constantly for the purity of the soul, but my body does not always listen."

David stood for a moment longer, struggling to think of something appropriate to say, but in the end he turned and began to stroll toward the vessel's gangplank. Behind him, he heard a roar as Segunda started the Land Rover's engine and trundled back the way they had come.

David found the senior officer waiting on the foredeck. He was an Italian, dark and swarthy, whose suntanned skin looked startlingly brown against the pristine whiteness of his uniform.

"How nice to see you again, sir," he said. "You will find Mr. Stone waiting in his stateroom."

David's face was grim as he eased through the hatch and walked down the companionway. Anger was building up inside him, a cold, almost clinical anger which left his brain astonishingly clear.

He entered the cabin without knocking. Stone was

sitting at the table, writing out a report. He was wearing a sheepskin shirt and leather trousers with slashed pockets which looked, against the whiteness of his hair, oddly theatrical. Watching him, David felt incredibly calm. It was a curious transition, his anger settling like the switching off of some high-powered electrical charge, not gone completely, merely suspended, held in abeyance and ready to be called upon if necessary. It had come at last, the moment he had waited for, the moment when he would confront Stone with the infamy of his actions. This was the man he had learned to hate more than anything in his life, the man who had taken Anne, who had tricked and deceived him, who had lied, cheated, betrayed. And yet, staring at the narrow face masked by a pair of incongruous reading glasses, David was struck by how unimpressive the Englishman looked. The spectacles seemed to diminish his vitality somehow, imbuing his features with an almost gnomish air. He glanced up as David entered, his face breaking into a smile. "David," he exclaimed, "how wonderful to find you still alive."

David grunted. "I guess it must be kind of disconcerting," he said, "after all the trouble you went to to have me killed."

The smile faded on Stone's lips. He looked surprised and hurt like a man who had just been let down in some unthinkable way. "You don't seriously believe I had any part in that?"

"Why not? You had a part in just about everything else."

Stone's lips drew together, and tiny wrinkles formed at the corners of his mouth. His face looked older than David remembered, as if the strain of the last few days had aged him visibly. "My dear David," he sighed, "shooting you was the Argentine's idea. I was outraged when I heard about it. In fact, when they radioed through this morning that Segunda had found you alive, I was overwhelmed with joy."

David felt his resolution wavering. There was no mistaking Stone's air of affable assurance. He looked totally at ease, his arrogant face slightly softened by the inelegant spectacles.

"Why did you do it?" David whispered.

"Do what?" Stone demanded.

"This. The whole miserable set-up. Why did you do it?"

Stone shrugged. "Patriotism, of course."

"Call yourself a patriot?"

"My interests lie where they have always lain. With the future of my country."

"But you deliberately let me go on believing you were an Englishman."

"I *am* an Englishman," Stone insisted.

"Born in Buenos Aires?"

Stone gave an impatient gesture. "The place where a man leaves his mother's womb is unimportant. I have always been British, and I always will be.

"Then you're a traitor," David breathed.

"So the Argentines believe."

"There's no other explanation."

Stone stared at him in silence for a moment. His thin face looked remarkably calm, but behind the calmness David glimpsed a sense of disappointment, a trace of anger that matched David's own. Placing both palms on the table-top, Stone drew himself slowly to his feet. "Are you really so stupid that you don't realise what I have accomplished here?" he whispered.

"Sure, I know what you've accomplished. I know what you've been accomplishing for the past ten months. I've seen the evidence, remember. It was you who radioed the Falklands defence positions to the Argentine invasion fleet. It was you who helped to persuade the British government to axe HMS *Endurance*. It was you who informed the junta in Buenos Aires that Britain would be powerless to react in the face of an Argentine takeover. Everything you've done, everything you've worked toward has been for one purpose only."

Stone sighed. "What a dull-witted fellow you are, David."

"You deny it?"

"Why should I? It's perfectly true. But that's only part of the story."

"Okay, then let's hear the other part. I'm anxious to hear it, I really am."

David could feel the anger starting up inside him again, dimming his senses, but Stone seemed unmoved by his

hostility; taking off his spectacles he folded them carefully
and slipped them into his jacket pocket. His actions were
graceful and precise, as if he liked to apportion his attention
to one thing at a time.

"I've been telling the British Foreign Office for years
about the danger down here," he said. "No one would
listen. They were ready to negotiate the islands away.
They'd have done it too if I'd let them."

"Let them?" David echoed. "Are you trying to tell me
you deliberately lured the Argentines into this?"

Stone smiled. "It wasn't difficult. I used the simple rule of
all diplomacy—understand your rival and the way he
thinks. Understand his weaknesses, his prejudices, his
irrationalities. The Argentine character has one fundamen-
tal flaw, the spirit of *machismo*. All I did was create a
situation in which their true nature could find expression,
in which the prospect of a military takeover would seem
both attractive and feasible."

"You made the Argentines believe that Britain didn't give
a damn about the islands?"

"Why not? It was perfectly true. Maintaining colonies in
the 1980s can be an expensive business. I've suspected for
years that the British government would like to relinquish
its Falklands responsibilities. I was determined not to let
that happen."

"Even to the extent of starting a war?"

Stone shrugged his shoulders helplessly. "Naturally I'd
hoped it wouldn't get as far as an actual invasion. My intent
was to produce evidence of the Argentine design and nip
the thing in the bud, so to speak. We'd have done it too, if
time hadn't suddenly run out."

"What the hell are you talking about?"

"After you'd broken into Camp Digepol, David, the
Argentines contacted me by radio. A major Falklands
assault was imminent, they said. I was requested to report
to Camp Digepol for immediate instructions. You can
imagine my position. I knew we were already too late.
Whether you succeeded in freeing Pinilla or not, it could
make little difference to the Argentine invasion plans."

"Why didn't you get word to me, for God's sake?"

"How could I? You were somewhere inside the camp

perimeter. Anne had already set off on the skiddoo. I was unable to contact either of you direct. So I did the only thing I could do in the circumstances. I obeyed orders. Argentine orders."

"And left us to die at the whaling station."

"You're quite wrong," Stone stated calmly. "I knew the Argentines would send someone to pick you up. If they hadn't intercepted your SOS, I'd have found a way of letting them know you were there. Of course, I didn't realise they would use Martin Segunda. I had no idea they intended to kill you. I was utterly horrified when Segunda came back with only Anne."

"You expect me to believe that?"

"I'm not a murderer, David, whatever else you think of me. Segunda spared Anne because he knew she was my secretary. That's the only reason they released her into my custody."

David hesitated, the enormity of what Stone was saying making his senses swim. "So now you're hoping the British will retake the islands by force?"

"My dear fellow, they'll have no other choice."

"You'd let men fight and die to feed your incredible conceit."

Stone frowned. "Conceit? It's not a question of conceit."

"You think so? You've lied, schemed, cheated—all out of some crazy notion you call patriotism. I don't believe you, Stone. I believe you did it for personal reasons. Power. It's like a drug. You're too much like my father, you can't help yourself. Manipulating people isn't enough for you any more. Now you want to manipulate nations."

Stone shook his head curtly, his face flushed and intent. "You're wrong," he insisted. "I found the whole affair personally distasteful. But the Falklands are the gateway to Antarctica. That's where the real issue lies. If the Argentines can remove us from these islands, they'll have opened the way for a military takeover of British Antarctic Territories when the treaty comes to an end. Without its deepwater ports in the South Atlantic, Britain will be powerless to prevent them. It may not seem to matter too much at the moment, but by the turn of the century, when our energy sources are running out, the oil and mineral wealth of the

Antarctic Peninsula will be vital to my country's survival. That's what this dispute is really about. And that's why the Falklands have to be protected at all costs."

"Supposing the British fail to win them back, have you considered that?"

Stone's features settled into an expression of wry amusement. "You drove through the streets of Port Stanley just now. You saw the soldiers out there. Conscripts, most of them. Young boys barely out of school. Inexperienced, poorly-equipped. Against the best-trained army in the world, they won't stand a chance."

Reaching down, he toyed idly with the inkwell on the desk-top, his face gentler than David had ever seen it before. It was as if, now that his task had been accomplished, some of the force, the vital essence of the man had dissipated.

"Let me tell you something, David," he said. "When the United Nations debated the Falklands issue recently, almost every delegate voted in favour of Argentina. Tomorrow, you may take my word for it, the whole world will be behind Britain."

David's fingers crept to his side, tracing the padded outline of the heavy dressing. "My God, you've thought it all out, haven't you?"

"I've thought about nothing else for years. The future of the Antarctic Peninsula is too important to ignore. Lose the Falklands and we lose everything."

"So you decided to use me."

"Good God man, there was nothing personal in it. I'd have used anyone."

"And Anne? Did you use her too?"

Stone's features relaxed into a smile. "I didn't have to. She understood what I was getting at from the beginning. Unlike you David, she saw the need for duplicity, she didn't shrink from it when the moment came."

"Where is she now?" David demanded.

"Waiting to say goodbye. She's decided to remain in Port Stanley, at least until the crisis is over. This is her home, after all. She feels it's where she belongs."

David felt his heart beating wildly. "She's here?"

Stone nodded. "You'll find her in the wheelhouse."

In that moment, David's brain seemed to switch off completely. A strange tingling sensation started up his wrists and forearms, and he pushed past Stone, scrambling along the narrow companionway. Everything the Englishman had said was suddenly forgotten in the thought that Anne was waiting for him on the deck above. He was gasping audibly as he clattered up the narrow staircase.

He found her leaning against the metal azimuth, her face pale and carefully composed. He guessed she was unsure of her reception. She was dressed simply in a pair of jeans and a heavy wool sweater, and her blonde hair hung loosely around her neck. As he paused in the doorway, breathing hard, a sense of uncertainty overtook him. He was unsure of how to react. Outraged and indignant? He had a feeling he wouldn't pull it off somehow. He was a quiet man, unused to histrionic displays. And besides, she looked so beautiful.

"David," she whispered, her eyes scrutinising his face, "they told me you were coming. I thought . . . I thought you were dead."

He nodded slowly. "I ought to be."

"Thank God you're safe."

He moved toward her, advancing slowly as if half-afraid that any precipitous motion might cause her to disappear. She stared down at the side where the shirt was still stained with blood. "You're hurt."

Instinctively, he touched the dressing with his fingertips. "It's where Segunda shot me. The wound opened up again during the night. The Argentines had to put new stitches in."

"David, you don't think . . . you can't possibly imagine I had anything to do with that?"

"What do you expect me to think?"

"You must believe me. When Segunda arrived, I had no idea what he was going to do, I swear it. Magnus neither. He was just as horrified as I was."

David moved closer, his eyes scouring her face. She was staring back at him, her cheeks white, her eyes filled with a curious emotion. Not shame exactly. Regret rather. Sadness, contrition.

"But you were in this from the start," he whispered. "You and Stone together."

She nodded.

"You used me. You set me up and used me."

"It was my duty," she answered dully.

"To whom? The British?"

"That's right."

"For Christ's sake, you were lying to them too."

"I was trying to make them see sense," she snapped angrily. "They were going to give us away. They were going to trade us in like a piece of unwanted merchandise. Well now they'll have to take a stand, the people will demand it. They'll have to make a commitment and support that commitment with force if necessary. And when it's over, they'll have to accept us for what we are. British."

David looked at the ground. The anger he had expected to feel hadn't materialised. Somehow he didn't care any more. The damage had been done. It wasn't his affair any longer. And now that the initial shock of finding her had faded, he was already turning his mind from the past, focusing it on the future. "You're staying?" he murmured.

"I have to. It's where I belong."

"For how long?"

"Until it's over."

"And then?"

She shrugged. "God knows. I haven't considered afterwards."

He hesitated, feeling his stomach tense. "What about us?"

"Us?"

"All right then. Me."

She straightened, tracing one finger down the side of his cheek. The touch of her skin sent a shiver through his body. Her eyes looked gentle, filled with a strange understanding.

"Poor David. You'd never trust me again. Not after . . . after everything that's happened."

"Why not give me a try?"

She shook her head. "It wouldn't work. It's over now. I'm not even the same person any more."

"Maybe we can work it out," he insisted.

"No David, it's too late. You've been kind and sweet and very, very patient. But I have to plan out my future in my own way. No complications, no memories from the past. I like you a lot. But it's time for us to part."

David fell silent. He knew he had lost her. It was a strange feeling, oddly empty of emotion. He felt no pain, that was the curious thing. Only a sense of emptiness. Of amputation and impending loss. She would walk out of his life for ever, leaving only the haunting resonance of her presence, and he would be left alone again. Peace of a gentle kind eased through him, the peace that came with the ending of uncertainty, with the realisation that whatever had to be faced could be faced now, measured in all its aspects. A man built his life on a series of illusions, he thought, each one separate and remote, each making up a part of the whole. Tonight, this whole experience would be a section of his past he could portion off and forget. Except that he knew in his heart forgetting was not in his nature. He loved her so much, that was the awful part. She looked ripe in betrayal, or perhaps he was the one who was ripe, for the sight of pale skin tempered by her loosened hair, the swell of the full breasts beneath the woollen jumper brought back his anguish with a breathless force.

"Close your eyes," she ordered.

"Why?"

"Because I don't want you to see me leave."

He felt his chest tighten as he did as she instructed. Her lips brushed his cheek and he heard a scraping sound as the door quietly opened and voices reached him on the cool evening air. Boots clattered, weapons clinked, the heavy rumble of armoured vehicles drifted across the rooftops. He stood like that for a very long time, a feeling of wrtechedness gathering inside him. When at last he reopened his eyes, he saw the inlet, its white waves dancing, he saw the cathedral with its pointed belltower, he saw the Philomel Store with the road rising behind it, the troops marching, the flags fluttering, the hills green and gentle in the gathering flush of twilight.

But there was no sign of Anne.

EPILOGUE

Magnus Stone's predictions proved graphically correct. On June 14th 1982, after a brief but bloody conflict, the Argentine army surrendered to Major General Jeremy Moore of the British Task Force. Governor Hunt was knighted and reinstated as Britain's representative in the Falklands, and HMS *Endurance* was removed from the government's redundancy list and returned to duty in the South Atlantic. In November 1983, the Argentine military junta was replaced by a democratic authority and General Leopoldo Galtieri was arrested and charged with helping to provoke the war. Anne Danby remained in Port Stanley until liberation day, then rejoined Magnus Stone as his personal secretary. David Ryker's father died in June 1984 and he now runs his family's business concerns in the United States.

At the time of writing, the Falklands issue remains unsolved. Britain occupies the islands but Argentina, with that inherent single-mindedness, that totality of purpose she has displayed from the very beginning, continues to claim them.

While nearly a thousand miles to the south, surrounded by snow and ice and isolated for twenty-five million years, the source of Magnus Stone's solitary obsession, the oil and mineral wealth of the Antarctic Peninsula still lies waiting and untouched.

ABOUT THE AUTHOR

BOB LANGLEY, the popular presenter of "Pebble Mill at One" and "Saturday Night at the Mill," joined the British Broadcasting Corporation in 1969. Apart from his television career, he has written ten action-packed novels of adventure, including *Autumn Tiger*, *Falklands Gambit*, *The Churchill Diamonds*, *The War of the Running Fox*, and *East of Everest*—each to considerable acclaim in both Great Britain and the United States.

Born in Newcastle, in northern England, Langley and his wife Pat live in a cozy cottage in the picturesque Lakes District where he spends as much time as possible outdoors, hiking and planning his tales of adventure.

BANTAM
SHOP-AT-HOME
C·A·T·A·L·O·G

Special Offer
Buy a Bantam Book
for only 50¢.

Now you can have Bantam's catalog filled with hundreds of titles plus take advantage of our unique and exciting bonus book offer. A special offer which gives you the opportunity to purchase a Bantam book for only 50¢. Here's how!

By ordering any five books at the regular price per order, you can also choose any other single book listed (up to a $5.95 value) for just 50¢. Some restrictions do apply, but for further details why not send for Bantam's catalog of titles today!

Just send us your name and address and we will send you a catalog!